PADDY FACES THE DRAGON

The Portal of Evil

Monique Sivelle McCracken

PublishAmerica
Baltimore

First printing

Hardcover 978-1-4512-2563-1
Softcover 978-1-4489-4150-6
PUBLISHED BY PUBLISHAMERICA, LLLP
www.publishamerica.com
Baltimore

Printed in the United States of America

Since the return of Paddy and Daryl to the Promised Valley four elfic years ago, a l-o-n-g time in the elfic calendar, centuries have passed for mortals but time is still very young for elves.

At the age of nineteen Paddy was tall and slender. Now he is a strong Wizard in his own right and getting stronger each year. After an extensive period of training at the academy, his friend Daryl has achieved Knighthood. Tall with a strong muscular body, the Human/ Elf boy was ready to go on a quest with his Wizard friend, Prince Patrick.

Chapter 1

The worried Elven Kings from the north were reporting bad tidings to King Ariol of the South Realm of the promised valley. Darkness hovered at the edge of the Northern Realms and was spreading rapidly. Zoltar, one of the great Evil ones from earth realm had moved into the Elfic Realm to join in his evil plot with Xary, the last evil sorcerer of the elfic realm. Together they had gathered the dark forces and were plotting to get control over the Elfic Realms and the Dwarves' Kingdoms.

King Ariol immediately called his counselors for a conference with The Dragon Lord. The Great Lord Wizard from the Sapphire Mountain came down at once to talk with the kings of the Elven Realms and Dwarfs Kingdom.

The Dragon Lord gloomily said, "A great evil is spreading its darkness in the north. Villages have been burned to the ground and the inhabitants enslaved by Zoltar. People are fleeing with their animals and belongings. Trails of refugees are on the roads going to the south Realms for safety."

King Ariol shook his head. "Yes, we must stop Zoltar, at any cost, once and for all. Since he left earth he has become bolder and bolder. His battle on earth centuries ago with King Tyson, and the refusal of the

King to give Zoltar his daughter in marriage infuriated him. Unfortunately, that is why he came to our realm," said King Ariol, and he sighed.

His first counselor asked in surprise, "But how come, after so many centuries, he is still alive? He is not an elf?"

The Dragon lord replied, "He won't be for too long now. He is borrowing time from the realm and the evil he is creating around him. His power is getting weaker as the time passes. That is why he called upon Xary to reinforce his failing strength."

The Dragon Lord pensively stroked his long beard and continued, "I agree we must stop him, but it won't be an easy task. As weak as his power is, we have to neutralize it forever."

King Ariol asked, "How can we do that?"

"'The only way is to crown him with the Magic Crown of Sapphire," answered the Dragon Lord.

"Where is it? Who has it?" all asked.

"I do," replied the Great Lord.

"Then the problem is almost resolved."

"Oh no, it's not "answered the Wizard.

"Why? You have the crown," asked King Ariol.

"Yes, I do. But only a Mortal can touch it without being transformed into a mindless being."

"A mortal," they whispered. Hope left all the members of the council.

"How can we find a mortal, and why a mortal?" asked King Ariol.

Many centuries ago the crown belonged to a great Mortal king, a friend of the Elves. When he died he left his magic crown to his best friend, a gentle Elf King from the West Realm. One of his sons became hungry for power. He was wicked, and tried to use the crown for evil purposes. The crown killed him. The sad King called upon me to take it away from his palace. Since then the Crown protects itself against any attempt to steal it. No Elf can touch it without risking his sanity.

King Ariol pensively whispered, "We have two Mortals in our Realm changed by us into elves, my son Prince Patrick and his friend and squire, Daryl."

Quickly, the Dragon Lord replied, “Your son, Prince Patrick, born half elf, would be in great danger and take a terrible risk.”

All eyes in the council had lost their spark. The King’s first counselor said, “We must call them and present the situation.”

“You are right,” replied the King. He rang for the chamberlain and asked him to go at once get the young prince and his squire. Soon he returned with the two young Elves.

“Sit down please, Patrick,” said the king to his son. Respectfully Daryl stood behind his Prince. The Dragon Lord repeated the story of the Magic Crown and its power to destroy the Evil Zoltar who had now become too powerful because of the alliance he had made with Xary.

“I will do it, Father,” said Paddy.

“I know you will Patrick, but there is another way. Listen, Daryl was a Mortal, a full Mortal, unlike you my son, who are only half. Because of that he doesn’t risk his life.”

“If your Lordship will permit me to speak?” Daryl asked, respectfully.

“Permission granted, Daryl,” replied the King. The Dragon Lord’s sharp eyes were set upon the Elf.

“Prince Patrick can’t carry the crown, it’s too dangerous. I will do it,” said Daryl looking square in the eyes of King Ariol.

Paddy jumped from his seat, turned around to his friend. “All right, maybe you will do it, but I will come with you.”

Daryl, forgetting where and with who he was, cried, “Hooray!”

The King laughed. “I see we have two champions for our Quest, my friends, and two very good ones.”

Paddy quickly shook Daryl’s hand and winked at his friend.

The Dragon Lord said to the boy, “You have to be Mortal for a while, otherwise by touching the crown you will die or lose your mind, because you are an elf.”

A worried look flashed into Daryl’s eyes.

The Dragon Lord smiled. “Do not worry yourself, friend. When the quest is over, you will be again an elf.”

“I will have to go through all the ceremony again?‘

"No, you won't have to, man," Paddy replied and laughed. The young Wizard patted his friend's back, knowing the fear he had of facing a crowd.

The king and his counselors looked at the young Elves wondering why the laughter on such a serious occasion. The Dragon Lord looked at the boys. He knew. The Great Wizard, a twinkle in his eyes, said to Daryl, "Let's get it over with and make you mortal again, boy." The great one got up, his long robe billowing behind him. In a large gesture he moved his long sleeves and stood in the middle of the room, all eyes upon him.

"Does it hurt, man?" whispered Daryl.

"No, silly," Paddy nudged his ribs chuckling softly.

Daryl was not reassured.

"Come here in front of me." The Wizard smiled, reading Daryl's fear.

Chapter 2

Bravely he walked to the Dragon Lord. *Nobody must know how scared I am.* He squared his shoulders. *After all I am Prince Patrick's Squire,* he told himself.

The Dragon Lord's bony hands moved toward the young Elf who instinctively took a step back. Out of the Wizard hands a gentle mist came covering Daryl entirely. A soft light flashed into the mist and everything disappeared.

"That's all?" Surprised, the boy felt different. He was not any more in harmony with things around him. Daryl touched his face. The pointed ears were gone, his body was heavier. Outside, darkness had shrouded the park. Daryl sighed sadly. His night vision was gone, too.

Paddy read his friends mind, then cheerfully he said, "Don't worry, man, soon you will have it back.

Daryl smiled. "I know, but I already miss it badly. I got used to being an elf all these past years. You know, man, you don't appreciate things when you have them, only when you lose them and you feel the emptiness."

Paddy gave an understanding hug to his friend.

"Come. I will see you at The Sapphire mountain. There, Daryl, you will receive the Magic Crown." The Dragon Lord left in a flash of light, blinding everyone in the room.

"Wow." Daryl couldn't refrain himself. Sheepishly he looked at the King. Everyone was smiling. Paddy grinned at his old buddy.

Early the next morning, Paddy and Daryl left the palace quickly and silently. Paddy didn't wish to alert his cousin Stoy, who would want to come. They didn't want to have to protect the child during the quest. It was not a picnic they were embarking on. Lightly equipped with bows and arrows, Magic Shining Swords, elfic cape and boots, plus the elfic elixir and the biscuits (much disliked by Daryl) the wonder water and the magic salve, they were all set to go. It was a beautiful day with singing birds wishing them farewell and the sun shining on the morning dew like diamonds from heaven. Lightheartedly, they crossed the stone bridge and waved goodbye to the Palace and its protocol. Happy to be once more on a quest together, away from the etiquette of the court for a while, to be boys of nineteen. Free of all strain they dashed down the road, challenging each other. Daryl soon became short of breath. His mortal body was much too heavy to follow Paddy.

They stopped. The fields, deserted at this wee hour of the morning, made the Elfic Realm all theirs. Just like young colts loosed in the pasture they resumed their running. Daryl, now that he was no longer an elf, was too slow. Laughing he said, "I feel like I have lead in my pants."

With a chuckle Paddy replied, "I know man, it's not funny at all." The Realm was waking up.

The fields suddenly were full of laughter from the kids going to school and the songs from the adults. Dogs barked and the chickens, at the sight of their farmer friend bringing food, cackled joyously. Daryl said, "How nice and peaceful."

Paddy sighed, "Peace that Zoltar and Xary want to take away."

Daryl stopped in his elan and stomped the ground crying furiously "Never, never over my dead body!"

"Man, that is why we are going on a quest." Paddy laughed at the anger of his friend, who continued screaming.

"I will get him! I will put that crown on his ugly head." Daryl was red in the face.

"Okay, okay, we will man, we will."

They walked quietly for many hours, happy to be together. They found a nice spot to rest under a large tree and sat. Paddy took out from his bag the elfic biscuits. "Oh no, can't you do better man?" asked Daryl, looking worriedly at Paddy.

"No!"

"What do you mean no? You are not a Wizard anymore? Will we have to go through the quest on elfic biscuits." Daryl was disgusted.

"What's wrong with them?" Paddy had a mischievous twinkle in his eyes. He watched Daryl, who nervously twisted on the grass at the thought of going on the quest without a good honest meal all that time.

Nervously he replied, "Nothing. You know, man, the only thing I didn't like at the academy was those biscuits." He sighed and between his teeth he mumbled, "elfic biscuits."

"Good, because here are your biscuits. You don't want to starve, do you?""

"Of course not" Without looking, Daryl held his hand out. A delicious smell tickled his nose and something hot was in his hand. "Oh you! I thought you were no longer a Wizard man."

"I know what you thought. Relax, I still am, and more powerful than ever. I could have changed you into a human body, but protocol obliged me to give that privilege to the old Dragon Lord."

Daryl, with a note of hope in his voice asked, "Could you change me back into an elf?"

"Yes, I could, but I won't. It would be too dangerous for you. Later I will."

"Oh, boy, I feel much better, now that I know you can give me my elfic body back. I don't trust those old Wizards of yours. If you wish, man, I will eat nothing but those biscuits."

Daryl bit his lips realizing what he just said. Worriedly, he looked at his buddy. Paddy chuckled and replied. "Let's go. We have little time to waste."

The two friends traveled for hours and found a good spot to camp for the night. After a good meal Paddy rolled in his cape and said, "You won't have to eat nothing but those biscuits you love so much. Goodnight, man."

"Goodnight Paddy," replied the human with a sigh of relief.

The night was peaceful, trillions of stars shone in the velvety sky. A wee pretty girl, dressed in gold, with dark hair and transparent gold wings watched them. Then she sat lightly beside Daryl and threw gold dust upon him. In the morning the two friends woke, feeling rested.

"I feel wonderful," said Daryl.

"Good, so do I. But as you know Elves usually do," Paddy said with a chuckle.

"Don't rub it in, man. How about eating? I am starved." Paddy moved his hand conjuring a delicious breakfast.

With his mouth full Daryl said, "There is no better way of traveling, than having a Wizard at your side. Of course, that is, if said Wizard is your friend. Those old bearded guys can be nasty." A serious look was on his face.

Chapter 3

"I see, that after all, I am good for something other than feeding you and escorting you, brave squire," said Paddy, laughing.

"Oh, yes, in many ways man," Daryl slapped his friend on the back.

"Good, let's move. We have a long way before crossing the River Abundance, the border of my Father's Realm."

"Too bad we have to leave. It's a beautiful place." Daryl, changing his mood said, "But we will be back." Joyfully he jumped to his feet and started running. "I will race you, man. That breakfast of yours must move down and not sit on my stomach. I am heavy enough the way I am." A gentle breeze was whispering in the trees. Daryl in his mortal body felt light as a feather. "I do feel almost like being an Elf, man," he said cheerfully.

"You had a good night of rest."

However, even with all his efforts he couldn't beat Paddy. They resumed their walk, only stopping for a bite.

With a tone of regret Paddy said, "Here is the border of my Father's Realm."

"I hate to leave. Let's go across tomorrow, man. Can we sleep on this side tonight?"

"Of course. As you wish." Pensively they walked along the river. Here ends the pleasant part of their journey. "Who knows what's awaiting us ahead."

"See that splendid tree? That is a perfect spot for us to sleep under its huge boughs."

They walked to the tree and Daryl flopped down. They ate their meal in silence. It was almost dark and both of them were tired. They rolled into their capes and were immediately gone from the world. In the middle of the night Daryl had a strange feeling. Drowsily he opened his eyes. Stupefied, he watched gold dust falling like a gentle rain upon him. "What's this? I must be dreaming." He turned on his side and returned to sleep.

The morning was a little hit crisp. After a short breakfast, with hot chocolate to warm them for the journey, they left rapidly, searching for a ford to cross the river. The two young men talked soberly about the dangers they would certainly face.

Then Daryl remembered his dream. "Last night I had the strangest dream. I was sprinkled with gold dust."

Paddy stopped. "By whom, man?"

Daryl shrugged his shoulders. "Beat's me. I don't know; couldn't see."

Paddy was now very curious. "If it happens again, try to see who's doing it."

"Gosh; I'll try."

"Here is a ford." Paddy dashed into the shallow water. It didn't take long to go across and set foot in a scruffy copse. Gravely Paddy said, "Now we are no longer in my Father's Realm. We are trampling upon evil ground and we must be prepared for anything bad to happen."

Daryl looked sadly around. Then Paddy's sharp eyes spotted a large plume of smoke.

"I don't like that," mumbled the elf.

"What do you see? I miss my Elfic vision." Daryl squinted and stretched his neck almost pulling his head out of his large shoulders. Paddy replied, "Smoke in the north."

Daryl, practical as usual, said, "Bushman making charcoal."

"Not in this part of the realm."

They walked briskly north, in the direction of the fire, under the shabby trees.

"How far is the Sapphire Mountain?" Daryl was getting anxious to start the quest against the evil ones.

Paddy thoughtfully said, "Far enough. It will be days before we get there."

They left the meager forest for one with huge trees. At first it was nice, but the further they went into it, the worse it became.

Daryl disquietedly remarked. "I don't understand why we haven't seen birds, squirrels, rabbits, or any thing alive since we entered this forest."

"I know. I can feel an evil force here. So do the animals. Like the people, they too have departed."

Daryl looked about, "What do you mean, man?'

Paddy, worried, replied. "I fear Zoltar's hands are extended until here."

The feeling of being watched made them shiver and set their skin tingling.

Daryl angrily said, "Wow, the jerk. It's time I put that crown on his evil head."

"Not so loud, man. They, or one of their minions, could hear you. We must hurry before it's too late and the damage becomes irreparable."

With more purpose they walked on the rotten soggy ground which slowed them down, especially Daryl, whose heavy body sank much more than Paddy's. How grateful they were for their elfic boots. The detestable feeling of squashing creeping things under foot was most disturbing. Strange noises were all about; branches cracked behind them. They shivered as growls and hissing raised hair at the back of their neck and arms.

"Let's move faster, man. I wouldn't like to sleep here tonight" said Paddy.

Daryl shivered. "Me, neither."

The light coming through the high trees was very poor. For hours they trampled in the decay of this horrible forest. They became stiff scared because they were now followed by a grunting sound which never got closer.

Paddy said, "Whatever is following us waits for the night to attack."

Daryl sped up but his human legs were not going fast enough to get him away from the predators behind them. "Gosh, what a cheerful thought man," replied Daryl grimacing. They had been eating their biscuits on the run without Daryl complaining.

He knew too well that this was not a place for a picnic. Suddenly darkness covered the forest. Night had come. Daryl tripped on things which seemed to come out of the ground to ensnare his boots. Behind them several pairs of large yellow eyes were much closer. Daryl got frantic and asked with a quivering voice, "Where are we going to sleep? I can't see. I am not an elf anymore! Oh la la."

Paddy reassured his poor friend, "I know. I know. Remember, I am a wizard. If thing get too dangerous, I will help. We are going to find a high tree and sleep at the top."

Indignantly Daryl asked, "And how do you expect me to climb up a tree in the dark?'

"With my help. First, let's find the tree." Behind them the monsters growled furiously. "Here is what I was looking for." They stopped at the foot of a huge oak. "Stay still. I am putting a magic rope around our waists. Hurry, they are almost upon us, man."

Paddy pulled Daryl up. In the dark the poor human tripped. Daryl did his best but clumsily missed branches in the dark. He scratched his knee as his foot slid off from a limb. Nothing in the world would have stopped him.

Down below, trying to shake them off from their refuge, the monsters rocked the tree. Exhausted by his fight to climb up Daryl whined, "Can't you wish us on the top of the tree, man?"

No reply came from Paddy.

The growling was terrible. Furious at their failure to shake the boys down, they set the tree on fire, to roast them like chickens.

Chapter 4

"Wow! They want to kill us, don't they," groaned Daryl.

With a chuckle Paddy said "Don't worry, man. I am going to cool them off. Watch." The young Wizard lifted his hand and heavy freezing rain mixed with large ice pellets fell on the screaming bunch. Howling, they ran away. Immediately the fire was extinguished.

Daryl laughing shouted, "Boo…I don't think we will be bothered any more tonight."

"Maybe not, but don't bet on it. If they can, they will try. Just in case they do I will leave the freezing rain falling during the night."

"Good idea, but it will cool off the temperature. I am glad we have our capes to keep us warm."

They continued up the tree, climbing much slower, to Daryl's relief, to find a larger branch to sleep on. "I am starved. Those biscuits are for the birds! Even perched on a branch, I am not one of them."

"Right, let's have a nice warm soup to start. I am cold and starved, too." Paddy replied cheerfully.

Comfortably installed on a big branch, with a good hot meal on their laps, they forgot the icy rain bellow. The meal over both rolled in their capes. Half asleep, Paddy mumbled, "I'll keep the rope around us in case you fall off."

"Thanks, man. I wouldn't like to find myself swimming in icy water, rescued by the monsters, eager to thaw me out on a roasting fire."

Paddy chuckled. "Goodnight Daryl."

"Goodnight, Paddy.

The night was dark with no stars and only the sound of the freezing rain falling on dried leaves below was heard. The two young friends were asleep. The girl appeared and gently sat beside Daryl and showered him with gold dust. The young human tossed and fell jerking strongly on the rope.

Paddy immediately woke up. "Goldy, what are you doing here?"

The gold girl smiled. "I protected the young human against evil."

Paddy pulled Daryl back on the branch. Stupefied he looked at the young girl. "What a cute little girl. Who is she?"

Paddy replied, "Goldy, Fairy of Gold."

Curious Daryl smiled and asked, "What is she doing here?"

"Protecting you, my friend"

Aghast Daryl said, "Who, me, what for?"

"Yes, you, my old skeptical friend."

Goldy smiled at Daryl

"With gold, she is covering you with gold dust. It is she you saw in your dream."

"Gold dust! Wow. Gosh I am worth my weight in gold then, and I am big," Daryl laughed.

"Don't laugh, you will offend her. It would be bad for you."

"Sorry. I didn't mean any offence."

"If you have enough magic gold dust on you, your presence can't be felt or seen by evil. No one can hurt you."

"Gosh, it's a sort of invisibility, then."

"Yes. Only Goldy and I can see you."

"What about Zoltar or Xary?"

"They can't see you or feel your presence. Goldy is a powerful Fairy, and not a little girl, as you see her."

"What do you mean, not a little girl? She is a lovely little one!" Daryl smiled at the wee Fairy.

"Oh, no. When your elfic vision is restored, you will see her. Goodnight Goldy. Please keep watching over my dear human friend."

The little girl smiled and left.

"Wow! Never before has a Fairy protected me," whispered Daryl under his breath.

"I know, but you belong to the realm. Now, being human again, you are vulnerable to evil power. You don't have anything to protect or help you during the Quest, except me."

"That is plenty, and good enough for me, man."

"Thanks, Daryl. Luckily for you, you now have Goldy, too."

"I don't think I need a girl to protect me." He made a face shrugging his shoulders.

"Sorry, you can't refuse her help."

Daryl sputtered, asking, "Why not'?"

"I told you. It would he a great offence and dangerous for you if she turns against you."

"Gosh." Daryl stubbornly repeated, "I don't need a girl to protect me. I am big enough to do it myself." He turned and went back to sleep.

Paddy smiled, remembering Daryl's fights with his sister on earth. He chuckled softly. He hadn't changed. Girls were still not his favorite thing. However, he was lucky to have Goldy on his side.

The young elf grinned in the dark. "I wouldn't mind being the object of her attention."

Below, the freezing rain was still falling. The night had been quiet. Before they left, Paddy stopped the rain and warmed the frozen ground with a spell and started down the trunk. Daryl pessimistically asked, "Aren't you afraid the monsters will he waiting for us?"

"No. They are evil things from Zoltar and Xary. They only come out at night."

"Good, I am glad to hear that. Now how about helping me down?" Daryl sighed.

They flew down. Daryl's cape had kept its magic even after he became human. Through a dim light from between the trees green grass and small flowers had appeared growing around the giant oak. Paddy's magic rain and warm spell gave the once beautiful forest the chance to bloom again.

"See, Paddy, flowers. This is magic!"

"Yes, it is, but good magic."

They moved north. The swampy forest had a most unpleasant smell of rotten decaying matter. "I will be glad to get out of here," mumbled Daryl, trampling in the mud. He tripped on a hidden root and fell flat on his face in the disgusting stuff.

"Soon we will be out."

"Hope so. " Daryl shook the foul stuff from his hands and wiped his face clean with his cape. "Soon won't be soon enough for me, I tell you." He was stiff scared by the whispers around them. Bravely he tried, in a supreme effort, to ignore the disturbing sounds by walking faster, but it was impossible. The weight of his large human body was too great, so he fixed his attention on not falling again. His boots, sucked by the mud made each step a battle. Paddy, being lighter glided on the stuff. Darkness once more began to cover the forest.

"Don't tell me, man, we will have to sleep here again," whined Daryl.

"No. We can see the sky above us, man. We are going to be out any minute now." He was right. They were at the edge of the forest. From behind a terrible roar made them jump. Paddy turned around and was almost nose to nose with two huge yellow eyes shining in the dark. A giant Sorky, a large lizard with a tail as long and thin as a whip, faced them. The monster swung the whip above its head. Paddy screamed to his friend, "Move. Run, man!" At the same time the elf took off as fast as he could, but not fast enough. The monster's tail snapped ensnaring Paddy. It pulled the light elf up in the air shaking him like a rag.

Shocked, Daryl abruptly halted and grabbed his sword. "No, no, go away. I can manage," said Paddy.

Chapter 5

"Remember, man, it can't see me."

The monster tried to crush his victim by throwing him against a tree. Paddy quickly stopped the swing of the tail. Daryl silently slid under the beast and thrust his sword into its stomach. With a sharp "clack" the sword snapped in two. The magic of his sword was not strong enough. He couldn't pierce the carapace of the evil creature. The young wizard managed to get one hand free. He took his sword and cut the tail off the body. In a puff of smoke the monster disappeared.

Paddy fell down. "Ouch," he said, getting up rubbing his behind.

"Wow! What was that?"

"A Sorky, one of Zoltar's creatures."

"Oh, boy, I am glad your sword was powerful enough to destroy that beast and that we are almost out of this place. Now I don't have any sword. It was a good sword. She served me well at the academy," he said, sadly.

"No problem. Here is another one and by the way, thanks for coming to my rescue." Paddy had conjured a sword, a real beauty.

"You are welcome. What are squires for, anyway, if they don't help in time of need?" He looked at the sword. "Wow, thanks, man. She is grand. Mine was one I got from the academy, but I loved her feel in my hand." Delighted Daryl swiped the new sword in the air then he glanced behind. Apprehension enlarged his round blue eyes and he quickly slid the sword into the scabbard and walked away. Bright moonlight helped him to see the flat country covered with small bushes, and made his walk easy. They traveled fast. Paddy wanted to put lots of distance between them and the nasty forest. Daryl was silent, suddenly he said, "It's wonderful it worked. The monster didn't see me. I didn't believe in that gold stuff you know."

"You brave fool! You came to my rescue with that ridiculous little sword of yours, not certain of your invisibility?" Paddy slapped his friend on the back, "Wonderful buddy of mine."

"Of course, I couldn't let that horrible thing kill you!"

Paddy chuckled. "It wouldn't have killed me. I am a Wizard. Remember that, before you put your life at risk for me. Okay, man?"

"I will," whispered Daryl feeling miserable.

"Don't be sad. I must remind you once in a while, right? Look, here is a perfect place to rest and have a good meal. We deserve it. How does that sound?"

In the wink of an eye Daryl forgot his misery and clapped his hands happily. "Food. I am starved."

Paddy chuckled. He knew his buddy and exactly how to make him forget all his troubles. They crawled inside a thick hush. There, a bare place on the ground covered with dead leaves offered them a perfect spot to eat and sleep in security. With a sigh of pleasure they lay down. "How wonderful to rest and not on a branch. My bones and my spirit wouldn't have taken another night like the last one, man."

"You are right. First, I will put spells around the bush. That way we will eat and sleep, completely safe from Zoltar and Xary's creatures."

Daryl, pondering, watched the young wizard. How wonderful it was to have such a friend. The human chuckled. Who could have told him, when he was on earth, that little shy Paddy would one day be a powerful Wizard in the Elfic Realm. A realm he didn't believe in. He had thought Paddy had lost his mind.

The young wizard sighed with satisfaction. "There, now we can enjoy our meal."

It was a perfect supper. Daryl ate a lot. When scared, Daryl afterward always ate like a horse. Paddy watched him, remembering the times Daryl had been punished by his parents, going without dessert because of his mischief. How good it was to have his buddy back, just like in the old time when they were kids.

Much too tired they didn't talk. Quietly, they rolled in their capes and went to sleep. The day had been a trying one. Suddenly Paddy woke. His pointed ears quivered. Cries, howling, and shouting, resounded in the night. A band of Urks was passing in the distance. They were too far away to smell them. Reassured, he went back to sleep. Next morning, rested, they ate a solid breakfast. As they came out from their shelter they noticed large footprints around the bush.

"Wow! What is that? I am glad you had us protected last night."

"Yes, so do I. We have been visited. Urks, sent by Zoltar or his ally Xary. I heard a large band passing quite far away during the night. This was a small group, investigating, knowing someone was near. Because of the spell they couldn't feel our presence, so they left."

"I hope those monsters don't show up during the day." Fear was in Daryl's eyes.

"Unfortunately, they do. Zoltar, with Xary's help, has started to extend his evil hand to the South. I wonder what we are going to find in the North?" said Paddy thoughtfully.

They soon entered in hills with a forbidding look. A brown sickly mist floated around giving a strange appearance to the country. Hours later they arrived at a village where almost everyone was ill in bed with a mysterious sickness. A chill ran in the boys' bones as villagers, walking painfully, came to meet them. A pale tall elf moved forward, wobbling on his legs. Sadly he said, "I cannot say welcome strangers. You do come at a bad time. The entire village is sick, and our young children die, and as you can see, the adults are doing very poorly." The elf looked like being ready to give up the ghost. The sickly old one continued, "Us, the old folks, are barely alive."

"What a pitiful sight. Poor people" whispered Daryl sadly. Paddy didn't answer. He walked to the Elder's house. No one was there.

Quickly they went to the Chief's home indicated by the sick old fellow. Legs almost buckling under his emaciated body a short elf opened the door.

Paddy asked, "Are you the Chief Elder?"

"Yes, I am, for whatever that means now." A sad smile came upon his pale lips. "Welcome, strangers. Come in."

The boys entered in a nice room with the curtains closed. The Chief explained, "My wife is sick. Excuse the darkness. The light hurts her eyes."

Paddy extremely concerned asked, "When did this illness happen in your village, Chief?"

"Two weeks ago. Zoltar came to enroll our young men and boys in his forces. They refused. 'He can't take us by force,' they said. No, but his vengeance was terrible! Smiling cruelly he made a large circle of his arms, and put a spell of slow death upon the village, and then left, laughing and mockingly waving his hand."

"How many died?" Daryl asked. A look of fear was in his eyes.

"Ten youngsters. We the oldest, can fight the spell, but the wee ones can't. Bit by bit our strength is getting weaker."

Paddy thoughtfully asked, "Do you think, Chief, you could gather all your people, right now, on the square, sick or not? All of them. This is extremely important that all be there."

Chapter 6

"Why? The ones in bed are so sick," he replied, with tears in his eyes.

"Listen, Chief, I am a Wizard. I will remove the spell from the village, but I need everyone present. One missing and my work will be for naught."

"I will call my people." The Chief Elder opened the door trembling on his legs.

"May I help you, Sir?" asked Daryl taking his arm.

"Thank you, young man. Surely I need your help. I am not certain I can do it alone."

They came back later, the poor chief completely exhausted. "They will be here. It's going to be hard. My people are courageous. If only they could use the donkeys, but it will be too exhausting for them to harness the little beasts."

"I can help the ones who need it the most, and harness the donkeys, Sir," said Daryl, eagerly.

"Wonderful, man. Do it. Hurry," said Paddy.

"Thank you boy, one of us will have to come with you and show where the donkeys are." Daryl left with a younger elf.

Paddy helped the Chief and his wife to the square, where they sat waiting for the other villagers to arrive. Sadly he watched them holding onto each other, bravely dragging their feet painfully in the dirt. A few were in donkey carts with sick children. It was a pitiful bunch of folks. The Chief's children came out of their house, arms around each other. The oldest son was painfully carrying his little sister, the youngest child of the family. When they reached the square, Paddy the Wizard asked, "Is everyone here?"

The Chief counted his people and stopped. "No. Two are missing. Orf and his wife Zita. They live at the south edge of the village."

"I will get them, " said Daryl ready to leave. He had just returned with several donkeys and their families sitting in the carts. The human boy asked, "Who's strong enough to show me the way?'

"I will come with you," said the eldest son of the chief.

"Good boy," Daryl took his hand.

They left, the boy in the donkey cart. At the house of Orf and Zita, Daryl explained what was going to happen and that they had to come or the spell couldn't be broken. The old elves, helped by the two boys, climbed up on the donkey cart. They arrived at the square, trembling and shaking. Daryl helped Zita down gently and sat her on a bench beside her husband.

Daryl, smiling at the couple, said to the Chief, "Orf didn't want to leave his wife. That's why they were not here."

Benches had been brought into the square by the ones who could do the carrying and set in a circle. Paddy asked everyone to sit holding hands. The youngsters were to sit on the dirt holding hands forming another circle in the center of the large one.

The young Wizard walked into the center of the small circle and gently bowed his head. Whispering, he turned slowly extending his arms like wings ready to fly. Then he brought them up above his head in the shape of an arrow and let his elbows come halfway down. Once more the young wizard opened his arms horizontally. At that instant thousands of sparks came out of his fingers showering the elves with brilliant colors. Paddy turned fast and faster. Out of his fingers rushed a strong wind. Lightning encircled the village and the surrounding countryside. Paddy let his arms drop down slowly and bowed his head. The wind, the sparks and the lightning disappeared. A deep silence filled the village.

Suddenly the stillness was broken by the children's laughter, as they started playing in the circle. The adults were silent under the charm of the marvelous things they had witnessed. The little ones, screaming joyously, ran to their parents. "Look Mommy, Daddy, we are not sick any more."

The same miracle had been performed on the adults, now strong on their legs. They hugged each other. Paddy and Daryl smiled, watching their happiness.

"Man, you are wonderful."

"Not really. Any good Wizard would have done the same, and I am getting stronger."

"I am glad your power is increasing. I always marvel at your exploits. What about the village, man?"

With a bright smile Paddy looked at him and turned to the Chief Elder who was rejoicing with his family. "Chief, I have protected your village and the country around against any evil attack from Zoltar or Xary."

"Do you hear that, my good friends? We don't have to fear death or sickness any more. The young Prince Wizard of the Promised Valley has freed us from our bonds of death."

In unison the elves cried, "Thank you, thank you Sir."

The Chief said, "We want to honor our liberators. Let's celebrate this wonderful event and prepare a feast."

"What a great idea," said Daryl, nudging his buddy.

Paddy laughed joyously, letting the tension he had been under go. "Ah Daryl, you are a marvelous friend."

The women ran, holding hands, joyously exchanging ideas for the feast. The banquet was on its way to be prepared. The men, talking loudly, were putting up tiny lights entwined in the garlands of flowers brought by the giggling children. Night came. Under the brilliant lights set around the square the colorful flowers shone like precious jewels. The young girls, helped by the ladies, spread lace tablecloth upon the long tables with big bouquets at the center. Later on, to Daryl's delight, the delicious aroma of food filled the evening air. The celebration ended in a joyous dance.

Suddenly thunder and lightning were above the village. Sulfurous vapors filled the pure night air.

Terrified, the elves screamed, "Zoltar! Zoltar is going to destroy us!"

Paddy stood up and yelled, "Quiet, friends. Don't be afraid. Zoltar can't harm you, except to frighten you. Your village and the land around are well protected against his evil doings, and right now he is showing off."

Zoltar again shook the earth with thunder and bolts of lightning, all the orchestra of his great furor. He tried wind and rain upon the party without any more success. Paddy, tired of all that noise, moved his hand above his head. The noises stopped. The elves laughed at Zoltar's failure and cheerfully went on with their dancing until very late. Paddy and Daryl were to sleep at the Chief's home. Paddy said, "Thank you for your kindness. We will leave quietly, early in the morning, to continue our quest."

"Don't talk about kindness, Prince. We are in debt to you and are yours forever."

"No, Chief. You only belong to yourself. I gratefully accept you as my friends, but no more."

"Thank you, Prince. Goodnight."

"Goodnight, Chief."

Chapter 7

At the horizon, a few hours later, a gold line announced the coming of the sun. The village was deeply asleep. Silent as cats on the prowl, the friends left. Paddy's sharp eyes saw in the north the large plume of smoke they had noticed days ago. Zoltar's storm from the previous night had soaked the ground around the village. Deeply absorbed in their own thoughts they walked quietly.

Hours later the lush green country was far behind them. Sand dunes and rocks made walking difficult. Their feet bumped on sharp stones, or sank in the sand.

Suddenly Daryl screamed. "I am being pulled under by my feet."

Paddy yelled, "Quick, protected your face with your hood."

A giant sand octopus had his tentacles around Daryl's legs and seconds later he was gone. Paddy moved his arms toward where Daryl had disappeared. A whirlwind sucked the sand, showing the monster holding Daryl, who was struggling to get free. Paddy zapped the beast with a lightning bolt.

Helped by his friend Daryl shakily came out of the pit. With an unsteady voice he said, "What a horrible experience." The poor human was trembling like a leaf in a high wind. He fell on his knees.

"Yes, I am glad you had your cape on. Without it you would be dead, choked by the sand."

Daryl, aghast, asked, "But where did that thing come from?"

"They live in these dunes, and usually are harmless. Zoltar and Xary have made them vicious. It's too bad I had to destroy one. There are not many. We must be careful so this won't happen again."

Terrified, Daryl asked, "How will you know if there is one?"

"They make circles of five holes in the sand to let the air into their den."

"I didn't see them." Daryl's shoulders had a nervous shiver.

"Neither did I. We were not looking for them. Now, man, we know they can be deadly."

"But why do they live here? There is nothing to eat."

"Oh yes, lizards, salamanders, snakes, and all sorts of other creatures. This time he was going to have a good meal on you, you are fat and juicy enough," Paddy said with a chuckle.

Daryl made a grimace and gave Paddy a nasty look. He didn't like the joke. The human boy walked away, mumbling and suspiciously looking at the ground.

"Better stay with me, man. Don't walk ahead. Let me lead. I can see the holes better than you can. Now we are aware of this danger we can avoid it."

Daryl stopped dead and without arguing slowed down to walk beside Paddy. He was still sore about Paddy's remark.

They had been in the dunes, fighting the slippery sand for hours, and darkness had come. Daryl became worried.

"Where are we going to sleep? I don't want to have one of your friendly beasts dig under my bed, pulling me down to cuddle me on its bosom," said Daryl with a sour grin on his face.

"Don't worry, man. I am going to make a flying station for us."

"Just what I need. What do you mean by flying?" Daryl was not too keen about Paddy's idea.

"We will be up in the air in a sort of bubble."

"Did you notice, by any chance, that those things have long arms and surely will reach us up there." Daryl was in a bad mood.

"No, not with spells around the station." Paddy made the shape of a large hoop on the ground and raised his arms. "Stay close to me." Paddy mumbled mysterious words. Daryl found himself sitting high up in the sky on a platform with a transparent dome. Satisfied, Paddy with a smirk on his face said, "There. No one will come to bother us."

"Well, if you say so." Then his good spirits came back, and with a grin he said admiringly, "Wow. You are something man."

It was large and comfortable inside, long enough to stretch, high enough to stand on your knees. Most of all high up in the sky to prevent any attack. A big smile flourished on Daryl face. "I am starved. How about eating, man?"

At Paddy's command a good hot meal appeared. Tired they went to sleep on comfortable bedding. Stars shone on a deep blue sky, and a light breeze gently rocked the station. The boys slept.

Daryl awoke feeling sick. Putting a hand on his mouth he pleaded, "Paddy, will you stop this thing from moving? It's upsetting my stomach. I don't like it." But Paddy was asleep. "Come on man I am going to be sick." Daryl begged again, "Please make it stop moving."

The wizard didn't answer, evil was in the air.

Paddy's powerful eyes explored the sky. Among the shining silvery stars shone a reddish one. He whispered, "There you are, Zcltar." Quickly he sent stronger spells around the station and stopped it from moving.

"Ah, thanks, man" whispered Daryl.

Reassured the Wizard returned to sleep but not for long. They were brutally awakened by something shaking them furiously. The enormous paws of a dragon were embracing the dome. Daryl, terror in his blue eyes, and a greenish glow of fear upon his face, asked in a shaky voice, "Did you say, man, you had strong spells around the bubble to protect us. Wow, see that monster!" He shivered.

"Yes! Relax. I reinforced them, and they are extremely strong. I saw Zoltar watching us in the night. With the hope of destroying us he has changed himself into a dragon."

"But he is going to break the dome!" screamed Daryl.

"No, don't worry. His power is not strong enough to do it. He will be only frustrated," Paddy said, with a chuckle.

"What if Xary comes along and joins forces with him?

Paddy said, "Don't fret, go to sleep."

The monster realized he was going nowhere, and in a burst of flaming rage he left.

Paddy grinned. "See, I told you."

Daryl sighed, "I started to feel uncomfortable in the arms of that dragon. After the embrace of the octopus, that is too much love for me in one day."

"What's the matter, man? Don't you like to be loved? I must admit I didn't like it either."

"I hope Zoltar is going to leave us alone now."

"Don't count on it. Right now he is probably thinking how he can shake us out of the sky."

Paddy was right. A terrible wind cane up tossing them furiously. "I am going to be sick," whined Daryl, who had turned pale as a ghost. Lightning zapped the dome. Quickly they pulled their hoods down to protect their eyes against the glare from the lightning. Zoltar used the power of a tornado to crash the dome on the ground, but the only thing he managed to do was to roll the station and make poor Daryl sick. Paddy promptly touched him to stop his upset stomach. The sorcerer's rage was unleashed for hours. Then, with a last blast of thunder and lightning he left.

They were exhausted. With a flip of his hand Paddy cleaned up Daryl's mess. They flopped on their mattress and fell asleep. When they opened their eyes the sun was high in the sky. "How are you feeling, man?"

With a grin Daryl replied, "I am all right thank you. Ready to eat a good breakfast. After last night I am an empty bag, my stomach clinging to my sore ribs."

Their meal over, Paddy brought the station gently down. He didn't want to upset Daryl's stomach again. He dismissed their shelter. The force of the storm had changed the appearance of the dunes. They were almost flat. In his tempestuous rage, Zoltar had done them a great favor.

Paddy grinned "Thank you. Now I can see much further to avoid the Sand Octopus."

"Good." Daryl rubbed his hands in satisfaction.

"Yes, but we still have a long day to walk in this desert."

"That does not make me jump for joy. However with your eyes, we will escape Zoltar's pets."

Chapter 8

So they went on zigzagging to avoid the holes. On the horizon Paddy saw coming toward them a long line of people and animals. The young Wizard watched their progress closely fearing the Octopus would attack. They walked faster to join the party. When they arrived, Paddy said, "Greetings and salutations, friends. Where are you going, wandering in this dangerous sand?" he asked the Chief of the party.

"Dangerous? What do you mean, stranger? Our people have been crossing this desert for thousands of years!"

"I am sure you have, but Zoltar has put a terrible spell on the Sand Octopus. My friend, here, almost lost his life to one when viciously attacked."

The chief sighed, "That evil one is everywhere. He burned our village to the ground when we refused to join forces with him."

"Then that was the smoke we saw coining from the North."

"Perhaps. Unfortunately, he has burned many. We are fleeing from his deadly claws."

"Did you lose some of your people?"

"No, Zoltar, I presume, has other plans for us."

"That is possible. Remember what I just told you. He has put spells to kill on the Sand Octopus. Where are you going Chief?"

"South to the Realm of the Promised Valley. We know peace is still there."

"You are right, and it will be forever. I am Prince Patrick son of King Ariol of the Promised Valley. My father will be happy to receive your people."

The Chief Elder bowed to the Prince. "Thank you very much. If I am not too indiscreet, what are you doing, Prince, in this troubled part of the Realms?"

"I am here with my squire to return peace and order to the Realms."

"Just the two of you?" asked the Chief, baffled.

"Yes, we are quite capable of doing so." Paddy smiled. "Now I repeat, be aware of the Octopus. I am sure you know how to recognize where they are."

"Thank you. Yes, we do, Prince. We are used to going across this land. Don't worry."

"Have a nice journey. Please tell my Father you have seen us and all is well. Soon we will be at the Dragon Lord's dwelling."

"You mean the great one who lives in the high mountains? Farewell Prince." The party left waving goodbye.

One hour later they passed the burned village, and sadly walked away. A while later finally the dunes were behind them. The sight of a large river rolling through fields of wheat refreshed their eyes which had been burned by the heat that had been reflected from the sand. In the distance the towering Sapphire Mountains' heads in the fluffy white clouds were facing them.

"Soon we will be at the Lord's lair. The highest peak in that range is where he dwells," said Paddy.

"It's about time. I thought it was a fable, and that after all, it didn't exist.'

"Oh yes, man. You saw the Lord at my father's palace. He turned you to your mortal state again, don't you remember? The Dragon Lord is the Greatest, oldest Wizard of all the Realms, and he dwells there." Paddy showed the Sapphire Mountain."

Daryl red in the face for his stupidity replied, "Of course I do, hooray! I will get that Magic Crown."

Paddy smiled at his buddy. "You bet you will, and crown Zoltar with it, to his doom."

"What a pleasure it will be to do that. All those poor people with their villages burned down. It's horrible.'"

They crossed huge fields trampled, destroyed by the Urks. Horror written upon their faces they looked at each other and moved away, tired and depressed. After a while green hills rolled softly down under their feet. The country was cheerfully covered with bushes full of red berries to the delight of chirping birds. Painfully, they dragged their feet with the hope of finding a place to rest. At last, relieved, they walked into a luscious prairie marked by tiny game trails. The aroma from thyme and flowers filled the evening air, and both breathed deeply.

Daryl excitedly said, "What a pleasant place. We will find a comfortable spot."

Paddy smiled, watching a little rabbit munching a plant of thyme and another quickly rubbing his nose with his front his front paws. "This is perfect."

Daryl was showing a splendid bush in horseshoe shape, as if to say, *This is going to make a nice shelter, man.*

"Good." Paddy flopped on the ground. "Ah! My feet are worn out," he said.

"Wow, I am done, finished, too." Daryl joined Paddy on the grass and stretched his arms and legs. "Gosh, how nice and peaceful it is here, no evil around."

"For good reason, man. This is the Lord's domain. The evil ones wouldn't dare to come with their minions."

"Look, look," whispered Daryl. Curiously a little family of rabbits was watching them. Small quivering noses and black mustaches were up in the air with long pink ears up. Daryl smiled. "Aren't they lovely?"

Paddy moved his hand slowly toward them, and a large patch of clover bloomed beneath their feet. Surprised, the little ones sniffed it and quickly ate, now completely unconcerned about the intruders.

The young Wizard sent a spell of silence. "There, they won't be scared by our talking and will stay with us."

"Thanks, man, I love them. When father was killing one, I always ran away. They are gentle little creatures and so pretty," said Daryl.

"I know. Now it is our turn to eat. I think we are hungry, too."

Paddy laughed "You bet I am? I am starving!" Daryl licked his lips. "Well here it is."

A delicious odor came to Daryl's nose. "Wow! You are the best cook I have ever known, man."

Paddy laughed. "It's not I, silly, but the chef at my Father's Palace."

Mouth full, Daryl said, "I will have to give him my compliments when we return."

Paddy with a chuckle replied, "Do that. But you eat his cuisine every day at the Palace. He will think you are nuts."

With a twinkle in his eyes he replied. "Ah yes, but it was not the same. When you eat under protocol, etiquette changes the taste." He chuckled.

"I don't understand you, man."

Daryl laughed. "So what's new. You never did, remember?"

Paddy sighed as he thought about all the things Daryl had done when they were young boys on Earth Realm. It was true that he couldn't understand his friend, but he loved him just the same.

Their meal finished, they talked and laughed in the silent company of the little ones eating what was left of their clover. Hop, hop, quietly they went away. Full, Daryl yawned, pulled his hood down, rolled in his cape, and fell asleep. Paddy, too, did the same.

In the moonlight, far away in the velvety sky, shone a white puffy cloud, surrounded by thousands of stars. The white cloud came closer, large and fluffy like fresh snow. A whirlwind rose and gently took up the sleeping friends. Later they opened their eyes in a splendid room of gold and green velvet.

"Where are we?" Paddy wondered. "I don't feel any evil around us, only happiness." A bell rang and a young boy with a tray of food entered.

"Where are we, boy?" asked Paddy. No reply came. After putting the tray on a small table the young fellow bowed, smiled, and silently left.

"I don't like that. Let's go and look for ourselves." Paddy pulled on Daryl's sleeve.

"One minute, first things first. Let me eat those crescents and drink my chocolate, please."

Paddy grinned and said, "If I were you, I wouldn't do that before we know who's keeping us here."

Daryl sighed, looking with envy at the hot chocolate.

Paddy walked to the door and found that it was not locked.

Chapter 9

The hall where they had entered was in white marble and gold. From the far end of the hall songs, laughter and music reached them. "What's that?" said Daryl.

"I have an idea, I think."

Paddy frowned as a large fellow came out from a side door and said, "I am Buloo, Genie of the Cloud of Happiness."

"No, not you again. What are you doing here'?" asked Paddy sharply.

"I need you. Come and see." The Genie opened a door. In the center of a large room turned the magic carrousel Paddy knew too well. Children, boys and girls were laughing.

Flabbergasted, Daryl asked, "Who are those children? Where do they come from?"

"I made them happy. I need you to help."

"Doing what? Stealing them from their parents?" asked Paddy with anger.

"Only from those who have too many," replied the Genie, smiling.

The carousel was not full and showed many empty places.

"What! Do you think that is a reason?" Paddy was furious.

"Yes, they are happy here. My carousel is not full. I need you to help to get more children. You are an elf. You know where to find them."

Paddy replied, "You cannot put enchantment upon us elves. It won't work. The children will only be crying. You have put a spell upon the other children to be happy. Remove the spell and let them choose and they will gladly return to their families."

"No, no, certainly not. They are happy here, and they make me happy, too. They have good food, lots of fun, and friends."

"Friends? How can you call them friends? They don't even speak to each other. Do you really think this is enough to be happy? You are not going to keep them here. I won't permit it." Paddy was getting furious.

"How can you make me return them? I am a Genie! You are nothing!" He laughed, and his jelly stomach bounced.

"Oh, yes! That's where you are wrong, my fellow! I am a Wizard, and will have them returned at once to their homes!" Paddy, to make his point, threw a bolt of fire at the Genie's feet.

Surprised, the big guy jumped back. "Why did I bring you here?" he screamed, and as if were controlling a puppet, he tried to overpower Paddy as he gestured with symbols in the air.

The young wizard laughed, because the genie's power was not strong enough to do anything to him. Harshly he said, "That is your problem. Now, let's send those children home."

"No, no, you can't do that," pleaded the Genie, crying.

"Oh, yes, I can and I will. Find other toys to play with, and I hope for your sake that you will never cross my way again. Twice is plenty for me," Paddy growled. He faced the Carrousel, and raised his hands. Instantly the room was silent, no more children. Only the sobbing of the Genie and the music filled the empty room. The children were gone, back to their families by Paddy's magic. The teen Wizard once more moved his hand leaving the Genie to his grief.

They returned to their camp and quickly departed. Paddy watched the cloud, ready to respond in case the fellow should become hostile. From above, a soft rain came down. The Genie was still crying about the loss of his pleasure. The young friends walked away briskly.

"Let's stop. I am starved Paddy! This morning, you didn't want me to eat my breakfast at the Genie's place. I can't continue on with an empty stomach." The rain had stopped, and Daryl sulked and sat on the trunk of a large dead tree on the grass.

Paddy laughed. "You always surprise me, Daryl. Your stomach, indeed, is your master."

"Yup, and a demanding one, man."

"All right." The young Elf sat beside him on the dead tree. The aroma of breakfast tickled Daryl's nose. A good meal lay between them. "Ah, now you are talking, man, that's better." Daryl rubbed his hands with pleasure. His cheeks bulging with food, he looked far away at the tall proud Sapphire Mountain standing in the midst of the clouds. Doubtfully he asked "Do you know how to get there, man?"

"No. But we will find a trail. Don't worry."

"Ah."

Filled with a good meal they quickly left. After several hours of traveling in a pleasant country of pine trees, where the ground was covered by needles, they felt the urge to have fun. Challenging each other, laughing they slid down the hill. For a few minutes they forgot their cares and just enjoyed themselves. Then they carried on and speedily approached the mountain and found a narrow opening in the hills with a steep trail leading to the foot of the mountain itself.

Darkness now was upon them. Paddy searched for a cave where they could spend the night. "Here is a place that is perfect for us." It was a small cave with a sandy floor. They both lay flat and stretched their tired legs on the cool sand. The long day had been taking its toll on them. Their brief meal over, hoods down, they rolled in their capes. With the sweet perfume of pine and lulled by the gentle sound of birds saying goodnight, minutes later they were deeply asleep.

The next morning they were surprised to find themselves in a large room soberly furnished, with gold velvet drapes on the windows. "'Now, where are we? Not again at Buloo's, I hope," said Daryl.

"No, this is the dwelling of The Dragon Lord."

"How do you know, man?"

"I am a wizard, and this is wizard ground."

"Ah."

The door gently opened, and an old Elf, followed by a young one pushing a silver cart entered, with a large breakfast.

"Greetings, Prince Patrick and Daryl. I am Yarny, Chamberlain of his Lordship, The Dragon Lord. His Lordship will receive you later. I will be back to escort you to Him," he said.

"Thank you, Yarny. Please convey my salutations to his Lordship," said Paddy.

The elf bowed to Paddy and left with the boy. Anxious to see the Dragon Lord, they ate quickly. Paddy paced the room waiting for the return of the Chamberlain, who, to their great disappointment, came back one hour later.

Respectfully he bowed to Paddy. "Prince, if you please, follow me." He walked out going through halls of green and black marble. Along the walls were bronze candelabras standing on dark ebony chests and large green chairs with a small table on the side. Several wooden doors, beautifully carved with flowers and birds, opened mysteriously along their passage. Daryl nervously watched over his shoulder. At last the Chamberlain stopped at a heavy bronze door with engraved runes and symbols.

The old personage touched a gold leaf on the left side of the door. Silently it opened, showing a very large room with dark red velvet drapes, and oak furniture. Simplicity prevailed. Gold torches on the walls gave a soft light. An extremely large double glass door opened onto a huge balcony of black granite facing the luscious valley below.

The Old Wizard was standing by the window, watching a shadow coming slowly from the north. Without turning his head toward the visitors he said, "Welcome Prince Patrick and Daryl, human friend. I am glad you have arrived. Zoltar, with Xary's help, is fast extending their darkness to the south."

"The south," whispered Daryl shivering.

"Yes, My Lord, we have encountered some of their handiwork," replied Paddy.

"The moment has come for you, Daryl, to receive the Magic Crown of Sapphire. Come with me. We must not waste any more time." His large white robe billowing behind, The Dragon Lord walked to a carved panel in his chamber. Mysterious words spewed out his mouth, a small door silently opened to a steep flight of stairs.

Chapter 10

The Wizard took a torch from the wall and it immediately flared to life. They went down to the bottom of the stairs to another small door. Once more the Dragon Lord whispered secret words, and the door opened making a screeching noise. Quickly, the Lord erased the disturbing sound with his hand.

In the darkness, upon a pedestal of gold, resting on a red velvet cushion, the Magic Crown of Sapphire softly shone under a crystal dome. The Dragon Lord brought from inside his long sleeve a dark velvet bag with a gold string and abruptly said, “Here Squire, put the crown in this bag.” Daryl, aghast, looked at Paddy. A shiver ran down his back, and hesitantly he took the little bag. The two Wizards anxiously watched the mortal.

Daryl approached the pedestal, and fear appeared in his eyes. Barely breathing, with shaking hands, he removed the crystal dome, set it upon the ground, and took the Magic Crown. Quickly, the human boy placed it into the velvet bag and sighed as he pulled the gold strings. Then Daryl, with trembling knees, bent down, took the crystal dome, and replaced it on the pedestal. Proud of himself, now smiling, he walked to the Dragon Lord and stretched his arm out to give the bag to the Wizard. “Here, your Lordship, I did it.”

"You certainly did, friend." The Wizard backed up. "No, I must not touch it, only you can. Now, tie the bag around your waist. Listen, when close to Zoltar remove the bag. Not before! Only at that time, otherwise Xary or Zoltar will feel the presence of the crown."

Daryl carefully tied the bag around himself.

"Hear me well, Prince Patrick. Under no circumstances must you touch the crown. If you do so, it will kill you, or maybe worse, make of you a brain dead Prince."

The Wizard, the mortal, and Paddy turned around and climbed up the small stairs to the Dragon Lord's chamber. As they entered a large shadow darkened the room. On the large balcony at the open window stood a huge dragon blowing a jet of fire at Paddy, not knowing Daryl was the bearer of the magic to destroy him. Quickly the Wizard gestured and snuffed the flames before the young elf could react. The dragon flew away, but the Lord ran to the window, spread his arms, and in one leap was on the ledge of the balcony. With a terrible roar, a dragon, twice as big as Zoltar, flew away.

Daryl watched the two monsters fighting in the sky with amazement. The young Wizard didn't dare interfere. That would have been an insult to the Lord. They disappeared from the boys' eyes behind a large black cloud created by Zoltar to hide. Bright red, orange, and blue flames pierced through, and smoke filled the air. Badly burned, roaring with fury, the evil one left. The big dragon made a majestic landing on the balcony and changed back to the Dragon Lord under Daryl's admiring eyes.

"Wow! Gosh, what a battle you fought, your Lordship," said the mortal, amazed by what he had seen. Smiling the tall 0ld Wizard looked at him. "Zoltar knows you are on a quest after him and wants to destroy you, Paddy. He doesn't know that you, Daryl, are the real danger. Because of Goldy's magic he can't see you. Neither does he know about the Crown you are bearing."

"Does he know what we are plotting against him?" asked Paddy.

"No, only that you want to stop his evil doings. Don't talk aloud about your plans, he may hear you. We don't want him to know your Squire is with you. He has to believe you are alone. Speak to Daryl in silent elfic tongue. Daryl, you can still do it. I haven't removed it from you knowledge as you will need it for the quest. In my dwelling he can't hear us. He has no power whatsoever here. That's why he attacked from outside. One more thing. He can't read your minds, either. Prince Patrick put a spell of silence around you. The less he knows about your intentions, the better."

"I will, your Lordship. It is comforting to know that he can't read our minds," replied Paddy.

"Depart immediately for the Dwarves kingdom. Zoltar is taking care of his wounds for the moment. King Orug will help you to get to the Evil Valley." The Dragon Lord moved his hand, and quietly the door of his chamber opened. The old Chamberlain came in. "Farewell mortal. With Prince Patrick you are in good hands. He is young but already a good Wizard."

"I know, your Lordship."

The two young friends bowed to the Dragon Lord and left. Quietly the door closed behind them. Without a word the old elf took another stairway, not the previous one they had traveled with the Lord. The little party descended for a long time to a small landing where another set of stairs greeted them and continued its course down further into the bowels of the mountain.

The ancient one spoke. "At the bottom of this stairway you will find a door with Elfic Runes. That is your way into the Dwarves kingdom. Farewell, Prince. Good luck, Mortal."

The Chamberlain bowed and turned around, taking the torch with him and leaving the young men in the dark. For Daryl, a human, it was pitch black, but no problem for the elf who could see in the dark. The human boy quickly fumbled in his pocket to find his elfic stone. "There I have it. Now I can see something." He secured the leather band around his forehead.

"The old guy surely does not talk too much."

Paddy smiled at the remark. "Let's go, Daryl. We won't accomplish anything by staying here."

"Nope"

The long stairs were winding down like a corkscrew. Daryl's elfic stone gave a little blue light cheering up the way. Walking in the darkness of those Wizard's corridors was not (and had never been) one of Daryl's favorites hobbies. "I will be glad to get out of this rat hole," he mumbled.

The Dragon Lord's dwelling was at the top of the highest peak of the range so it was a long way down. The stairs wound their way through the mountain. Strangely enough the air was light and not stuffy. The Dragon Lord had provided a safe environment for the young men to travel. At last, hours later, they reached the bottom of this endless staircase. As they had been told, a bronze door was facing them with Elfic Runes engraved upon it.

"Wow, my human legs are buckling underneath me. I thought I would never see the end of that descent."

"I believe you, man. Now, let's see what these runes tells us." The young Wizard walked to the door. "These runes are very old, probably several thousands years. Sit down, Daryl, be patient. It will take a long time before they make sense to me."

In a few minutes Daryl was asleep, and Paddy tried to understand the meaning of the engravings, but had no luck. Finally it became clear. "I see, how stupid of me! " shouted the elf.

Surprised in his sleep, Daryl jumped. With foggy eyes he looked around. "What is it? What's the matter, man?"

"The runes. I was reading them the wrong way. How clever. They are written diagonally."

Rubbing his eyes Daryl asked, "What do they say?"

"The brave heart will go through."

With rounded eyes Daryl asked, "That's all?"

Paddy repeated, "Yes." With a strong push and a loud screech the rusty hinges opened the door. A musty smell came out.

"Phew, it stinks. I hope it won't be like that all the way, man." Daryl wrinkled his nose.

"No, when other tunnels merge the air will improve."

"How do you know that for sure?"

"This is Dwarf territory. They are very good at making air flow clean in their Kingdom."

Followed by Daryl, Paddy walked into the tunnel and the door screeched again as it closed. The air was less than pleasant, and they pulled their hoods down. Daryl's little blue light softly shone through his hood into the darkness. The tunnel went straight for hours then it turned sharply right. They arrived in a large cave where they could see three other tunnels. Daryl removed his hood curious to see if Paddy's theory about the air being better when the tunnels merged. To his amazement the air was good. "You were right, man. It smells better here! Must we play head or tails to know where to go?"

Chapter 11

"Not really, but almost. As a good guess, let's take the middle one. I hope it's the right choice." Paddy removed his hood. The ground, full of pits and holes, made walking treacherous. It seemed the tunnel had been long abandoned. They traveled several hours, when suddenly Paddy disappeared into a crevasse followed by Daryl. Their elfic capes flew them down safely, but to their surprise they plunged into a river of hot water. "A hot spring! Wow! I am glad it's not ice, man," said Daryl.

"So am I."

They looked around. Nothing! Only a sort of gully where the river flowed.

"I guess we must swim until we arrive somewhere," said Paddy.

Daryl loved swimming. "Well, we were due for a good bath," he said with a chuckle.

For more freedom of movement they removed their capes and stored them in their backpacks. Paddy offered Daryl a small silver crown to secure the light on his forehead. "Thanks, man. I don't need that. I have my leather band." Paddy felt silly that he hadn't realized that Daryl had already put the light on under his hood.

Excited to be in the water, Daryl swam like a fish. The river got larger. Along the shore was a small sandy beach. The water turned turbulent and extremely dangerous. Paddy's sharp ears caught a loud noise from ahead. He yelled to Daryl. "Put your cape on with the hood down. Hurry."

Daryl struggled to pull the cape out of his bag. He had just finished securing the hood on his face when he was swallowed by an enormous mass of water and engulfed into a huge water fall. So was Paddy. They were tossed like pieces of straw. The Magic Elfic capes kept them away from rocks where they would have been crushed to pulp. At last Daryl took control. Now the water was less violent and by getting away from the falls, the noise had diminished.

Paddy swam close to Daryl. "Are you all right?" Then he pointed to Daryl's side. "Do you still have it?"

Yup, clinging unto me like a babe to his mother."

"Boy, that was a dandy waterfall. I thought it would never end," said Paddy.

"So did I, man, Without our capes we would have drowned."

"No, I would have helped us. There is a. law in Wizardry. Before we act we must fight our own battle. If I used my power needlessly, I would lose it."

Daryl, with a chuckle, said, "I see. We have to be dead before you do something."

"Not quite, silly." Teasingly he added, "Almost."

The water, now quiet, was deep and dark. Thanks to his hood, Daryl still had his blue light on his forehead. "I wish we could stop to eat. I am starved. Tired, too. I bet night has come out"

"You are right."

"How do you know that for sure?'

"My Wizard's sense tells me lots of things that you can't feel or see."

Sarcastically, Daryl asked, "Does your Wizard's sense tell you we are going to find a place to sleep? Or we will sleep in the water like fish?"

"Ha, ha, you are becoming a Wizard! We are going to sleep in the water. You said it." Paddy laughed.

"Stop it, Paddy! I am dead beat. It's not funny." Daryl was now in a bad mood.

"Sorry, man. We should find a cave not too far from here. I can see it." In a last effort they swam to a sandy beach with a cave which was quite large. Daryl flopped on the sand while Paddy surveyed the cave.

"I don't feel any evil, only prints in the sand which I can't identify."

They entered the cave and Paddy served them a large supper and watched his buddy, now full and tired, roll in his cape and fall asleep. The young Wizard sat for a while probing the prints. Feeling no evil presence, he, too, went to sleep.

Silently little shadows crawled on the sand and slowly approached. Their large gentle brown eyes looked at the boys. Unafraid, quietly they lay down.

Paddy woke up feeling a presence in the cave. Close to him two little brown bodies were asleep. He smiled. Here was the answer to the traces in the sand. "What are these two Otters doing here?" he whispered. However, not reaching any satisfactory conclusions, he rolled in his cape and returned to sleep. In the morning the two little visitors had left. When Daryl woke up Paddy told him about the young Otters.

"Wow, that's strange. Usually they live in open air and not in underground streams."

"I know. It's what I thought, too."

After breakfast, continuing their quest, they returned to the warm water. An hour later, the two little playful Otters were splashing around them. Paddy and Daryl entered in the game.

"Where are we going to eat?"

"Spread your cape on the water and sit on it."

"But I will sink, man."

"No, I promise you won't. Try it."

"All right." Daryl took his cape and tried to do what he was told, surprisingly, without arguing. Paddy was used to doing that since he was a very young elf. He sat on his cape in one jump. Then, laughing, watched Daryl struggling to get on his.

After many tries, spitting water, he finally made it, and said, "Go on, show off, give us something to eat now. After all that sport I am famished."

Daryl like a starved wolf engulfed his food. The little Otters tried to get their attention by pushing from under the capes with their heads. Paddy conjured some fresh fish. They didn't touch them.

"Have you ever seen Otters refusing fish?" asked Paddy.

"Nope. Try goodies. Maybe they have a sweet tooth like me."

Pastries and chocolates flew from Paddy's hands. The little Otters jumped catching them before they touched the water.

"How about that. I just said that as a joke, man! And see, they eat sweets."

"Yes, something is strange, very strange. I must grab one when we are in the water or when they are asleep."

To the great joy of the Otters the boys played in the water with them. Several times during the games Paddy tried touching one and missed. Even for an Elf, they were too fast. Night was coming, and they were on the lookout for a place to sleep along the river. A sandy beach beckoned them, and quickly they swim to shore. 'The little Otters watched them and joyously joined their new friends.

"Come, little ones. Come, we are going to eat. What would you like to have?" asked Daryl.

The whiskers on their small black noses quivered, their gentle brown eyes shone.

"What does that mean?" We know they don't like fish." Daryl scratched his head. "Do you understand any of this, Paddy?"

"We'll see." The Elf softly touched the head of the little Otter beside him and he rested his hand on it. "It's what I thought," he said.

"What is it, man?"

"Zoltar's doing, again."

"What do you mean?"

"Those two little Otters are the young daughters of King Tory, King of the Realm of the Changeling Elves."

"What are they doing here?"

Chapter 12

"Yata says that she and her sister were playing in the stream by the Palace. Their favorite game was changing into otters. Zoltar was watching, and he made it impossible for the girls to change back to elves. He took great pleasure in deporting them here, providing only basic food."

"That is why they were so happy to eat candies and chocolates. Poor little ones," said Daryl.

"Yes. Their father has refused to work with Zoltar. This is his revenge."

"That is terrible. What are you going to do, man?"

"First, I must know if their parents are still alive. Then I will act." The teen Wizard sat at the shore's edge. Daryl and the two little Otters watched him. In the dark the young Wizard glowed like a lamp with a large halo shining around him. Then a tall young elf appeared. The two Otters got so excited they jumped and rolled in the sand. The Wizard and the Elf were talking when huge flames entered into the halo and tried to burn them to cinders. Paddy quickly shielded the Elf and himself. The young Wizard responded to the attack with lightning bolts. A terrific explosion occurred snuffing the flames. The halo returned and slowly the light dimmed, and the tall Elf left.

The Otter's stopped their exuberance. Happiness was gone. From their gentle brown eyes big tears rolled on their wee faces. Paddy came back and sat by the little ones. Slowly he put his hands on their heads and said, "I am going to send you home right now, little girls. Your parents are waiting for you." They ran and rolled joyously. Paddy used that great moment of happiness and moved his hands. Pouf! They were gone.

"There, Zoltar's evil doing is undone. They are back with their family. Xary and Zoltar no longer have the king's daughters as hostages to force him into his plot."

"But, he will get them again."

"No. I told the king that from now on strong spells are protecting the family."

"Hooray! You are a Prince, man!" Daryl laughed and jumped, clapping his hands.

Paddy chuckled. He loved to go on a quest with Daryl. They were both, like in old times, chums. No Prince, no rank, no protocol—only two good friends sharing the same adventures.

"Now that you have done your good deed, let's eat! All this excitement has made me hungry."

Paddy laughed. "You are always starving, man, excitement or not. I don't understand how come you are not like a hippopotamus!"

"Yup, I guess you are right. But I love the hippopotamus. They have such big mouths. Lots of food can go in there." Daryl laughed to tears.

The night had been quiet. They woke in a happy spirit ready for more adventures. Breakfast over, they plunged into the water. Their little playmates had left a void, and they missed their joyous company. Much later the air became very hot.

"What's happening? We are in a sauna!" said Daryl.

"I don't like what I hear."

"What, man? I hear nothing."

"I know, but I do. It sounds like a hissing kettle. Something unpleasant is ahead of us." They swam silently and slowly as they approached the noise. Red lights flashed against the dark roof of the tunnel, and the water pulled them faster to the growing sound.

"Another waterfall," shouted Daryl.

"Yes, and more, ending in a very unpleasant place."

"Where, man?"

"In a volcano."

"What!"

"You heard me. Let's swim to the left, and maybe we can walk along the small shore and avoid the dark water sliding into the crater."

After a terrible battle in the turbulent water, they managed to go across and set foot on a narrow path wide enough to walk one behind the other.

"Let's hope it will stay like this," shouted Paddy.

Before going over the edge, the churned water became as smooth as oil. As it fell into the pit the noise it created was like a thousand claps of thunder. Brilliant red light shone on the walls of the crater and the heat from the steam forced the boys to turn their faces away.

"Wow, how are we going to get across that, wise man?"

"I don't know yet."

So intense was the temperature that they pulled their hoods down and closed their capes tight around them. The Elfic boots protected them from being injured by the burning rocks. It was a hard task to reach the edge of the crater.

"Do you see some way where we can make it?"

Paddy didn't answer. He was too busy surveying the side where they stood. His sharp eyes noticed a narrow ledge going around the crater "Yes, I see a way out, dangerous, but possible. See that ledge? I will put an iron rod along the wall, and we will grab it with our capes. The cape will take the shape of gloves."

"Gosh, can't you do better than that, man. You mean we will hang above this pit of fire?"

"Yes, almost, but with our elfic boots to help us, our feet will be safe resting on the ledge. We will be fine, man. There is no other way as you can see. Don't panic, that's all."

"How nice. I always wanted to be roasted like a chicken. I just love the idea!" Daryl grinned at Paddy.

The teen Wizard faced the wall and raised his arms. From his fingers fire came out in long flames. He moved his hands along the burning rock, touching it slowly with his mind's-eye, then he dropped his arms. The flames from his fingers vanished.

"There, that should do. '" Paddy said with a sigh of satisfaction.

Daryl looked at the rod in disbelief. "You are crazy man! I can't believe you want me to hang up there. I can't do it! I thought you were joking." He was almost hysterical.

"'Calm down, man. I will put a spell on you to take away your fear. When we are on the other side, I will remove it."

"Thanks, I can use it."

Paddy touched Daryl. "Come. Now you are all set to go."

Paddy went first followed by Daryl, who suspiciously looked at the rod. Elfic capes were closed, hoods down. They couldn't be touched by the burning heat. When he grabbed the rod, to Daryl's amazement, his cape immediately took the shape of gloves. Like spiders spinning their webs they moved very slowly. Daryl didn't dare look down. Even with the spell he had doubts abut his fear. He kept his eyes glued on the wall in front of his nose. Once he slipped and hung dangerously in the air. How grateful he was for Paddy. He didn't even panic. "How wonderful. How come this is happening? Zoltar doesn't know I am here. Evil can't see me," he whispered.

Ahead Paddy saw Daryl's feet letting go, and he halted ready to help. When he saw that Daryl was able to continue he carried on. Arriving at the end of the rod he lightly jumped to a large rock a little distance from the burning pit. He waited for Daryl. The volcano below roared and spat fire and steam.

Daryl put his foot on the rock. Looking down victoriously he said, "I did it, thanks to you, Paddy." He sighed, and with a boyish grin he asked, "Would it be possible to keep the spell during the quest, by any chance?'

"No, Daryl. To grow, you have to keep fighting the challenges. It wouldn't be fair if I took that opportunity away from you. Sorry, man."

Chapter 13

"But you just did it?"

"Yes, because the danger was too great. You knew that, when your foot lost its grip. What happened, man?"

"Don't know. I think I lost faith. Too bad. It was swell not being afraid."

"Come on, you have never been a chicken. I was. Never lose faith, you hear me. It is part of life being afraid and conquering it, man."

"You are lucky with your power you are never afraid."

"Oh, yes, I am! There are times where I am scared just like you, and you know how scared I was on the earth realm."

"I won't bother you any more with that nonsense then. Where to, man?"

Paddy lightly touched Daryl, and the spell was gone. "Come, Walk carefully. The ledge is narrow. I can see a passage not too far from here." Their Elfic boots clung to the rock, and they moved slowly. Daryl's heart more than once jumped in his throat, water ran on his forehead and back. He knew that the heat was not the only cause for this outpour of perspiration.

"Hang on. We have arrived," shouted Paddy. Daryl sighed. Paddy's human chum was wet from head to toes. Still under the great stress he had gone through, Daryl walked gingerly into the cave. With a trembling hand he removed the hood to wipe his face.

"Don't do that! You will burn yourself as sure as with boiling water." Paddy quickly pulled Daryl's hood down.

"Sorry, man, but I am so wet."

"Don't worry. Your cape will take care of that. Soon you will be dry as a bone. Come on."

The cave was large. The intense heat had disappeared. It took them a while to cross it. "I hope there is a tunnel to get out of here." Daryl had a flare of bad temper.

"Relax man. Because of the many Dwarf kingdoms in these mountains, there are always tunnels. They lived here for centuries and turned it into a swiss cheese," replied Paddy laughing.

"All right, but why do they always dwell in caves?"

"Not always, most of the time, yes, they do. They find the precious metals that they need for the marvelous work we know them for. Our fine jewelry is made by their artistic hands. When the metal is not found any more they move to other area."

"Wow! They are gypsies, then."

"No, silly. It takes centuries before the resources of the mines are exhausted."

They found a tunnel going away from the heat. Daryl removed his hood. His cape had dried him up. They went deeper into the mountain. The tunnel they were in had been long deserted. No one had worked here for the longest time.

"We will stop when we find a place, for the night."

"Good, my stomach tells me it's time to eat, man."

"I know!" Paddy laughed. They continued searching, then Paddy saw a large hole up above in the wall.

"Ah, this will be perfect."

The young human man, stupefied, looked up and asked, "Will you be kind enough, Sir, to tell me how you hope to get me up there?"

"With your cape, silly"

"My cape, that's right! Since I became a mortal, I have forgotten all my training as an Elfic Squire. It's terrible."

"Don't worry. It will come back later on. About the cape, open your arms, and give a kick to the ground like this."

Up went Paddy, followed by a muttering Daryl, "I didn't remember I could do that!"

Paddy smiled. They were in a small cave carved in the rock. Paddy explained," "The Dwarves, when their work day was over, came here to sleep."

"I see, but how did they climb up here?'

"With a ladder made of rope and wood hanging down during the day. At night when everyone had climbed up into the shelter, the foreman pulled up the ladder, and they had their meal. They were perfectly safe for the night."

"Clever chaps, those Dwarves."

"Yes, very much so."

""How about eating, man? I am starved and dead tired."

With a mischievous grin Paddy said, "I thought you had forgotten! Here it is."

Shocked, Daryl cried, "I, forget to eat? Are you out of your mind, man?"

With a chuckle Paddy moved his hand, and a hot plate fell on his chum's lap.

"Ah, this is the reward of a hard day," gourmand Daryl said, and licked his lips.

"I agree. I am starved, too, and tired."

They ate their meal silently, and when they were finished, they sighed and rolled in their capes. Daryl touched his side and moved the Magic Crown to a more comfortable place for him to sleep.

During the night Paddy heard noises below. Cautiously he looked down and whispered, "Oh, no." He moved his hand hastily and hid the cave with a spell. A party of Goblins underneath were sniffing and arguing furiously.

"I smell elf presence," screamed a young skinny one excitedly, and a big fellow growled affirming that he could, too. Suddenly the odor vanished. "You are a band of fools," yelled their leader and a fight resulted with blows flying from everywhere, pulling hair and biting.

Paddy, chuckling, watched the bunch, escorted by their leader vigorously booting their pants finally leaning over and rubbing their bruises. Paddy returned to sleep. In the morning he told Daryl about the incident of the night. Daryl was disappointed "Why didn't you wake me up? I love to see those guys fighting. They do it with such ardor."

"Promise, next time I will. They were so funny I had a hard time not to laugh aloud and cheer."

"I know," replied Daryl with regret. Such sport was not offered every day to watch.

"“This means, man, we have to be careful. They are around in the tunnels."

"Good, I will have a chance to see a fight."

"Come on, now, be serious. Remember, thanks to Goldy they can't see you."

"That's right! Then I can be in the middle of the fight!"

"Don't push your luck, man, you could be hurt."

Daryl replied with a chuckle. "They can't see me, and they can't smell me, either. I am a mortal! Oh this will be fun." Joyously he rubbed his hands with anticipation.

Chapter 14

Breakfast over, they flew down. On the ground were the remains of the battle, tufts of hair and pieces of cloth. Along the way they saw above their head several small shelters made by the Dwarves. Traces of Goblins were all about, but no sign of them.

"I wonder where they are?" Daryl scratched his head.

"Not too far. This has probably been their hiding place since the Dwarves left," replied Paddy.

They went through caves where the Goblins had camped, but still found no one in sight. "It is as if they have deserted the place. I am sure they are somewhere, all together, for a reason," whispered Paddy.

From not too far away, his sensitive ears picked up the loud noise of a crowd. "Hush! Listen."

"What is it?"

"I think we will know soon." Suddenly the tunnel turned sharply, revealing a large cave where hundreds of Goblins were gathered around a huge fire-pit, where something grilled on a heavy rod of metal and thick smoke filled the cave. It was difficult to see.

"Oh, no!" whispered Daryl, frightened by the number of Goblins. He backed up and held his elfic stone.

"This is what I was afraid of," murmured Paddy. "What are they doing here?" "Zoltar and Xary must have called upon them to reinforce their evil battle."

"You think Xary is with them, too? I am certain they have enrolled cheerfully in the evil intrigue."

"Look who's amid them, the master of darkness himself," whispered Paddy.

"Is Xary here, too?"

"Not yet, but he will be. Take my word for it."

The Goblins were talking and screaming. The excitement was obviously close to starting a fight.

"It wouldn't take very much to start a real battle," said the elf.

"Nope, and I can help." Daryl silently walked into the middle of the crowd. He had extinguished his elfic stone. The flames from the fire were enough for him to find his way. No one noticed him. Chuckling, he gave a Goblin beside him a strong whack. The guy acted as if he had been skinned alive. He screamed and kicked the next fellow who fell on his back under the crushing feet. In one jump he was distributing blows all around. On earth Daryl had been a good football player. He enjoyed the game avoiding the violent blows flying around. Soon the cave became a furious battleground. Paddy watched Daryl coming back laughing. Then Xary appeared in a dark red cloud. He gave a hand to his evil partner to stop the brawl.

"Good for you, Daryl. Let's go. Knowing Goblins, it will take a long time settling the matter." They could see a furious Zoltar, with the help of Xary, trying in vain to kill the riot. The sorcerers finally threw bolts of lightning at random at their feet. Startled the savages stopped, furious. They looked at the two evil ones, and then their furor turned on the Wizards. Xary and Zoltar just had time to shield themselves with invisibility. Frustrated, the Goblins returned to their fight almost immediately. The cave was gray with smoke.

Paddy used that time to walk quietly along the wall. Daryl went first, continuing to inflame the battle as he went through, booting the Goblins in their pants. They were too preoccupied to smell an Elf amidst them. Zoltar and Xary reappeared, their eyes flashing flames of rage. Xary, trying to restore order, screamed like a demon. Zoltar had enough of the riot and threw bolts of fire into the crowd, this time not sparing the wild bunch, burning several of them so severely they howled with pain. They got the message and stopped.

Paddy and Daryl left unseen, chuckling. Daryl had started a good fight. Only at a safe distance, they stopped and sat on the ground resting for a few minutes. After a while they went their way, continuing their journey in thoughtful silence.

"Too bad Zoltar stopped them. I had such good time. I surely enjoyed myself. I have wanted to boot them for so long, and now I did it!" Daryl laughed loudly and cheerfully said, "Thanks, Goldy."

A whisper, that only he could hear, replied, "You are welcome."

Daryl smiled.

"What are you smiling at, silly. You were lucky Goldy's spell worked."

Worried, Daryl looked at Paddy in surprise, 'What do you mean? I never thought it wouldn't."

Walking behind, Daryl mumbled. "And if it hadn't worked, oh la, la."

Paddy chuckled.

Hours later Daryl's stomach growled.

"Are we going to find our way out? I have had enough of these tunnels and caves." Daryl gloomily looked around.

"Of course, we will. The Goblins do it. Come on, man, shape up."

A small cavity was just above them. Without a word Paddy moved his hand. Daryl was mumbling unhappily "I guess when my stomach is empty and growling, I do see things differently and I am not funny," he grimaced.

"Sit down. This will help your humor and satisfy your stomach." A delicious smell of roast meat came to his nose.

"How did we get here?"

Paddy with a chuckle said," You were too busy complaining when I conjured us here, that's all."

"I already see things in a different light. I feel better." Daryl's good mood had returned. Their meal finished, they flew down and left.

Paddy wanted to be out of there soon. The place was quite unhealthy with the Goblins crawling everywhere. He didn't want to face a band of raging monsters. As he looked ahead, he saw an opening in the ceiling of the cave.

"See, here is our way out. You can be sure the Goblins are not using it. We won't meet them up there."

"Excellent, those guys can't fly." Daryl laughed. "Let me go first. Remember, thanks to Goldy, I can't be seen by evil."

"Be my guest, man."

Daryl forgot that Paddy was a Wizard and could be invisible at any time. The mortal opened his cape, gave a kick to the ground, and flew up. He landed in a very large cave. A little blue light shone softly. It was as quiet as in a mole hole. Daryl leaned down, calling, "You may come. It's all right."

"Thank you." Paddy landed beside him. The Elf walked to the other side of the cave where he found a well kept tunnel with sand on the ground. Iron rings were on the walls, but there were no torches and no signs of activity.

"This is strange. The Dragon Lord said we would find the Dwarves here in the mountains." Daryl looked around, puzzled.

"I am afraid something terrible happened to them," replied Paddy.

For the longest time they walked in deserted tunnels and caves where lovely engravings, paintings, and carvings silently waited for the return of the Dwarves. Iron tables and benches were still in place.

"Do you think they left?"

"Yes, they have," said a small voice coming from underneath a bench. A young Dwarf appeared. The wee fellow was wearing a cheery green vest, red pants, and brown boots. On the top of a crop of black hair was a yellow bonnet with a big white pom-pom. At the sight of the elf, his weary little face bloomed with a happy smile.

"What are you doing here by yourself, boy?" asked Paddy, surprised.

"I was far away from home busy doing some chores when everybody left. I am certain they didn't realize I was missing, otherwise they wouldn't have left without me. I don't know where they are." The little boy's smile disappeared and big tears rolled in his brown eyes.

"Oh, poor little chap," said Daryl

Chapter 15

"What's your name?' asked Paddy.

"My name is Ryan. I am the youngest son of the master goldsmith.

"When did they leave?" asked Paddy.

"I think it was four days ago. It's difficult to know when you don't have a thing to give the time. All is dark here."

"You haven't eaten for four days!" cried Daryl, horrified.

"Not much. Because of where I had gone to do the chores, I had food with me. I made it last."

"What were you doing, with no one with you?" asked Paddy.

"As young boys this is part of our training" he said proudly, and added with a smile, "Girls don't have to."

Paddy, concerned at this piece of news, said, "I see." Actually, he didn't see at all, and he sighed and shook his head. With all the perils of these days, how could parents send a young boy alone in endless tunnels for training?

"Tell me, do you know, why they left?" asked Paddy.

"Not really. Zoltar and his friend, Xary the evil one, have been after King Orug for months to join forces with them. The King refused. Zoltar angrily said that he would be sorry for not doing so."

"Then what?" asked Paddy.

"I don't know. Since then I have seen many Goblins and Urks. They eat people you know. They are in our tunnels," the boy said and shivered. "This is probably Zoltar's vengeance. I am so scared of them. That is why I am hiding." Ryan once more shivered in fear.

"Poor little chap." Daryl patted him on the shoulder.

"Let's use a table to have a good meal. I am sure Ryan can use it," said Paddy.

"Wonderful idea," Daryl rubbed his hands. "Sit down, boy."

"But I don't have a thing to offer" the boy replied, almost in tears.

"That's alright. I am going to treat you." Paddy smiled......"Watch." With wondrous eyes Ryan saw Paddy snap his fingers and bring upon the table all the goodies he loved. "How did you do that?" His mouth fell wide open.

Daryl with a chuckle replied. "He is a Wizard, boy."

"A Wizard." Ryan was excited, then sadly he said, "We have a Wizard, too, in our Kingdom."

Paddy cheerfully said. "You do? Wonderful. Let's eat first, young friend. We will talk about what to do with you. The boy ate so much that Daryl had a hard time following. Laughingly the mortal said, "Wow, you beat me, small one. I never thought it could be possible. I give up."

Paddy laughed to tears. The young Dwarf, still eating, watched them in surprise.

Daryl asked, "Tell me something, boy. Do you eat always that much?"

The human rounded blue eyes were popping out of his head. "Oh no, sir, only when I am very scared or lonely, and I have been plenty of both," he replied.

"That explains it all." Paddy patted the boy's back. They waited patiently for Ryan to finish. "Are you done now Ryan?" asked Paddy.

"Yes, sir."

"Feeling better?" asked Daryl with a large grin on his face.

"Oh, yes, thank you, sir. Much, much better."

"Fine, let's talk then. My friend and Squire, and I, are going on a Quest to stop Zoltar and Xary's plot," explained Paddy.

"Oh!" Ryan's eyes sparkled. "May I go, too?"

"That is what I was about to ask, Ryan. Would you like to join us and show the way out?" Paddy smiled at the boy.

"Yes! Yes! I will be the hero of our kingdom!" He clapped his hands jumping excitingly.

"Wow! That is an enthusiastic response." Daryl laughed.

"Fine. I will contact your Wizard to inform your parents about your well-being and that you expressed the desire to join us in our quest against the evil Sorcerers."

"Wonderful!" shouted Ryan, dancing joyously around Daryl.

The teen Wizard left Ryan to his exuberance. They watched him as he gently glowed in the dark. Beside him appeared an old Dwarf. "That is our Wizard," whispered Ryan to Daryl. After a while, the Dwarf and the light quietly faded away. Paddy came back smiling. "There, now you belong to our party."

Amused, his new friends watched Ryan throwing his yellow bonnet up in the air.

"Let's move away from these Goblin infested tunnels. I presume you know your way out, Ryan?" asked Paddy.

"Yes, S-i-r! " The little Dwarf proudly pointed left. This was his first help in the quest.

"One minute boy, you can't see in the dark," said Paddy.

"No, Sir, but I know my way around."

Daryl, all this time, had his elfic stone on his forehead.

So far, the Goblins hadn't found their traces. Ryan, knowing the place like his own pocket, took the lead and went through tunnels and secret doors known only by the Dwarves. Hours later, at last, they were outside. A bitter wind greeted them howling through the mountains. The night, with her black cloak, had come down, covering everything. Poor Ryan. To protect him against the terrible cold he had only his green vest. He was freezing.

Paddy immediately gave him a cape. "Here, boy, put this on. It's an Elfic Cape. They are very useful, and you can do many things with them."

"An Elfic cape for me, thank you, Sir. I know the power of your wonderful capes. The old folks tell stories to us young ones about the marvelous things of your Realm. My dream was to have one."

"Enjoy it then, and make good use of it." Paddy ruffled Ryan's bonnet which fell on his nose.

The little boy wrapped himself in the cape, put his yellow bonnet back on his black hair, shouting, "I am warm all over!" A happy grin shone on his small frozen face as he pulled the hood down.

"I am glad. With weather like this, we need these capes," said Daryl pulling, his hood over his face, too.

"I can see through my hood!" screamed Ryan.

"Yes, boy, it's marvelous," replied Daryl, cheerfully.

"Where are we?" asked the elf to Ryan.

"At the foot of the Blue Mountain, my home. Below is the Happy Valley."

"Good! We will have some happy time then." said Daryl with a grin to Ryan.

"Oh, no, Sir. The darkness has extended its shadow there, too."

Daryl touched the Magic Crown under his cape and whispered. "It will not be a long. Wait until I crown his evil head with Glory."

"We better find a shelter for the night," said Paddy.

"Yup, but where?" Daryl removed the blue light from his forehead. Keeping it would be very dangerous. Too many eyes could be watching, and not friendly ones, either.

Chapter 16

"I know a secret place where my friends and I played," said Ryan.

"Good. Show us where. It's freezing here," Paddy said.

The boy followed by Paddy and Daryl walked on a small trail. Daryl, for fear of losing Paddy in the dark, or even falling, hung onto Paddy's cape. Ryan, sure of his way, led without any hesitation. Then he stopped in front of a very large rock, bent down and touched the ground on the right. The big piece of granite turned upon itself revealing a small cave, and Ryan walked in. Paddy and Daryl followed. Quickly, Ryan touched the side of the door. It closed quietly. He pulled a torch from the wall, lit it, and secured it into the iron ring by the entrance.

Proudly the boy said, "You never know if Goblins or Urks could be prowling around."

"This is an interesting hiding place, Ryan. How did you find it?" asked Paddy.

"I found it, that's all."

"Yes, but how?" asked Daryl.

"Well, I was searching for special stones that are found only in this part of the hills when I saw a the big rock that was exactly like the one I was looking for. Excited, I grabbed it and pulled. At that instant, the rock moved, showing the entrance of a cave. Terrified, I hid myself, but nothing happened! No one came out. I approached and looked inside to see if anyone was there. No, not a soul. I went in. That's all. Since then it has been my cave," he said with a large smile.

"But your friends know about it, no?" Daryl asked.

"Yes, they do, but not how to get in," giggled Ryan.

"How did you manage that," asked Paddy laughing.

"Well, it was simple enough, Sir. I stopped them at the foot of the hill, and they only came up when I made the cry of the owl."

"Well, this is a pretty smart boy, man," said Daryl.

"Did you look to see if other caves were behind this one?" asked Paddy.

"Yes, Sir, and I didn't find anything." Ryan sat on a small chair brought there with the help of his friends. The boys had modestly furnished the place. Ryan shyly said, "I am sorry that they are too small for you."

"Don't worry. We will sit on the floor," said Paddy.

"How about eating, man. I am starved," whined Daryl. They sat legs crossed on the floor happily eating their meal provided by Paddy. Ryan on his chair was twisting, embarrassed. He looked at the boys on the floor and joined them.

Paddy laughed, "Use your chair, Ryan."

"No, Sir. It's not proper for me to sit on a chair while you sit on the floor."

Paddy smiled as he was thinking the little chap had been well brought up. "Thank you Ryan. You may sit where you want."

"I'd love to sit with you, Sir"

"Now, how about eating this wonderful food. I am starved," replied Daryl. Joyously they ate the food provided by Paddy. The meal over, Ryan's eyes got heavy and he fell asleep. Daryl carried him to the small bed and covered him with his tiny cape.

"Do you think, man, there is another cave?"

"I think so. I don't see why the Dwarves would have bothered themselves with a secret lock here, if there was not another cave somewhere."

Paddy walked around, his sharp eyes scanning every crack, every inch of the walls. Nothing, "This is strange," he whispered still searching. His eyes came to the corner where Ryan was asleep. Above the bed on the wall was what he had been looking for,-Rrunes, Dwarves' Runes. "Here it is," Paddy said aloud.

"What is it, man?"

"See, we are told how to open the passage." He read, "When the ring is around its neck, it will open." They looked everywhere. "There is no ring. The secret lock must be behind Ryan's bed," said Paddy.

"Let's move it then." Daryl walked to the foot of the bed. Without waking the boy, they grabbed the bed and moved it. There, inserted in the wall, was a polished panel of granite upon which had been carved a beautiful Swan stretching its neck up. At its feet lay an old rusted ring attached to a small chain hanging on a rusty nail.

"So what"

"Don't you see man?"

"Nope."

"I have to put the ring on the neck of the Swan."

"How can you do that, silly. It's flat on the wall."

"Watch and see. Here is good magic, man." Paddy took up the ring from the floor and touched the Swan's beak. At that very moment the head moved out from the panel of granite. Now Paddy could put the ring around the neck. Silently, a slab of stone opened in the floor showing in the darkness a flight of stairs going down.

"I'll be darned! How about that!"

"Here is our route for tomorrow, man," said Paddy cheerfully.

"Cool man, cool. Now let's go to sleep." Daryl rolled in his cape on the floor, and he was asleep. Paddy removed the ring from the Swan's neck. The Swan's head resumed its place flat on the slab and the trap in the floor closed.

In the morning when Ryan woke, Paddy explained to him what they had found. The boy got excited. "The old folks talked about a lost secret passage leading to a magic city, the lost City of the Swans."

"That would explain the Swan carved on the wall. I think we are about to find the lost city," said Paddy.

"Gosh, man, do you believe that story?" asked Daryl, skeptical as his usual self.

Ryan couldn't stay still, waiting nervously for Paddy to open the secret passage. Breakfast over, Paddy walked to the wall followed by a very, very excited boy stomping the ground, repeating, "Oh boy, oh boy, oh boy. Wait until I tell my friends about this!"

Paddy laughed. "Slow down, Ryan. First, we have to find the city." Paddy took the ring and touched the swan's beak. Like the previous night, slowly its head came out of the wall. Ryan, mouth wide-opened, eyes popping out of their sockets, watched as Paddy put the ring around the delicate neck. The floor quietly moved showing a flight of stairs. Ryan put his little hand over his mouth.

"The door is opened. Now we must find the lost city," said Paddy going down. Ryan ran behind the Elf, followed by Daryl. Above their heads the floor closed soundlessly. It was pitch-dark. Daryl took out his Elfic stone mounted on a leather band and secured it upon his head. Ryan, not as fortunate as the human boy, hung onto Paddy's doublet.

In his kingdom to go about in the dark tunnels, caretakers had the job of lighting torches everywhere and going around watching they stayed that way. Paddy realized the young Dwarf's handicap. Quickly he reached into his pocket.

"Here, Ryan, and please let go of my doublet."

Chapter 17

"An Elfic stone for me? Thank you, Sir."

Daryl helped the boy to tie the leather strap around his head.

The stairs turned endlessly like a corkscrew. Daryl skeptically asked, "Do you think, man, we will find the end of it?"

"Eventually, yes, but be patient, Daryl."

Ryan, excited about the fabulous city, quickly explained, "The old folks said that the city is very deep down by a lovely lake with beautiful, speaking white Swans, and because of the warm water of the lake they have great vegetation."

"You know a lot about that fabulous city, don't you, Ryan," said Daryl.

"Yes, Sir. My people teach us many things about our present world and about the past, too."

"You show that you have a good knowledge of us Elves" said Paddy.

"Yes, Sir."

The stairs were still winding down. As they approached closer to the end of their descent the stair went straight. The young elf saw something shining below. It was water. A few minutes later he said, "We have arrived."

"But where?" asked Daryl.

"At the bottom of the stairs," laughed Ryan.

Bent with laughter, tears rolling down their faces, the two old friends looked at each other slapping their knees. They were for a few seconds two youths back on earth realm. "You are right. Ryan. We are at the bottom of the stairs," replied Paddy, choking, laughing, wiping the tears from his eyes. Ryan baffled by this outburst of laughter was looking at them worriedly.

An underground river as calm as oil faced them with a lovely swan shaped boat rocking gently, moored to the bank.

"Wow, that is quite a boat," whistled Daryl admiringly.

"The Swan people, the Swan people!" Ryan had forgotten all about the burst of laughter from his friends. "We have found the lost city," he screamed clapping his hands.

"Gosh, boy, you are going off your rocker," said Daryl with a chuckle.

"Hey! Not yet boy, not so fast," said Paddy. They climbed on board. Carefully, slowly the boat left the dock.

"It's moving! We are going to the lost city!" cried Ryan.

"Yes, we are moving, but I don't know if I like that! All this magic makes me nervous," replied Daryl.

"Why? It's wonderful," giggled the young Dwarf.

After a while the boat moved much faster. The water became turbulent and from ahead a loud noise of churning water reached their ears.

"We are heading for a large water fall," cried Daryl. Quietly the Swan opened its wings and flew over the crashing water. Daryl's mouth fell wide open. "How about that man, this blows my mind! Now we are in a flying boat."

"Magic, man, magic!" laughed Paddy. Ryan screamed with joy. They flew till the body of water calmed dawn. The Swan landed quietly folding its wings and continued its course.

"This boat has a mind of its own," mumbled Daryl, not at ease at the thought of all that magic. His mind had completely changed. He was not thinking like an elf any more. This was troublesome for him. Paddy hadn't said a word for a long time, neither had Ryan. The young fellow was way too interested and not a bit afraid. He wanted to remember everything and be able later to tell his people about this marvelous journey. His eyes shone like stars in a summer sky.

The young Elf watched him smiling. Now, for centuries to come, thanks to Ryan, the story would be in the Dwarves chronicles and told to the young ones in winter nights gathered around the fire.

The boat slowly approached an amber dock shining under an invisible source of light and stopped. Amazingly it was as clear as if the sun had been shining. They climbed out of the boat and took a path of white sand. Birds of various kinds and colors chirped flying in beautiful trees. Fawns and does were playing on the green grass.

"Wow! How can there be a place like this at the center of the earth?' asked Daryl.

"I don't know yet, but I will. So far I don't feel any evil," replied Paddy.

Ryan was very quiet. .It didn't matter to him, why, and how. His only concern was that his people had talked about it, and he was here to testify that they were right. Strange flowers bloomed everywhere. The path passed like a pale white ribbon through another soft green lawn. There, white Swans quietly groomed themselves. A crystal Palace with large bay windows shone in the light. At the bottom of a large stair, an old man with a long white beard and dressed in gold waited.

"Welcome to Swan-City strangers. My name is Maira, Chamberlain of Prince Kazan and Princess Orora, his wife. Please follow me."

They went up the stairs and through beautiful halls. People smiled at them. They arrived in front of a large oak door. The Chamberlain rapped, a young page opened to let them in. The room had ivory furniture trimmed with gold. No drapes hung on the large bay-windows. A harp, strummed by invisible hands was playing soft music. The Prince and his wife were talking quietly on a sofa. Both wore long white shimmering tunics. On their heads diamond tiaras shone like evening stars.

"Greetings and welcome, Prince Patrick and friends."

"Thank you for your welcome, Prince."

Curious Paddy asked, "How do you know my name?"

"We were expecting you and your party."

Paddy didn't answer, observing everything with keen Wizard's eyes.

A small voice beside Daryl asked, "How did you know we were coming, Sir?'

"We have been expecting you for a very long time, my little friend," the Prince looking at Ryan replied.

"Who, me?" The boy, baffled, looked at the prince.

Smiling, he added, "Yes, you. When you found the cave, we had great hope that you would find the secret door leading to the city."

"You were expecting me. But why, Sir?' asked Ryan aghast.

"It's a very long, sad story," replied the Prince. "Please, all of you, sit down. Now listen. Once upon a time, in a Realm of happiness, a young Prince and his Lady lived, envied by an Evil One. He wanted to get power over that Realm. After a long battle, evil triumphed, and he won. The evil creature as a vengeance created a crystal mountain to keep them there forever, the Prince and his Lady, and friends. He cursed the court with a terrible curse. Every night they all would be changed into Swans and come back as people only at sunrise the next morning. He provided a lovely world for his victims. Sunshine pierced through the crystal mountain top and a large lake was created for the swans. Plenty of plants, flowers, and birds existed, too. With a sardonic smile they were told this was to be their realm forever.

Chapter 18

One day our old Wizard counselor said, "I have found a way to break the spell, my Prince, to remove the curse, and at the same time destroy the evil one. We must find a young boy Dwarf and bring him here. The boy will fly upon the Prince's back with a diamond crown in each hand. At precisely midnight, the boy will cross his wrists upon the swan's neck then quickly open his arms and throw the crowns into the middle of the lake." Prince Kazan smiled as he said to Ryan, "This, my little friend, is our story and the way to destroy the curse. For so long we tried to have you come." Prince Kazan shook his head.

Excited, Ryan jumped to his feet. "I'll do it. Are you sure, Sir, it will work?"

"Yes, we are, boy."

"It will work, Ryan," said Paddy. Prince Kazan smiled.

"Thank you for your confidence, Prince Patrick."

"It's not only confidence, but knowledge. I too, am a Wizard." Paddy chuckled at the face the Prince made. "A very good one." Ryan's eyes shone, proud to have as a friend so special a person.

"Will you please show us what you can do?" asked the Prince, a little skeptical about the talent of so young an Elf.

Daryl, smiling proudly, said, "Wow them your power, man. Be a dragon!"

"So be it, Daryl," The elf walked to the bay window. With a sharp cry Paddy jumped on the window and flew away as a huge dragon. Daryl knew that his friend's roar was laughter. Seconds later, a large shadow covered the light coming from outside. Paddy was back. He hopped onto the floor.

"Very impressive, Prince. Maybe you can talk with our own Wizard and join forces to make sure everything will be done the right way," said the Prince.

Daryl nudged Paddy in the ribs. "Wow, man, you surely did it." Paddy pushed him. "Be quiet, you bad egg."

Daryl moved away, mumbling. "All right, all right."

Kazan rang a crystal bell. A few minutes later, an old skinny personage arrived. Ryan whispered to Paddy, "Why are Wizards so old except you?"

"They started young like myself, boy."

The Prince introduced the young Wizard to the ancient one who looked at Paddy doubtfully. The Prince smiled saying, "Be reassured, my old friend, the boy is a strong wizard. He proved it to us. Go in peace." Having much to talk about before midnight, immediately the mighty ones, old and young, excused themselves and left.

Daryl and Ryan escorted by a young page left for a nice room with big velvet sofas. "The young Wizard will join you later," said the page.

"Good enough for me, but is it possible to have a meal please? I am starved," asked Daryl. With a twinkle in his eyes he winked at Ryan.

"Certainly, Sir," the young boy quickly left and came back a few minutes later followed by a domestic carrying trays of food.

"Wow! This is a fast service." Daryl laughed with pleasure.

Giggling, Ryan watched Daryl putting away the food quickly in his large stomach. Never had he met anyone who could eat so much at any time of the day. Their meal over, they lay down, and in a few minutes they were asleep. Paddy joined his friends. Sighing he lay on a sofa and stretched his long legs. Exhausted, he fell immediately asleep.

Eleven-thirty rang at the Palace's tower. The Elf jumped to his feet and cried, shaking Ryan awake. "Hurry boy! We have no time to waste. We must go to Kazan's at once."

In seconds, the little Dwarf was at the door. Daryl painfully woke up and dragged himself out of the room. Half asleep, he followed the two running down the halls. When they arrived, the Prince and his Princess were changing into Swans.

"On the swan's back, hurry Ryan," shouted Paddy.

"One minute! I have to get the crowns from the Swan's heads." Quickly Paddy grabbed the crowns. "Here they are, hurry Ryan!"

With the crowns in his hands, light as a feather, the boy Dwarf jumped onto the bird's back. With a sad cry, the two beautiful Swans took flight from the balcony over the garden, then flew above the lake.

Paddy, in his mind, heard Ryan rehearsing what he had to do. He felt his nervousness. "Calm down, you can do it." The boy relaxed. Paddy continued watching him. Carefully Ryan made sure that he was exactly at the center of the lake. "There, you are in place." shouted Paddy. Quickly, Ryan crossed his wrists upon the swan's neck, opened his arms, and threw the crowns in front of him into the lake. The water below churned. Big waves crashed upon the dock breaking the boat. The mountain trembled and cracked. Quickly, the Swans flew to the palace. Paddy and Daryl were waiting anxiously for their return. Ryan jumped clown from the bird's back.

The Princely couple was changing back and forth from Human to Swans. It was a frightening thing to witness. The mountain crashed in a tremendous noise of shattered crystal. Hastily the young and old Wizards threw strong spells to protect everyone. Without their power, the place would have been their tomb crushed under tons of crystal. A terrible cry shook the broken universe. A huge dragon with flames bursting from every part of his carcass fell from above buried under a mountain of crystal. The evil one had been destroyed.

It was night with beautiful moonlight shining a pale ray on a dark pile of rocks. The Prince and the Princess, with the three friends stood aghast upon a luscious green hill with the old Wizard and the people of the court who he had protected by spells he had spun around them at the moment the crystal dome collapsed. The Swan City was a pile of rubble. No more lake, only dark rocks.

A beautiful valley quietly slumbered below.

"We were deep in the bowels of the earth! How can we be here?" asked Daryl, looking around.

"Remember, man, you are in the Elfic Realm, where all is possible, and the sorcerer did build that mountain," replied Paddy with a chuckle.

"That's right, I think like a mortal," he replied sadly.

The Prince said, "Friends, we have to say goodbye. The sorcerer who kept us prisoners for centuries is now dead. He put all his power into this evil work. When the mountain crashed he was destroyed with it. Now we are free to return to our Realm. Ryan, you will always be remembered. Your name is now in our history, because you have restored happiness to our people and to us."

The Prince took from his hand a ring, and said, "Ryan, when you desire to visit us, rub the stone of the ring, and you will be in our realm at once. Put the ring on."

Ryan looked. It was so big. "But, Sir, it will fall off." However the boy did it, expecting that it was going to fall on the ground, but, no, the ring took the size of his small finger.

The Prince smiled. "Ryan, you are like a son unto us. We will be waiting for your visit. Goodbye for now." The Princess kissed him. Ryan's smiling face got as red as a poppy.

Prince Kazan joyously cried to his faithful friends of exile. "Let's go home!" Gently he took his wife's hand. In a burst of light they were gone.

Astonished the young men looked at each other and Daryl whispered, "Gosh, I'll be darned!"

The moon in the velvety sky shone softly. The feeling of being in an unreal strange world was almost unbearable. Suddenly the strain of the past hours fell upon them. Daryl yawned showing his white teeth. Ryan arched his back, stretched his arms above his head, and fell to the ground asleep.

Chapter 19

"Boy, I am tired. When you came to our room, man, I was sound asleep," said Daryl.

"Well, let's do like Ryan," replied Paddy, who rolled in his cape, instantly falling asleep. Daryl soon did the same. Ryan, much too excited, woke as fast as he had fallen asleep and sat for the longest time looking at his ring. The deep green stone softly shone under the moonlight. He couldn't close his eyes! All the wonders of the past days, like a carousel, were turning, dancing in his mind. Then his head nodded. Gently he lay down on his right, and in one breath he was again asleep.

Two cruel eyes were watching in the serene night. Paddy, too tired, had forgotten to protect them. In his sleep the young Wizard felt evil approaching. He woke up facing a horde of flaming eyes encircling them. Paddy at once was on his feet. Arms extended sideways he turned like a windmill under a high wind. The ground shook. Daryl opened his eyes and looked around, seeing Paddy, who was turning like a windmill. Terrified, the young mortal realized why Paddy was frantically dancing in the middle of the night. He was protecting them with spells.

Fangs out, eyes burning with fire, the monsters ferociously howled.

Drooling they ran to attack their prey. Paddy now sat quietly beside Daryl and Ryan, who was still asleep. Daryl worriedly asked, "You sure, man, they can't touch us?"

"Absolutely, not with those spells watching."

The monsters, arriving full speed, reached the barrier of spells and they began howling louder. Not with joy this time. The shrieking bunch was badly burned. Their fur was burned by lightning and sparks bursting from everywhere. They left screaming, running away faster than they had come.

"See, man, I told you," laughed Paddy.

"Wow, I am glad you woke up in time."

"So am I. They won't be back, and if they do, they will receive the same treatment," Paddy said, with a chuckle.

"No chance they'll do it then," Daryl laughed.

Paddy rolled in his cape and went back to sleep. Daryl looked in the dark and curled up close beside Paddy. "What a night," he mumbled closing his eyes.

In the morning the sun showed its face. They had slept very well. Ryan opened his eyes and cheerfully said, "We are going to have a lovely day."

"Yes, boy. I am starved!" said the human, with a big smile.

"Me, too," laughed Ryan.

"All right, all right, breakfast is coming."

Ryan ran around, then stopped to look closely at the ground "Did you see the footprints here?"

"Yes, we had visitors during the night," replied Paddy.

"What kind of visitors? They must have been very big."

"Yes, Zoltar's creatures. Nice chaps, indeed. We invited them in, but they didn't want to come," said Daryl making a wry face.

Ryan laughed to tears.

"Come on now, eat, boy, instead of laughing at me!" said the human, pretending to be cross.

"I'm sorry, Sir, I didn't mean to offend you," said Ryan looking sadly at Daryl.

It's a joke boy, I just teased you," said Daryl ruffling the boy's hair.

"Really?" Ryan's eyes lit up.

"Of course."

He jumped to his feet and danced on the monster's tracks.

The bright sun in the sky was promising a nice warm day. Daryl checked the crown. "Yup," he replied adjusting his belt.

"Yes, if we don't have more nasty tricks from our friends Zoltar and Xary," replied Paddy.

Ryan giggled. "I know Daryl likes to be scared," he said mischievously.

"Be silent, you naughty boy," thundered Daryl's, with a voice big enough to impress the Dwarf.

Surprised Paddy looked at him. Then he saw Daryl ready to burst into laughter. "Good, for a moment I believed you were truly angry. Stop scaring the boy with your outbursts, silly guy."

"Are you kidding, man? I used to do it with my sister. I had lots of fun."

"He is not your sister. Look at Ryan's face, stupid."

Daryl slapped his knees, laughing, "I surely fooled you both."

"Enough playing, man, we have work to do, or did you forget."

"Nope, I will be glad to get rid of this thing and be an Elf again."

"You were an Elf? How come you are not anymore?" Ryan looked at Daryl with round eyes.

"Too long a story, my little friend. Let's go," Daryl said and smiled.

Ryan left, going after a butterfly, then he came back as fast as he had left.

"What's the matter? Are you already tired of running in the sun," asked Paddy.

"No, Sir! I just want to know what happened to the birds and the animals living in the Crystal mountain? Have they been killed?" he asked worriedly to Paddy.

"Not at all. The old Wizard protected the people and all living creatures within. They are in their Realm, Ryan."

"Ah good." Joyously Ryan returned to chasing after another butterfly.

"Nice little chap," remarked Daryl smiling.

The sun shone, warming up everything. After so many days in tunnels and caves it was a real treat. Ryan had stopped chasing butterflies. His face was red and he had big droplets of sweat on his forehead.

"You better put your cape on to cool off," advised Paddy. Surprised, Ryan did it.

"It's wonderful. I am not hot any more." Quietly, he walked beside his big friends.

The valley had large trees with delicious fruit. No shepherds, no animals were to be seen. Nature was still, and the pastures were deserted. All the villages along the river were silent.

As they passed through one of the deserted villages Paddy remarked, "Zoltar's creatures have been working here. Everybody has fled. Let's be careful. Probably they are still around."

"That monster is destroying peace everywhere," said Daryl.

"Yes, and it will be like that until we get him," replied Paddy.

They left the village walking silently. No more joyous outbursts from Ryan. Staring at his friends faces, he realized they were not teenagers engaged in a pleasure party. After a while they sat under the shade of a tree along the river. A delicious lunch was served. Paddy, knowing his buddy, pressed them to finish. They were not at a picnic. The urgency of the quest demanded their diligence. The elf wanted to be in a more protected area for the night. It was hard in this beautiful day to think that evil waited in the dark to destroy them. They moved faster. The lovely river shone under the sun.

"What a perfect place to go fishing!" said Daryl with envy.

"What's fishing?' asked Ryan curiously.

"You mean you don't know what fishing is?" Daryl looked at Ryan with unbelieving eyes.

"Honest, I don't."

Paddy, amused, followed the conversation for a moment, then he became a bit annoyed and asked, Look, man, how do you want the boy to know? Have you seen a river and trees in his Kingdom?"

Chapter 20

“Nope, I guess you are right. Well, Ryan, when the quest is over, I will teach you to fish.”

“Sounds like fun.”

“You bet it is! Shake hands on it to seal the deal.” With a solemn look on his face Ryan placed his wee hand in Daryl’s hand. Paddy watched them with a grin.

“We must find a ford to go across the river,” said Paddy.

“Maybe we will find a boat along the shore,” replied Daryl.

“The folks must have left them here. Look for both, ford and boat,” advised Paddy.

“You know now what a boat is, Ryan,” said Paddy.

“Yes Sir. It’s the thing that took us to the Swan City.”

“That’s right, but it’s not as fancy and not flying, boy,” replied Daryl laughing.

“So, let’s look for one then,” said Paddy.

They had walked for a while, when Ryan running ahead shouted, “Here, look, there is one tied at a post.”

Daryl ran to check it. “Good, it’s a nice one, too.” The human got busy loosing the knot. Paddy was watching the water. His sharp eyes noticed at the center of the quiet river some strange activity.

"Everybody on board!" cried Daryl laughing.

Since he had been (for the first time) in the boat going to the Swans city Ryan loved it. Joyously he embarked, followed by Paddy. Daryl was in his element. With a strong push, he sent the vessel away from shore. Quickly, he jumped in and grabbed the oars. "Here we are en route for a leisurely cruise," laughed the human boy.

"Keep your eyes opened, man. I don't like what I see. Remember all our moves are being watched," replied Paddy.

"Sorry, I was only trying to make the journey fun for Ryan."

"I know that, but I must be the watch dog of the party. It's not always a pleasant task," replied Paddy giving a slap on Daryl's back.

The river was large. To reach the middle took a long time. Paddy's eyes were still watching the center of the river.

"Daryl, row away from that agitated place. I don't like it, I feel evil there."

"But the water is very quiet. I don't see anything."

"I know, man, do what I say, please."

"Okay, I wis—" Daryl didn't finish his word. The boat was grabbed underneath and thrown violently upside down in the air by a mysterious force. They were heading to crash on a large rock formation on shore. The three passengers hung on, heads down. To stop Zoltar, Paddy shouted magic words. The boat rocked in the air and turned wildly. Two powers, good versus evil, were fighting. Suddenly the evil force let go. Paddy had won. He mumbled, and slowly the vessel stopped its spinning in the air. It went down on the water in line with the shore not far from a landing point.

"Wow, I guess it's needless to ask who did that," said Daryl shocked.

Ryan during the battle had wisely retired under the bench. As he crawled out he looked around with frightened eyes.

"Relax, Ryan, it's over." Daryl tried to steady his voice.

Paddy realized that his poor mortal friend was trembling. Angrily he said "I knew they were there, I felt evil presence in the middle. Are you both okay? The sorcerers are gone for the time being."

"Yes, I am. But, being human, things like that shake me up badly.

Let's go to shore." Daryl took the oars, rowing like mad and carefully avoiding the rocks. They arrived at the beach sound and safe. Ryan without a word quickly jumped off the boat, the boy had gotten the scare of his life. Wordlessly, they sat for a while on the green grass, then Paddy's voice sounded. "Let's go."

They left the valley. Ahead was a badland, bushy with rolling hills, big boulders, and deep gullys. Rapidly, the sun disappeared. It was time for the party to find a safe place for the night. "I am starved," complained Daryl. "Those emotions have made a big hole in my stomach."

"In mine, too. Scared or not, Sir, you always have a big hole in your stomach," Ryan giggled.

"Yes, but if you ask Paddy, he will tell you that when I have been badly scared, the hole gets much bigger, and right now this is the case."

"Same for me. This is the only time when I eat a lot," Ryan said soberly.

"Yup, then both of us will eat a lot." Daryl laughed

"Yes," replied Ryan. Paddy had followed the conversation and with a chuckle said, "First we must find a safe place."

After climbing down a deep gully to come out this chasm, they had to climb up a huge rock. From the top they saw upon the crest of the next hill a clump of large trees standing up like a small fortress. "Looks to be the perfect place for us. We will eat under the trees and sleep in their bushy branches," said Paddy.

Ryan danced and cried excited, "Wonderful. I never slept in or even climbed up a tree before."

"I am not as enthusiastic as you are at the prospect Ryan. Trees are for birds and monkeys, but I am neither one of them. My bottom is too heavy for that," replied Daryl making a grimace.

They walked for a while to arrive under the trees. Ryan looked at Daryl giggling. He sat on the grass and Paddy served a big meal. Daryl was in a mood to eat, and so was Ryan. The boy, with a large smile, watched the human and chuckled. No one will believe him when he tells his friends about Daryl's appetite.

They talked for a while and got ready to climb up the tree. Paddy gave a hand to Ryan. When on the first branch, the boy went up like a born squirrel. Ryan's dream was fulfilled! How many times had he wished to be up there looking down at the big world below! His friends like himself were too small to reach the lowest branches.

Daryl, heavy with the amount of food he had gorged himself on, had a hard time climbing up. He tried again and again and couldn't make it.

"Do you want me to push you up?" Paddy asked, laughing

"Nope leave me alone. I can do it by myself." Daryl was grouchy.

"All right, I am going up then," The elf leaped lightly from branch to branch and joined Ryan.

"Where is Daryl?"

Paddy replied with a chuckle, "Down below."

"Why? Is he afraid of climbing trees?"

"Well, he does not like it for sure, but this doesn't seem to be the problem right now. The truth is, he ate too well." Paddy laughed followed by Ryan's clear giggling.

"Poor Daryl, you can't leave him alone down there, Sir. What if Zoltar's monsters were to get him?"

"No, I am not going to." The young elf moved his hand.

"Here, you made it." Paddy grinned.

"You know perfectly well I didn't. You did it for me. My tummy was much too heavy for that sort of exercise." Daryl laughed, patting his stomach. "Any way thanks the same. I didn't cherish the idea of staying down there with Zoltar's pets for company."

Ryan giggled.

"Never mind I am going to remove the branches below. We don't want to be disturbed by the pleasant surprise of Goblins dropping on us for a visit during the night." The noise of falling wood reached them. "There, we can rest in peace now. Goodnight guys."

Ryan had found the perfect branch to curl up on, as did Daryl and Paddy. The night was without a moon, and soon the three travelers were sound asleep.

Chapter 21

In the darkness eyes were watching and waiting. Quietly, the creature crawled to the tree and slowly oozed its way up. Paddy felt its presence too late. At the speed of lightning, the monstrous reptile struck, and an evil laughter shook the night.

Daryl woke up. Paddy was terribly white. "What's the matter? What happened? Why are you so white?" asked his friend.

"I have been struck by a serpent. It was Zoltar, turned into a snake. My power has been drained out of me."

"Goodness! What can I do? Are you going to die?" Daryl was frightened. He didn't want to lose his buddy.

"No, relax. He has neutralized me with his venom. The power I had left is none to speak off. That is why he left"

"What are you going to do? You can't stay without power."

"I must go to the Fountain of Power and drink of its water."

"Where is it?"

"Quite far in the west. The voyage is going to take us away from our journey to the north."

"How do you feel? Thanks goodness your color has returned."

"I became white under the shock of my power seeping away from my body."

"Can you sleep? I will watch. You should rest now."

"Thanks, man. I accept the offer. I am tired."

"Goodnight, . Sleep well." Daryl leaned against a branch. Tense, he listened. How he wished he had his elfic eyes to see in the dark and his sharp ears to hear. He sighed regretfully he smiled, remembering that thanks to the lovely little Goldy he couldn't be seen by evil. The rest of the night was calm.

As a promise of a bleak day, a pale morning light showed up at the horizon. Ryan opened his eyes and gave Daryl a large smile.

"What are you doing, sitting up like a sentry watching what?" Daryl realized that the by was not aware of the tragic event of the night before. He had to tell him about Zoltar's attack on Paddy. Gravely Ryan listened.

When Daryl was finished the young Dwarf said "We must leave right away! Prince Patrick can't stay like that. Let's go!"

"Slow down, young man."

"I am not a man, I am a Dwarf."

"All right, no offence. For me a boy is a man,-Dwarf, Human, or Elf. Okay? Just wait for us."

Paddy woke up. "What's all that chattering about?"

"Our young friend was ready to take the road for the Fountain of Power, I think, without us," said Daryl with a chuckle.

"We are going, but together." Paddy patted Ryan's bonnet. From Daryl's backpack came some elfic biscuits which were quickly eaten. With the help of their capes they flew down and left going west. A heavy rain was falling making their walk difficult. Tall wet weeds tangled around their boots like snakes. Because of the weeds Daryl carried Ryan on his shoulders. To their misery. a strong head wind started blowing. Ryan could have been lost in that jungle of tall grasses.

After a while.Ryan tried to be brave. "Thanks, Daryl. I can make it."

"I know you can, but we will go faster if I carry you."

"I guess you are right." Ryan sighed. Time was extremely important. He knew that. With Ryan upon Daryl's shoulder they moved much faster. The big human boy fought wind and weeds furiously, anxious for his buddy. It was hard to see through the heavy rain. Everything was bathed in a gray veil and had an unreal, unpleasant feeling. The only certitude for them was that they were climbing up hills and lots of them, trampling in that miserable weather. Without stopping, a bite of biscuits was their meal. Daryl moaned and groaned, (but not too much) because of the dreadful situation Paddy was in. All day long the rain poured down, and the wind blew strong. The night came upon them

"Why don't you give us a proper shelter, man? We are tired to death. Gosh, I can see a nice fire to warm our wary bones."

"You are right. We certainly deserve it." The young wizard moved his hands. Nothing happened. He tried again.

"What's wrong, man?" Ryan hadn't said a thing. He only watched Paddy with sad eyes.

Don't you remember the Prince has lost his power?" His voice came down from Daryl's shoulders.

"I am stupid, really stupid! I am so used to Prince Paddy having power that I forgot he had lost it! Well, we have to sleep under our capes and eat our biscuits." Daryl grimaced at the thought.

"It's better than nothing," said Ryan cheerfully.

"You're right. Truth comes out of babes' mouths," laughed Daryl.

"I am not a babe," said Ryan, offended.

"No, you are not," replied Daryl. "I just hope during the night no one is going to come waking us up."

"Not likely. Zoltar knows I am powerless, useless in his book."

"The night is very dark and quite bad. We can be missed by anyone passing," added the young boy.

"I still have my sharp elfic hearing and eyes. But you are right, Ryan."

"Good. let's get set for the night then. Hurry, we have these wonderful elfic biscuits to eat," said Daryl.

Paddy chuckled. "Well, man, you will have to live on them for a while."

Daryl, disgusted, turned his head and said, "I am afraid you are right."

Ryan crawled under Daryl's cape, which took immediately the

shape of a small teepee. The temperature inside was nice and warm. After eating his biscuit, Ryan curled up and went to sleep.

"Goodnight, Daryl."

"Sleep well, man." A few minutes later Daryl was asleep. In the middle of the night the shaking ground woke him up. Paddy reassured his friend. "Don't worry. It's just a large band of Urks passing at about half a day's walk from us."

"Wow, lucky. We could have been trampled by them."

"Yes, man."

Scared, the young human sat for a while. He mumbled, "Paddy's power is not here to protect us any more. I must stay awake and watch."

"Don' t worry. Daryl. Go to sleep," said Paddy who had followed Daryl's thought in his mind "I still have a bit of power left. That is why I could hear you and the Urks. It's just not enough to conjure what we need or fight Zoltar and his acolytes, and they know it."

Worrying, Daryl finally fell asleep. A few hours later when they opened their eyes, the morning was still bleak, but the rain had stopped. With a grimace, Daryl ate his biscuit. Ryan giggled watching him.

"Let's go, we have a long day. Hopefully tonight we should be at the Fountain of Power," said Paddy.

A strong wind from behind pushed them helping the three walk faster. Ryan had tumbled several times. Without a word Daryl tossed the boy upon his shoulders. This time he didn't protest. They continued walking munching on their cookies. Paddy was well aware of the great danger they were in. The elf saw, high above the clouds, a large bird following them.

Chapter 22

"We are watched by the evil ones. A creature of theirs is spying on us, or maybe it's even Zoltar. They have found our trace," said the Elf.

"Where?" asked Daryl.

"See that black bird?"

"Nope, I don't see anything."

"I am sorry. I forgot you don't have your elfic sight any more."

"I know! Don't remind me. I will be glad when this is over."

Daryl touched the crown making certain it was still here. Smiling he nodded to Paddy.

They left the field of tall weeds for an area of rocks with clouds of sand and dust flying all over. Quickly, they pulled their hoods down. Perched on Daryl's shoulders, Ryan did the same.

It was twilight when from behind a huge boulder came an enormous hairy, smelly beast. His head had horns all around. He bore as a terrible weapon a large harpoon between his eyes. He stood up, poised on his hind legs, a giant. His outstretched front paws were armed with claws ready to tear apart anyone challenging him—a real killer. From his foul mouth, full of long sharp brownish teeth, a terrible roar spewed. In the dusk his yellow eyes shone. The monster moved slowly toward its prey, anticipating its victory.

Frightened to death Daryl screamed, "What are we going to do? You can't fight this without power, man! It will kill you!"

They ran behind a boulder. "I still have my Magic Sword." Daryl put Ryan on the ground. The little guy was so small that he could hide any place. The beast, furious, came at them full speed and violently pushed the big rock aside. Terrified they jumped back now facing the monster. It disgustingly drooled over it's prey. Huge paws grabbed Paddy and held the struggling elf just above his sharp teeth with the big horn pointed at him ready to harpoon him. The beast couldn't see Daryl beside him. Goldy's magic protected him from the evil beast, and Ryan was too small, hidden among the tall weeds. Paddy had his sword out pointed at the yellow eyes, but he couldn't reach them. The beast's arms holding him far from his eyes were too long. Paddy's magic blade, feeling evil, was firing lightning.

Helplessly, Daryl and Ryan watched the horrible tragedy. Ryan tried to distract the beast by screaming and thumping his little feet on the ground. His voice was too feeble to be heard above the terrible growling. In despair, the young Dwarf realized how futile this was! His face red with rage, furiously he continued to thump his feet turning at he same time around the monster trying to attract its attention. Daryl poked the beast with his sword, which was like an insect's bite to the monster. Ryan was still raging, and suddenly he found himself twice as big as the monster. Taking Paddy from the beast's paws he put him on the ground. Then he grabbed the horrible thing by the scuff of the neck and threw it on the rocks near by. Howling with pain, the monster disappeared in a puff of smoke. A few seconds later a small Dwarf proudly smiled at the feet of his friends.

"I didn't know you were a changeling, Ryan. This is wonderful," said Paddy, shaken, pulling on his doublet.

"Wow! I am glad you are our friend, Ryan." Daryl patted the yellow bonnet.

"But I didn't know I could do that! It just happened when I was furious, because I couldn't help you."

"You certainly did, boy. By now I should be dead. The evil ones knew I couldn't fight the beast without power, and they sent one of their strongest creatures," said Paddy.

"Do you suppose maybe he doesn't know you have lost your power? This could be the reason why he sent so strong beast after you. But it doesn't make sense! Why would he have laughed when the serpent struck you?" asked Daryl.

"I guess he was happy in his own sinister way. We were at his mercy, and he had scared us."

"Good! Then he will think this is your doing," replied Ryan.

Paddy smiled at the young boy and said, "Yes, powerful and wise Ryan. One thing, he is going to leave us alone for a while. By that time my power will be restored."

Daryl helped Ryan upon his shoulders. The wind continued blowing fiercely. Daryl covered Ryan under his cape, and off they went walking faster. They were in great danger. Maybe when the evil Wizards attacked again, Ryan wouldn't be able to help. That depended on what Zoltar or Xary would do next. They entered a nice grove with moss on the ground. The wind had stopped blowing as they approached and the dark blue sky shone full of stars. At the center of a meadow stood a large formation of granite with a grotto. In the granite a sparkling diamond half-moon shape had a spout of gold with a trickle of crystal clear water.

Paddy whispered, "The Fountain of Power," and he moved quietly toward the luminous spot. They had arrived.

"This is the Fountain of Power? You are kidding, man! It's merely enough to fill a glass. This is going to restore your power? I can't believe it! A teeny-weeny thing like that." Daryl pouted in disgust.

"Don't worry about the size. A few hours ago you had proof that size could be deceiving." Paddy walked to the fountain asking them not to move. Doubtfully, Daryl and Ryan watched in the clear night. The young elf stopped at the tiny fall. There Paddy made strange signs, and a goblet of gold appeared on a crystal shelf beside the diamond. Paddy took it, filled it, and drank. When empty, the goblet vanished, and he filled his hands with water and poured it over his head several times. His friends, amazed, saw Paddy glowing with sparks coming out of his body. He was on fire, burning like a torch. A few seconds later it was over. Smiling, the teen Wizard came back announcing, "I am again a Wizard."

"Wonderful! I am going to drink, too," said Daryl running to the fountain.

"No! You would be burned to ashes!" Paddy's hand was stretched out to hold him back.

"Why? Let me go!" cried Daryl, disappointed.

"Because you are not a Wizard."

"But you were not any more.'"

"I still was. Only my power had been cancelled. By the signs I gave, the fountain recognized me as such. Come on, Daryl, I am going to treat you to a feast."

Chapter 23

"Hurrah! No more biscuits!" Daryl forgot all about his itch to become a Wizard. Paddy cast a spell of invisibility upon the fountain. They sat away from the magic place in the grotto. Paddy quickly conjured a delicious meal. Outside the night was black.

"Why are all the stars gone?' asked Ryan.

"The magic of the fountain is at rest now. We will sleep here. I am going to cause the grotto to be invisible."

After a terrific meal Daryl rolled in his cape, and Ryan curled up underneath at his side. "Goodnight, Paddy, and thanks. It's surely nice to have your power back, man."

"You are welcome. Goodnight guys." Already asleep, the little boy didn't reply.

The next morning the wind was still down. The night had been quiet, and a delicious aroma of a good breakfast woke everybody.

"Ah, it smell so good. Tell me, Paddy, why the evil ones don't come here to get more power?"

"Only Wizards of Light can use it. If the Wizards of Darkness were drinking or even touching the water, they would be burned to cinders. Believe me, man, they know it."

"Good, I am glad they can't."

Their meal over, talking joyously and happy, they left the grotto in good spirits resuming their direction north. The terrain of crushed rocks was hard under foot. The bad weather had not returned. Ryan, like a young pup, ran back and forth. A few hours later they left the rocky region to be in a marsh. Many birds perched on tall legs, and with beaks as long as swords, pecked in the muddy water.

"What are they doing?' asked Ryan, watching them curiously.

"Fishing and eating," replied Daryl.

The little boy went running, splashing all around, laughing moving his tiny arms to scare the birds. Flapping their wings noisily they flew away.

"It's nice to be a young boy," said Daryl with a chuckle.

"Yes, we had a good time, too, in Earth Realm, didn't we?" Paddy laughed at the thought of their mischief.

The marsh was very large, and walking was a tiring business. The sun disappeared on the horizon, the birds had returned to their fishing.

"Where are we going to sleep?" asked Ryan trembling with cold.

"Well, I don't know yet. Put your cape around you to get warm and dry boy. It would be nice if we could find a dry spot away from this watery ground," said Paddy. As far as his eyes could see, it was wet land. The elf carefully scanned the marsh's surface. "Good, I see a small island on the right.

"How far?" asked Daryl.

"Not too far, about fifteen minutes away."

Ryan's teeth had stopped chattering. and he didn't shiver any more. The elfic cape had done a good job. He was dry. The island was small and covered with birds that left screaming at their approach.

"Let's have a nice warm soup, man. We are frozen," said Daryl. After a good hot meal, they rolled in their capes and went to sleep. It had been a trying day. Ryan quietly crawled under Daryl's cape.

A loud sound of flapping wings woke Paddy. The birds had returned and savagely attacked the sleepers. Without the protection of their elfic capes, they would have been pierced through by the long beaks.

Daryl was about to remove his hood and look outside, when Paddy cried, "Don't do that!"

Under the sharp injunction Daryl jumped. The young Wizard quickly moved his hand. The terrible flapping stopped. Only quiet sounds reached their ears. The human curiously looked through his cape. The birds were busy grooming their feathers, and one by one they had crouched on the ground. Heads under wings they went to sleep.

Daryl yawning whispered, “Good birds, good birdies. Let’s do the same. Sleep well, Paddy.”

The rest of the night was peaceful. In the early morning the birds left the island. Ryan woke, looked around excited, and shouted, “See! See here, the birds are fishing again!”

“Of course, they have to eat.” Daryl laughed. Then, puzzled, he turned to Paddy, “What happened last night? Why did they became wild like that?”

With a chuckle Paddy replied, “It was not a bad idea at all from the evil ones. They sent a spell to attack, harpoon, and kill with their long beaks.”

“They never miss an opportunity to make life miserable for us. Just wait.” Daryl patted the crown on his side.

Paddy quickly grabbed his hand and said, “Zoltar is trying his best to get us.” He touched Daryl’s belt and put a finger on his lips.

The boy replied with a grin, “Don’t worry, Paddy.”

The human boy added, “Yup, those birds were ready to harpoon us, but we are not the fish they catch every day.” Daryl chuckled, “One thing thanks to Goldy, they can’t see me or hear me.”

Paddy smiled, “That is true, man, but let’s not take a chance. Better speak elfic tongue, okay?”

“Fine with me, man, but what about Ryan?”

Paddy with a chuckle said, “I will open his understanding.”

Paddy touched Ryan bonnet. Curious about the conversation between the young men. the boy asked. “What happened with the birds?”

Paddy told him about the night attack. “They knew we are getting closer.”

Daryl made a terrible grimace, and Ryan laughed heartily.

“Why are you laughing, little friend?” asked Daryl offended.

Ryan still giggling said, "Your face, you made a such funny face."

"Well, my face is my face, funny or not, that's all," he said and grimaced at Ryan.

Paddy refrained from laughing and said, "Come on, guys, we must get out of the marsh."

They walked for the good part of an hour in the soggy soil and finally reached solid ground. Once more Ryan was all wet, and without any concern, like a puppy getting out of the water, shook himself splashing everybody.

"Thanks, pal," said Daryl. Paddy laughed, and dried Ryan with a spell.

"Thank you, Prince Patrick. It's nice to be dry. Why do you speak that funny language, and how come I understand it?"

"You are welcome, boy. Your cape would have done the same thing, but I am faster. It is with my help that you understand the Elfic language." Paddy grinned at him said, "Watching you enjoy paddling in the water, one would never thought you loved to be dried."

"Oh, but I do," replied Ryan, shocked.

Bleak weather undermined their spirit of adventure. In the north lightning flashed into the dark sky. Ahead, a mountain range was still to be climbed before they reached The Evil Valley, the dwelling place of Zoltar and Xary. They walked as fast as possible fighting their way through bushes of thorns and rocks. A nasty cold rain drenched them. It was almost dark when they arrived at the foot of the mountain.

"We are too tired to look for a shelter. We will have a cabin with good food and fire, and at last get warm," said Paddy. The elf moved his hand, and a small log cabin appeared. The back of the little shelter was against the rock.

"Hooray!" cried Ryan clapping his hands.

Quickly they ran to the house and opened the door. "Wow," said Daryl delighted at the sight of a fire burning in the chimney, and a table served with a steaming meal. Paddy quickly closed the door leaving rain and wind outside. The young Wizard gestured and made sure that he protected the cabin with strong spells. Pleased, he joined his friends. Daryl, satisfied, his back turned to the heat was rubbing his large bottom.

Paddy watched him. Smiling he said, “We can relax and rest from our fatigue.” Grinning to Ryan he sat on a comfy chair and stretched his long legs to the heat.

Chapter 24

The smell of food made Daryl's stomach growl. Quietly Paddy got up and went to sit at the table. Daryl, with a happy grin, followed his friend. Little Ryan, in one light leap, jumped on his high stool. No sound was heard, only the sound of the spitting fire in the chimney, the forks and knifes in the plates. The meal over, they sat by the fire. Tired, young Ryan rolled in his cape on the floor and fell asleep. Not too long after, both elf and mortal did the same.

The first part of the night was quiet. Just after midnight a large thing came and sniffed around the shelter. A few minutes later others joined him. A savage thumping crushed the ground. Paddy woke and looked through the small window. Ten large Urks rose up and started howling. Furious, they tried uprooting the house from the ground. Paddy smiled, glad to have protected the house with strong spells. Of course, the diabolic creatures could feel their presence. The elf returned to sleep by the fire, leaving the beastly brutes to their frustration.

The day was still bleak on the following morning. With the first light, the Urks had departed. Daryl looked outside at the falling rain. "I wouldn't mind staying inside by the fire, man."

"I know. Not too inviting, is it? I wouldn't mind either, but we have pressing business to attend to."

Gloomily Ryan looked out. In silence he sat at the table eating his breakfast. They left the warm shelter regretfully, and, hoods down, stepped into the rain. Paddy dismissed the cabin. Slowly men and boy searched at the bottom of the mountain for the trail leading to the pass. Everything was engulfed in a veil of water. For several hours they trampled in the mud. Finally, they found what they were looking for, behind a bunch of prickly bushes.

"Here it is guys. Our search is over," said Paddy.

"Good, I am not Ryan. I have had enough of being drenched with cold water for nothing. It won't be fun going up in this kind of weather," said the human.

With the abundant rain the ground was mucky. Rocks and pebbles viciously rolled loose under foot. Daryl worried about losing the crown. He held it tightly at his side and mumbled something in his hood.

Paddy chuckled. He could hear Daryl in his mind. He, too, would be happy when the quest was over. So many were suffering because of Zoltar and Xary's evil doings.

The trail became worse. Many times Ryan fell nose down in the mud. When he moved one step, he was pushed back by the rolling water and slippery stones.

Daryl watched the boy fighting endlessly. The human bent down, picked him up, and sat him upon his big shoulder under his cape. Ryan exhausted whispered, "'Thank you, Sir. I couldn't have fought any longer."

With the altitude came the cold. How thankful they were for their elfic boots and capes. Like a pack of wolves the wind howled around them. To add to their misery, the rain turned to heavy snow.

Daryl came closer to Paddy. Worried he asked, "When are we going to be out of this storm? Is it far to the pass?"

"I don't know, man. I hope it will be soon." Paddy held his hand up to stop. Above the din of the screaming wind, a noise as terrible as a thousand charging horses shook the mountain.

"That is not the wind. It is an avalanche!" Paddy yelled too late. In a fury tons of snow rolled into the abyss. They didn't have time to take cover. They were taken for a ride inside a gigantic snowball, bouncing, rolling, crushing on its way trees, shrubs, and whatever else was in its path.. Then, at last, the silence. The horrid voyage had stopped! The ghastly ride had ended, but where?

"Are you hurt, Daryl?"

"Nope, only bruised."

"And you, Ryan?"

Ryan's voice came out from Daryl's cape. "I am all right, Sir, only shaken up.

"So are we, Ryan. The important thing is that we are all alive and well," Paddy replied.

"What a ride. How are we going to get out of this cocoon man?" asked Daryl.

"Easy. Watch." Flashes burst out from the Wizard's fingers destroying the snowball. A few seconds later they were free and in a valley full of flowers and singing birds.

"Wow! Are we back in our Realm, Paddy?" asked Daryl.

"No, this is not it."

Rubbing their ribs, they got up stretching legs and arms. A field of wheat gently swayed in the breeze. Laughter reached their ears, but they couldn't see anyone.

"Where are they?" asked Daryl.

"I think I know where we are."

"Where?" eagerly asked Ryan.

"In the Realm of the Invisible Elves."

"Just what we need, people we can't see," mumbled Daryl.

"But you can, man. Remember, Goldy gave you the gift of invisibility. So you are in their Realm," laughed Paddy.

"What? That's right! I see them on the other side of the field. They are cutting the wheat."

"Good. Don't forget to make use of your gift, Daryl, or you will lose it."

"Thanks, man, for reminding me about it. I had forgotten."

"They are surely a busy bunch," said Paddy.

"You can see them, too?" asked Ryan.

"Of course. I am a Wizard."

"What about Ryan?"

"No, he can't," replied Paddy.

"Will they see us?" asked Ryan.

"Yes, boy, they can see you," said Paddy.

They approached the group where elves worked diligently. The chattering and laughing stopped. "Hello, greetings, friends. I am Prince Patrick from the Elfic Realm of the Promised Valley. Daryl, my squire, is a human from the Earth Realm, and young Ryan is from the Dwarves Kingdom of the Blue Mountain. They are my friends and comrades."

"Welcome, Prince Patrick of the Elfic Realm," replied the leader. "I am Irca, elder of the Invisible Elves Realm. Come, please, I will escort you to our Chief Elder."

Curious shining eyes followed them. They walked in the valley and while talking arrived at a small village tucked in a quiet meadow. The wood houses, painted different colors, were lovely, shining under the sun like jewels.

"Wow, those houses are beautiful," said Daryl admiring the little village.

"They surely are."

"What houses? I see only trees in a meadow," replied Ryan, disappointed.

"It's really too bad. There are many smiling children looking at you," said Daryl.

"I don't see them," replied Ryan sadly.

"Can't you do something for him, man?"

"This is their Realm, and, yes, I can, but only with the Chief Elder's approval."

"Please, Sir, will you ask him?" Ryan's eyes shone.

"Yes, I will," replied Paddy.

Paddy introduced himself and explained that he was a Wizard of his own realm, and that was the reason why he could see them, and that Daryl had received from a fairy of the elfic realm a special gift to be himself invisible to evil. Paddy then looked with sympathy to Ryan and presented the request of the young dwarf to the Chief.

Iork, the chief elder, had a commanding stature. He was extremely impressive—tall, slim, with long straight blond hair touching his shoulders. A large gold belt around his waist held a light green tunic reaching his knees which were covered with white satin tights. His feet had gold boots. He looked kindly at the shining eyes of the small Dwarf. Smiling he said, "Permission granted, little one."

Chapter 25

Paddy touched Ryan's eyes. At once he could see the colorful village and the smiling children. "Oh, thank you, may I go and play with them, Sir?".

"Of course, child," replied the Chief Elder.

Happily Ryan left to join the youngsters waiting for him. Eager hands pulled their new friend away. Poor Ryan, since the loss of his family in the mountain, hadn't had much fun with the elf and the human teen who were too much preoccupied about their important business. The boy had a glorious time with the children.

In a few words Paddy explained the quest they were engaged in.

Iork replied, "Fortunately, Zoltar or Xary can't do a thing to us. They know of our Realm because they are Sorcerers, but they are powerless against us and can't act through their creatures. For them we are invisible. Only I have the power to say you may see us. Believe me, I won't!"

The children took Ryan to the secret place of their own where they hid their most precious treasures, a splendid crystal rock shining with the colors of the rainbow. Some very large purple and green scales from a dragon, an old spinning wheel spinning by itself, several big lizards, snakes. and a huge turtle named Gurtry. There were also all sorts of other items dear to them.

"We take turns feeding Gurtry and the other animals," explained the children. "After a while we let them go. It's fun to catch new ones," they giggled, "but Gurtry always comes back."

They stayed with those nice people for two days. Ryan needed a break. Daryl specially enjoyed the food, the music, and the dance.

Then Paddy said, "We are sorry to leave, but continuing our quest is very important. Zoltar and his accomplice become bolder every day."

Iork replied, "Yes, it's not because the evil ones can't touch us that we must be selfish, boy."

Paddy gently touched Ryan's head, and the spell of invisibility was gone. "Oh, I don't see the children anymore," said Ryan sadly.

"I know. Sorry that was a temporary gift permitted by the elder, Ryan."

An elf was appointed to escort them and to show the trail going up to the mountain. Daryl remembering the bad weather said, "It's a shame we have to go there again."

"The trail is not bad. We use it to go to the other side often," replied the escorting elf. Courteously he bowed to Paddy and left the party wishing them a safe journey.

The weather was pleasantly warm and the trail wide enough for them to walk abreast. Ryan ran searching for unusual rocks and plants. It was a good day. "With the avalanche, Zoltar must have lost our tracks," said Paddy.

"Let's hope he won't find them until I crown him!" mumbled Daryl between his teeth. The trail got wider and to everyone's joy Paddy had enough room to conjure a little shelter. He quickly cast spells upon it. With the altitude the night was extremely cold, and a fire in the chimney was a must. Entering the house, they found two lovely guests looking surprised, a mountain goat and her baby.

"Oh, no, the evil ones have found a way to get in," shouted Daryl running for the door.

"Relax man there is nothing evil about these animals. When I conjured the shelter, I didn't notice them on the trail."

"Are we going to keep them here for the night?" asked Ryan getting closer to pet the baby goat who bleated.

"Well, I don't know, let me talk to the mother," replied Paddy. The young wizard looked into the mother's eyes, and then he said to Ryan. "Be happy, boy, she agreed to stay with us. I will provide food and water for them."

"I am so glad. Thank you, Prince Patrick." The baby goat bleated softly. Ryan sat beside his new friend. The little animal put his head on the boy's knee. The mother quietly lay down beside them. Paddy smiled at the charming picture. Daryl complained about being starved.

"Okay, man, here is a good meal for all of us, The day has been long and hard. We need it." A delicious smell filled the room. The agile goat got up to eat the hay provided by Paddy.

"May I eat here, with my friend?" asked Ryan.

"Sure, boy." Daryl filled a plate and brought it to Ryan. Curious the little goat sniffed it, sneezed, and got up to suck his mother's milk. When finished he came back to lie down by Ryan. The mother continued eating, enjoying every mouthful. The young boy and the baby goat had fallen asleep. Tiptoeing, Daryl went to get Ryan's plate. He covered the boy with his cape, then returned to sit with Paddy.

Both elf and human were tired. They rolled in their capes and went to sleep. Nothing happened that night. Probably Zoltar and Xary thought they had perished in the avalanche. The next morning the sun shining through the window woke the party.

"Wow, we surely slept well," Daryl said stretching his arms with a big yawn.

Ryan and the baby goat jumped on their legs to look outside. "I think it's time to open the door for our guests," said Paddy.

"Oh no, they will go," cried Ryan alarmed.

"Of course, Ryan, they can't stay with us," replied Paddy.

Without a word Ryan went to the baby goat, kissed him goodbye, and with Daryl's help opened the door. "Have a good day, gentle friend. Be careful, please." The goat nuzzled Ryan and left with his mother. Before disappearing at the bend of the trail going down the valley, he turned around to look at Ryan. Sadly the boy waved goodbye.

After breakfast Paddy, dismissed the little cabin with a flip of his hand. A warm sun shone, the birds chirped happily in the bushes white with snow. Briskly, they walked away on the quiet trail.

"We are spoiled by this beautiful weather," said Daryl throwing a snowball at Ryan who had begun to look unhappy. The boy turned his head and grinned at him. "Cheer up boy, your little friend will be better off in the valley."

Ryan sighed whispering, "I guess so."

Paddy watched dark clouds gathering menacingly above their heads. "I don't think the good weather is going to last long. Look guys, see what's approaching from the north."

The birds left, flying south. The sun suddenly disappeared behind a large black cloud, and a big gust of cold wind arrived. Shivering, they quickly pulled their hoods down. "I am glad the baby goat and his mother went toward the valley of the invisible Elves," said Ryan, now much happier.

"Good, because soon we are going to be in miserable weather, boy," replied Daryl.

Grumpy Paddy added, "Zoltar found us." He looked at the sky getting darker. The strong wind pushed Ryan so hard in the back that he fell flat on his face. "Better you come with me, Ryan. This is not weather for you. I will carry you until it gets better," said Daryl.

Chapter 26

"No, thanks, Sir, I can manage." The boy stood up and grabbed Daryl's cape just in time to avoid being blown into the ravine.

"Don't be stubborn, Ryan. Let me help you."

With a big sigh Ryan let Daryl pick him up. The heavy human fought hard to stay on track, while the light elf walked painfully bent against the unleashed elements. Fortunately, the trail was wide enough to prevent them from being blown into the abyss. The thunder rolled angrily in the dark sky. Lightning streaked the ground around them.

"Zoltar and his friend Xary are trying to get us with their heavy artillery," yelled Paddy.

"Thunder and lightning have never been my favorite things," yelled back Daryl jumping aside to avoid an electric zap.

The noise of the storm rolled in the ravine growling like a mad beast in its cage, and the thunder boomed against the high walls of the mountains. The rain came down with a vengeance.

"I hope we are going to find a cave," yelled Daryl.

No answer. The elf was catching other noises beside the wind and the thunder. A large body of something or someone was coming down the trail ahead of them. Paddy shouted, "Stop! Hurry, hurry, put yourself flat against the mountain. Give me Ryan. Remember, Daryl, don't panic. You are invisible to evil. I am going to shield Ryan."

As the elf finished talking, just in time they found a place to tuck themselves in a large crack, a sort of chimney. A howling band of Goblins arrived and stopped in front of them. Daryl almost panicked, but suddenly his arm was locked n a vice by Paddy's hand. Sniffing in the storm they smelled the elf, and as always they argued and fought like demons. Many were lost in the process falling into the abyss. Daryl remembered the fun he'd had in the cave. They couldn't see him! So, quickly he pushed Paddy' hand from is his arm and entered the fight. Cheerfully he distributed blows at random making the matter worse. In the heat of the battle, half of them disappeared into the chasm. Others, screaming in the storm, forgot what the fight was about, and left running.

Daryl continued booting the ones closing the rear. "Well, I've had my sport and fun for the day," he said, satisfied, laughing, rubbing his hands, and sweating a little bit.

"Zoltar is not going to be very pleased by the loss of so many Goblins, and Xary will not excuse that loss either," said Paddy with a chuckle.

"Yup, too bad, those nasty ones should choose better allies," replied Daryl still laughing.

Ryan was mighty quiet. The little fellow had been scared out of his wits. Night had come and now they were walking in a deep darkness. Daryl couldn't use his elfic stone for fear the sorcerers would see him. Paddy, afraid of loosing him and Ryan in the storm, had linked his friend by a spell unto him. With the help of his night vision the elf looked for a place to set camp. Then he saw a piece of rock, a large extension of the mountain, a huge arm crossing the trail high up above their heads. "Here, this will be the perfect place for us to sleep."

Daryl asked, "Where? I don't see anything of the sort."

"Of course you don't. You can't see in the dark! It's above your head. Give me your hand. I will take you and Ryan up there."

As they left the goblin battleground Ryan quietly returned under Daryl's cape. Paddy grabbed his hand, then the human and the boy found themselves floating in the air. Gently they landed on mossy ground. "How nice it's so soft," said Daryl putting Ryan upon his feet.

"Yes, but right now with all that rain, it's soggy. That why it is soft," replied Paddy.

The wind was howling fiercely around. The young elf made a circle with his arm and dried the place where he caused a small cabin to appear. Not fearing to be seen by anyone, Daryl put his elfic stone on his forehead. So did Ryan. Daryl looked at the size of the cabin and said, "But, man, the wind is going to blow us and this little accommodation away."

"Don't worry, I secured it with spells. We can't have a stronger house, I don't know the strength of that rock."

No more argument from Daryl was heard. They walked in, glad to be out of the rain and the cold wind. At the center of the small room, in a circle of stones burned a cheery fire. Around it was a large wooden bench with comfortable cushions. Sighing with pleasure they sat. Ryan had been quiet for the longest time. Paddy grew worried and asked, "What's the matter, Ryan? You haven't been very noisy those past hours."

"Nothing, Prince Patrick. Maybe this quest is too much for me. Sometimes I would love to be with my family, like any boy should, that's all," he replied with a big sigh.

"You are very brave and your family will be proud of you, Ryan. Your friends will envy you when you tell them of your prowess," replied Paddy.

"Do you think so, Prince Patrick?" The boy's eyes shone.

"Of course Ryan. Would you like me to send you back to your family? I can do that you know, but we will miss you."

Ryan smiled.

Paddy, worried, watched him.

Daryl shook his head approvingly.

Paddy thought, *The boy has been through a lot in a short time.*

The human looked at his old earthly friend, they smiled at each other. Ryan was still quiet pondering what Paddy had just said to him. No decision had been made by the youngster. He sat at the table for a good meal, perplexed. He didn't know what decision to make. He loved the quest and missed his family, too.

The meal over they rolled in their capes by the fire and went to sleep. The wind howled outside, and the rain beat wildly at the window.

Slowly in the night, the arm of stone moved and curled itself in the shape of a gigantic hoop. With a powerful thrust, the hoop was in the air. The cabin hadn't moved. Soundly asleep, Paddy didn't realize what was happening.

Ryan, restless, got up and through the little window looked outside. Screaming he gave the alert. Startled the young Dwarf stood at the window. "We are flying! Look, look!" yelled Ryan.

"What's the matter? What do you say, boy?" asked Daryl rubbing his eyes.

Ryan excitedly thumping his foot replied in a shrilling voice, "I say we are flying."

Paddy in a light leap was on his feet looking outside. "He is right, Daryl. We are flying in a large hoop of stone. It is incredible, man, but true."

"What? Flying in a hoop of stone? You are kidding, man!" Daryl jumped and looked outside. The human burst in a thundering, "Wow!" They were in the sky among the stars, brushing planets, going through the galaxy at a vertiginous speed. Daryl mumbled, "It's a dream, of course."

"No, Daryl, it's real. But, by what enchantment are we in the sky?

Wonderful, wait until I tell that to my friends," Ryan laughed and clapped his hands. The boy had forgotten his longing for home.

"Where are we going, this time, at this speed?" asked Daryl baffled.

"We'll see. This is not Zoltar's doing, neither Xary's," replied the elf.

Skeptically Daryl asked, "How do you know, man?"

"I would feel evil, and I don't."

Daryl raised his brows. "Ah."

It took the best part of the night to arrive where they were going. Ryan's nose was glued to the window. The speed decreased gently. The hoop entered fluffy white clouds and emerged in a brilliant sun to land on a pad polished like a mirror. Workers left their busy jobs to meet the flying noiseless hoop. A small saucer arrived gliding almost at ground level. The glass dome opened, and a tall young man dressed in a silver jumpsuit stepped down. He removed a tight-fitting silver helmet, and long black hair spilled out. Smiling, he said, “Welcome to the Planet of Light, Prince Patrick and friends.”

Chapter 27

"Who are you? Why are we here?" asked Paddy dryly. The young Prince was not accustomed to being treated this way.

The man bowed. "Come with me, please. You will receive answers to your questions." He courteously showed the saucer.

They climbed on board. Immediately it flew away by itself, this time higher in the sky. During the short voyage no words were spoken. Ryan's eyes were not big enough to see all he wanted to see. Mind you, It was only blue sky, nevertheless he was watching in case he should miss something. They flew above a splendid edifice of white onyx with windows in crystal reflecting the bright light of the sun. Silently, they landed on a shining terrace with beautiful trees around. The glass bubble opened.

The tall man bowed and softly spoke showing the way to a door which silently opened. "Follow me, please." They entered a large luminous hall. The young man once more bowed and without a word left. An oppressive silence fell upon their shoulders.

"Strange, what's the meaning of this? Are we supposed to find our way in this Wizard house?" asked Daryl troubled by the course of the events.

"I don't think so. Just wait. I am sure someone will come."

Just at that instant a little man ran to them, puffing red in the face, apologizing. He was dressed in dark blue tights and a white shirt. A silver cape floated gracefully behind him. Upon his long red hair a silver cone-shaped hat had a dancing dark blue feather at the top, giving him the appearance of a clown. The long supple plume brushed his shoulders, flying around like a wild bird at each move he made. "Please excuse me. I should have been here to greet you. It was only when the bell rang in the hall that I knew you had arrived. I am sorry." He bowed, the dancing plume touching the ground.

Ryan almost lost his composure and put his hand over his mouth as a burst of laughter was ready to escape. A sharp glance from the elf stopped him. Daryl bit his lips, with tears shining in his eyes. Quickly he bent down to pull at his boots.

Paddy composed himself and, in his best Princely behavior, said, "Don't trouble yourself my good man. It's of no importance. We want to know what we are doing here, and why we have been brought to this place without our knowledge and consent," replied Paddy

"Please, come with me." As the little man bowed the plume once more touched the ground, and he didn't answer. He turned around to guide them. They walked away with the strange and marvelous feeling of going through light itself. A great peace filled their hearts. Fear and worry had left Daryl's troubled mind. They crossed many halls, climbed up delicate stairs of light. At last they arrived in front of a large archway with doors made of thin transparent gold like a veil. The personage bowed, and the plume once more touched the ground. There was no laugh from the boys who were fascinated by the golden doors. The man left. Mysteriously, one door opened.

At first they were blinded by the light filling the room. A pleasant voice spoke. "Welcome Prince Patrick. Welcome Daryl and Ryan. I am the Lord of Light and Peace." A slim man dressed with a long shimmering silver gown faced them his hair was white as pure snow and his sharp eyes blue turquoise.

"Thank you, your Lordship." Paddy bowed. "I am confused. In my realm I have met other Lords of Light"

"Yes. They are my sons, Prince, sent by me to your realms to help in time of need." The blue eyes shone pleasantly.

"But they are so old," Paddy said. "They have been in our realms for millennia."

"I know, like myself, as old as the world. You wonder why you have been brought to my Realm."

"Yes, your Lordship," replied Paddy still puzzled by the whole thing.

The great Lord smiled. "In my Realm dwell only the righteous ones. We have been watching you for a long time. You and your friend Daryl are worthy of living with us. So I sent for you."

Paddy jumped. "But, your Lordship, you can't do that. In my Realm they need us. We have a quest to finish. If we don't, my people will be doomed," replied Paddy alarmed.

"I have not been informed of this by my sons. Please speak. I will judge if this is a worthy cause and act upon it."

Paddy told all about the quest and Zoltar and his evil partner and their diabolic doings. How Daryl was the only one able to destroy him with the magic Crown of Sapphire. The Lord of Light listened attentively, sharply looking at the two young men. Ryan was all ears and eyes.

"Your Lordship, I am needed in my Realm," replied Paddy with a smile. It was the first smile since they had left the mountain unexpectedly.

The Lord of light smiled, too. "I know that you are brave, kind and honest. It would appear that your place, young Prince, for now, is among your people."

"Thank you, your Lordship. Please, will you be kind enough to let us continue our quest?" asked Paddy, a little worried.

"Indeed. I see that you must return quickly to your Realm. I don't have any right to keep you away from your duty. One day we will meet again, boys. Your wish will be granted. Farewell for now; Prince Patrick, Daryl and Ryan."

The light got so bright around the Lord that for an instant they were blinded. When they were able to see again, he had vanished. The little man entered. His feather was still dancing around his face. No giggling from Ryan. On the terrace, their pilot waited for them. Without any comment they returned to the flying hoop, and went back to the Elfic Realm.

Being on board for hours going at a vertiginous speed, suddenly darkness shrouded the hoop, and vapors of sulfur choked them. Then they found themselves attacked from everywhere by diabolic creatures from space. The monsters were on the arm of the hoop trying to prevent them from reaching the safe refuge of the mountain. The battle was fierce. Entering the house was impossible. Daryl tried using his sword, but against evil he had no power. Paddy called the strength of high wizardry and managed to free them from the evil snare by sending spell after spell of destruction. In a big explosion all was finished. Stunned they entered the cabin, and, exhausted, collapsed on the floor. The hoop resumed its course. They arrived next afternoon. The arm of rock slowly stretched itself out at the same place from which they had left. The rain was still pouring, and the wind howling.

"I prefer this nasty weather, man, to the Realm of Light. I am not ready for such perfection." Daryl chuckled.

"Neither am I. I understand what you mean, man," replied Paddy.

"If we had stayed up there, I wouldn't have been able to tell my story to my friends. I would have been very unhappy," said Ryan.

"Why? Because of your story?" asked Daryl.

Surprised, Ryan looked at him. "No! I really don't mind that much about my stories. I love my family, and I want to be with them."

"You are right, Ryan. I didn't think about that. When I was a young Lad, I didn't appreciate my folks because I thought they didn't love me. I was such a troublemaker. But now I realize how much they did to put up with me. I don't have any family of my own here."

"How sad for you Ryan look at him with sympathy.

"I guess so," sighed Daryl, with regrets about all the mischievous things he had done to his sister and parents in the earth realm.

Paddy looked at him, and smiled. "Come on, man, no sad thoughts." He gave his buddy a nudge in the ribs. "It's time to leave, guys."

After dismissing the little shelter they flew down. Ryan resumed his place under Daryl's cape. Bent under the wind and the rain, they walked away. The trail was still going up. The temperature had dropped even more, and it was bitterly cold. They pulled their hoods down to protect their faces against the freezing rain.

Chapter 28

It became extremely difficult to walk. Their elfic boots helped them greatly to stay safely on track. Ryan, under Daryl's cape, was thankful for the human kindness. They fought this bad weather for several hours. At last Paddy spotted a cave on the side of the trail. "Night is coming fast, we should stop here. Maybe tomorrow the weather will lift," said the elf.

"I agree, a warm meal and a dry place will be appreciated." Daryl grinned at Ryan who had jumped down from his shoulders

The cave was spacious with soft sand. exhausted they dropped down. Their tired bodies were now feeling the hard walk on the icy trail along with the battle against the nasty weather. Ryan stomped his feet.

"We better have a fire going," said Paddy. The elf immediately closed the entrance with spells to keep the wind and rain out. Then he conjured a big fire and beside it put a huge pile of wood for the night. They sat around warming up their frozen bones.

Rested, Daryl became famished. "How abut feeding us, man. My stomach is growling dangerously."

Paddy laughed. "I was waiting for that one. I thought you had forgotten about eating."

"Are you insane? Me forgetting eating Never, I was only recovering from the cold."

"I see, and you, Ryan, still cold?" asked Paddy.

"I am fine, thank you, Sir. But I would like, please, to have a hot soup to warm my insides. They have turned to ice."

"Here it is, Ryan."

In the boy's hands appeared a large bowl of vegetable soup steaming hot. "Oh, thank you, Prince Patrick, Just what I need."

Daryl smiling at his little friend said, "Eat, you need it." For once the human forgot his stomach and with real pleasure watched the boy eating.

"Here, man, eat before it gets cold." On Daryl's lap appeared a large plate. "This is the reward of a hard day of labor, guys," said Paddy. Only the sparks from the fire and the noise of Daryl's mouth working with ardor on a big bone full of meat was heard. Ryan, his soup finished, rolled in his cape by the warmth of the burning wood and fell asleep. Their meal over, the two friends did the same.

"Goodnight, Paddy"

"Goodnight, man."

In the morning Ryan was red with fever. The poor boy had caught a bad cold, and he was coughing his lungs out. Paddy gently rubbed his forehead to make the fever disappear, and for the cough made a special herb tea to drink. The boy curled up into his cape and fell asleep at once. He woke at noon and said, "I am hungry, I feel fine."

"Are you sure?" asked Daryl worried.

"Yes, honest, I am fine now."

Daryl asked Paddy. "Is it true, man?" The boy was very dear to him.

"Yes, as if he had never been sick." The weather outside was nasty. "Do you think we should go? Ryan could be sick again."

"Come on, man, he is all right."

They left and Daryl, just to make sure the boy was not going to catch cold, took him under his cape. The snow had been falling during the night. "We are getting closer to the pass. We should see the Evil Mountain from there," said Paddy.

"Good, it's about time. I am impatient to crown His Majesty."

"You will soon, man, you will."

The snow was blowing wildly. It was almost impossible to see anything around. Paddy tied himself to Daryl with a spell for fear of loosing him and Ryan in the blizzard. The great danger of falling into the abyss was there, too. Heads down they moved slowly. Hours later they arrived at the pass. The snow there blew fiercely and the wind screamed like a loose demon.

"Zoltar does not want us to see his lair or how to get there, " said Paddy.

"We are stuck,"said Daryl.

"No, don't worry. I will see through his spells."

The teen Wizard faced the mountains and moved his hand slowly in front of his eyes, just as if he were wiping the steam off a window. The mountain range appeared to Paddy. At the center, dark and foreboding, stood the highest peak, the dwelling of Xary and his guest Zoltar.

"There it is," whispered Paddy.

"Where, where?" asked Daryl boiling with impatience.

"Sorry, man you can't see it with your human eyes."

"I can't either," said Ryan looking through Daryl's cape.

"No, you can't, boy, you are not an Elf," said Paddy/

"I know! I am a Dwarf," replied the boy joyously.

"I can't do the blasted deed fast enough, man. I want my elfic body back." grumpily growled the human.

Paddy smiled, remembering how Daryl on earth didn't believe in Elves. "Patience, you will be an elf soon."

It was almost dark. Paddy found the perfect place to put up a small cabin. When he had finished protecting their shelter, he rubbed his hands with satisfaction. "There, now we may relax. With the fire burning in the chimney we are going to enjoy a good hot meal, how about that?"

Daryl sat on the floor and Ryan crawled beside him. "Splendid!" replied Daryl without any joy.

"What's the matter, Sir?" asked Ryan looking at Daryl.

"Don't worry, boy. He will be all right, Just a bit down the weather because he isn't an elf anymore."

"But you will be again, Sir." Ryan put his small hand on Daryl.

"Yes, I know, but at times it gets me."

"Here is something to set you on the right track." On the floor in front of Daryl, appeared a large steaming plate. With a large smile he forgot his depressed mood. Food was the best magic for him. Paddy grinned at him. He knew his old pal well. The meal over, they rolled in their capes and went to sleep. Outside the storm raged. Zoltar tried hard to blow the cabin into the abyss. The next morning the house was buried under a mountain of snow. Paddy chuckled. He said, "How childish of them to bury us."

"Good, then he has no more bad tricks in his bag," replied Daryl.

"Oh, yes, he has, and a lot, believe me."

The snow was still falling, and the visibility was nil. Paddy dismissed the cabin, and they left. Ryan was safely tucked under Daryl's cape. The boy wouldn't have been able to walk in that deep snow. "The mountain range is in the shape of a horse shoe. We are standing at the left of the Evil Mountain. The sorcerers' dwelling is in the center."

Curious and worried Daryl asked, "How are we going to get there?"

The young wizard smiled, "Well, by following the trail, man, until we reach their lair."

Daryl made a grimace, "Sounds too simple for being safe, man."

Paddy laughing gave a big slap on his friend's back, "You are getting wise, Daryl."

"Yup!"

Chapter 29

Paddy's sharp wizard eyes scanned the trail. In the middle, a strange dark blemish covered a big part of the way they had to go through. Paddy pensively said, "I see across the trail that there is a dark pot on the white snow, but there is nothing here to make a shadow."

"Let's go see what's going on out there. Anyway we can't stay here forever," said Daryl leaving with decision.

"Hey, slow down, man, be wise." The young Wizard stopped him, grabbed his arm, and took the lead, Daryl sheepishly followed. A mighty silent Ryan was still under his cape. It took a good hour before the human boy's eyes could see what Paddy was talking about.

"Wow, now I see it. How strange. There is nothing around here to create this large black spot."

"I know. This troubles me to no end. I feel strong waves of evil coming from this place."

Cautiously they approached. The shadow oozed toward them. Suddenly from out of the snow sprung a gigantic beast with three heads and the carapace of a lizard. It stood in the middle of the trail on four massive legs, and its monstrous tail switched furiously lifting from the ground a tremendous cloud of snow making it almost impossible to see. It spat flames from its three enormous mouths at once. The mountains shook and cracked.

"Wow." Daryl, jumped back in fear.

Paddy gathered all his power and tried to kill the monster. He couldn't muster enough energy. He sent lightning bolts and bolts of fire with no result. "This is the evil ones' last resource. They have joined all their power to conjure that monster. The beast guards the entrance of their lair." Paddy made a terrible face.

"What are we going to do? We must go into that place," said Daryl.

Quietly, he left. Evil couldn't see or feel him. When at the monster's side he waved to Paddy. The young Wizard didn't pay attention to his friend, but Ryan was watching. Paddy called once more upon his full power with the hope that this time he would be strong enough to destroy the evil beast. Concentrating his mind, slowly he lifted his arms and threw thin ropes of fire to ensnare the monster. Now, it was ensnared in a net of fire, Paddy destroyed one of its heads. It roared in pain and stretched one neck a long way out and grabbed Ryan. When the battle had started, the boy had left Daryl's cape.

" Ryan, it has Ryan!" cried Daryl horrified from behind the monster.

"Let me go! Let me G—O!" screamed the little one hanging at the monster's teeth. In rage he kicked as hard as he could. His face became purple, and he lost all fear. The monster was not holding a poor frightened Dwarf anymore, but something even larger then the beast. It was facing a gigantic porcupine like beast with horns all over its body. Two enormous arms grabbed the remaining necks and tied them together in a big knot. With a powerful swing it threw the beast into the abyss.

Paddy hadn't moved, knowing the evil was doomed. He smiled. Speechless, Daryl had watched the fight.

"There, it's gone," said Ryan who had changed to his normal self. Satisfied, he rubbed his small hands as he looked at his friends.

"Wow! Ryan, you are something! The evil Wizards must be furious. You have killed their pet." The human boy shivered, the hair at the back of his neck stood up.

"'I am glad you helped, Ryan. The evil ones combined power was terrible. The beast was almost undefeatable," said Paddy.

"I am happy I could, Prince Patrick."

"Now the way is opened. Let's go," said Daryl exhilarated by the battle, his fear gone.

"Just a minute, man. Let me check if nothing else is waiting for us out there." The young Wizard very carefully scanned the trail. "We may go I don't feel any immediate danger. Deadly evil is there, but not threatening us at this instant."

After not much difficulty they arrived at the wall of Xary's lair. A terrible whirlwind of fire caught Paddy and Ryan but not Daryl. The whirlwind opened the wall, and Daryl rushed in remembering that he couldn't be seen or felt by evil. That was the reason he was not taken into the fire with Paddy and Ryan. The evil ones didn't know he was there. Quickly, Daryl followed them in the whirlwind.

Invisible, Goldy watched the human and whispered "I am glad I helped him"

A triumphant cry rang n the courtyard. The fire had died down, leaving Paddy and Ryan unharmed. Laughing, Zoltar with Xary by his side showed themselves.

"Ah. Ah! Welcome to our happy home, silly young Wizard. You thought you were more powerful than our greatness and would destroy us, like you did that stupid Wargo. You have a lot to learn yet! Of course, that is if I let you live."

Ryan prudently hid behind Paddy. The evil wizards, enjoying their victory, laughed sardonically. Paddy was watching Daryl from the corner of his eye but didn't reply. The human savored that instant so desired by him. Quietly, he approached Zoltar flanked by Xary.

Daryl had arrived at the right side of the evil one. Slowly, he took the Magic Crown out of the bag. At that instant impatiently Xary pushed Zoltar aside screaming, "Move! Let me deal with him. I have had enough of that stupid Wizard boy!"

Too late, Daryl quickly had crowned the wrong Wizard. Zoltar saw the flashing of the crown. Screaming, in a burst of flames Xary vanished for ever. With a tinkling sound the crown fell upon the ground. A tremendous force shot through Zoltar, throwing him up in the sky where he disappeared, shouting, "You don't have me yet."

Gently Daryl picked up the crown and returned the precious jewel into the bag. "Not now, but we will.

Well done, man, let's leave the place. The ground is shaking," said Paddy. The gate of the lair was opened. Daryl grabbed Ryan who was stunned by all that he had seen. As fast as they could, they left the sinister place. The mountains around shook and cracked fiercely.

"Hurry up, man, lie down against the mountain, pull your hood over your face" cried Paddy.

Daryl's human body was too heavy. A gentle hand took his, and he was floating on a cloud of gold above his friend, with Ryan still in his arms.

The boy cried, "Sir, Sir, we are in the sky, in a cloud of gold."

Paddy covered his face and quickly crouched on the ground. A terrible shower of rocks fell around and upon him. Then there was a terrific explosion, followed by a great sound of rushing waters. The rain of rocks and the tremor stopped. He uncovered his head. The landscape had completely changed. The horse shoe had been broken through the middle, and the black evil mountain was no more. Daryl, still holding Ryan, found himself beside Paddy, almost deafened by the noise of a huge waterfall rushing into the newly created abyss.

"This is beautiful!" cried Daryl.

"Oh, yes, much nicer than the Evil Mountain," said Ryan clapping his hands and dancing away. "But how come we were in a cloud of gold, Sir?"

Daryl gave a quick glance to Paddy and smiled. He whispered, "Thank you, Goldy."

A sweet voice replied, "You are my friend. I love you very much, Daryl."

If only Paddy could have seen his buddy face. It was as red as a ripened tomato.

"We deserve a good rest and a good meal with all the trimmings you like Daryl. Let's go to the top of the pass. From there we will contact your family, Ryan."

Paddy patted the boy's bonnet. The boy jumped with joy shouting, "Oh boy! Do I have things to tell them." He was so excited he forgot the promise of a good meal.

"Yup, you certainly have, my powerful friend," said Daryl with a chuckle as he ruffled Ryan's hair.

They gave a last look at the new waterfall and left. It was cold. Heavy snow began to fall and soon it became too deep for the young Dwarf to walk. Daryl laughingly propped him upon his shoulders. At last Ryan was a young boy again with no fear. From his high station he stuck his pink tongue out catching the large snow flakes. The young adventurers were pondering the last events and Daryl his talk with Goldy. They went silently to the pass.

Daryl sighed, "How wonderful not to fear evil any more."

"For the time being, that is so. Just remember that Zoltar is still on the loose, man, and alive. We have to neutralize him, too. When? We don't know. Xary is destroyed. Wargo too. Two evil forces gone, one more to go. The Realms are not yet completely safe," replied the Elf.

"I know, man " replied Daryl.

A voice quietly spoke up, "I am hungry."

"Who said that?" laughed Paddy.

"I did!" Ryan looked worriedly at the elf.

"Yes, boy, I forgot. When you have been scared you eat a lot."

"I have been plenty scared, Sir."

"First, let's have a nice house with a big fire to get warm." Paddy moved his arm to conjure a cabin, "There, come in guys. Now, to celebrate our success, we will enjoy a good meal," They rushed inside. Ryan screamed, "Beds!" In one leap he was crashing on his. Three comfortable chairs were waiting for them in front of a large chimney with a bright fire, cheerfully greeting them with joyous flames.

"It is so nice to rest my poor weary bones. We haven't had such luxury for ages, man." Daryl fell in one of the large chairs, which complained under his weight with a loud squeak. He sprawled his legs in front of him.

"I agree," replied Paddy doing the same, followed by Ryan falling in a chair of his own size. For a little wile they dreamed looking at the dancing flames.

Then a voice broke the silence. "I am hungry!"

Paddy and Daryl laughed. For once it was not Daryl who was calling for food, but their friend Ryan. "Sit at the table, young wolf. I am about to serve."

The celebration of their victory over Xary was sweet to the young adventurers. Ryan went to sleep in his bed. Paddy and Daryl sat comfortably by the fire and talked for a while,

Daryl, caressing the crown in the bag said, "Too bad I didn't get Zoltar."

"Don't worry, we will. For now he is stunned. He won't do any damage for a long time. The Realms are safe for a while. Stay here, I am going to call the Dwarves Wizard and speak to him. They will be happy to know that Ryan is fine, Xary is no more and Zoltar paralyzed for centuries. Don't forget he is from Earth Realm. As a sorcerer he will be able to prolong his life by borrowing a bit of power from the Realms, but that's all. He will have to die."

The elf walked to the back of the room. Daryl turned around and watched him. The young Wizard glowed in the dark, and a gentle mist covered him. Then the old Wizard appeared, dressed in gold. They conversed for the longest time. Daryl soon fell asleep by the fire. Paddy came back and sat quietly beside his buddy. Invisible in the dark Goldy watched them. Smiling, she sprinkled gold dust on Daryl and vanished.

Early the next morning, Ryan, was up and excited. Paddy and Daryl were asleep by the fire in their chairs. Ryan paced the floor whispering, "Come on! Come on. Wake up, Prince Patrick."

Paddy chuckled, and said, "All right, here I am, impatient boy."

The Dwarf blushing said, "Oh! I am sorry. I didn't want to disturb you, Sir."

"Then, my young friend, never whisper near a wizard's ear. He can hear you."

Sheepishly the boy looked at him. Daryl, grinning, said, "Don't feel bad, the guy is only a wizard." He winked at Paddy.

"As you know, boy, last night I talked with your Wizard. Your parents have agreed that you may finish the quest with us. Later on, they will meet you in my realm."

Ryan clapped his hands, jumped, and danced, shouting, "Wonderful, wonderful. I am going to see the Elfic Realm!"

The elf smiled. "Yes, Ryan, but first we will stop at the Sapphire Mountain and return the Magic crown to the Old Wizard."

"When, when?"

"Today, after breakfast, we will be there."

"How? It's so far!" asked Ryan with wonder in his eyes.

"Have you forgotten that Paddy is a Wizard, young bird-brain," said Daryl laughing.

The boy frowned. "I am sorry. Please may we eat. My head will be clearer."

The two young friends, elf ;and human, smiled at Ryan. The breakfast was brief. Quickly, Paddy dismissed their shelter. The house gone, they stood in the soft fresh snow. Joyously the young elf said, "Dear companions of the quest, give me your hands." Ryan stood up on his toes to reach the Wizard's hand. Paddy whispered and with a loud cry promptly lifted up his arms above his head. Ryan flew up in the air and came down gripping the elf's arm. Abashed, he faced the old Wizard, who was smiling at them, seated in his big chair.

"Greetings, Prince. I was expecting you. Well done, mortal. Thank you for destroying the head of the evil trio. We have two of them down, Wargo and Xary. Unfortunately you know that Zoltar is still alive. Peace won't be entirely restored until he has disappeared from our Realms. Thank you, Ryan, the changeling. Your help has been invaluable."

The young Dwarf turned red. He was not used to such praises from a powerful Wizard.

The ancient-one said, "Let's return the Magic Crown to the cave. Please follow me."

Daryl with a large grin replied, "It will be wonderful, your Lordship. I will be too glad."

The old Wizard nodded. They went to a wall of the Wizard's room. The ancient-one, moving his hand, turned to Daryl. A panel in the wall quietly slid aside, showing the small stairwell going down, the same one that once he traveled with the wizard to get the crown. They stepped into the dark. The Wizard took a small torch to show the way. After a short time they arrived in the round cave they had left months ago. Daryl removed the bag from his waist. This time, without fear, he took the Magic Crown out. Before placing it back on the purple velvet shelf, he gently touched the stones, admiring this work of art. Sighing with relief he stepped back. Suddenly the crown in the dark shone like a hundred stars. "How beautiful," Daryl said. Then in the cave covered with gold he said, "Goldy, you are wonderful."

"The crown shines for you, Human. It knows you are from the same realm and worthy. No one from another realm could have touched it without dying instantly. The crown thanks you for your courage, and Goldy admires you deeply," added the old Wizard with a smile.

"Me! Wow!" Impressed by the fact that the Crown thanked him, a human, and that he had the attention of a fairy, the young man was spellbound. He knew he had a profound sentiment for Goldy and was grateful for her protection and attention....but, but!

They returned in silence to the Wizard's majestic room. The ancient-one smiling said, "I took the liberty, Prince, to send word of your coming. You are expected impatiently. Please allow me the privilege of sending you and your companions of the quest to your families and friends."

"With pleasure, Your Lordship," replied Paddy bowing his head courteously. The old Wizard whispered mysterious words and moved his bony arms above his head. For a brief moment the long gold sleeves of his robe, like large birds, floated in the air above the young people he said, "Farewell, my courageous friends."

Chapter 30

A blue sky and a delicious perfume of flowers reached their noses. "We are home!" cried Daryl. "I can't believe it! Fear is over! Wonderful! I hate sorcerers and their black magic."

Ryan looked at the castle, his eyes like saucers. Never had he seen such beauty. "The Elfic Realm," he whispered.

"Come guys, people are waiting for us," Shouted Paddy, as he ran to meet King Ariol, his father, and Queen Tara, his mother. They joyously came down from the balcony to greet their son. They embraced Paddy and Daryl. With a smile the Dragon Lord (who had already arrived) watched Ryan shyly standing behind everybody. The boy's father and mother appeared along with the Dwarf Wizard. The king came up with Paddy and the Queen. Ryan forgot where he was and flew into his parents arms with a cry of joy.

The two Realms celebrated the destruction of two great evils. Mitsou turning and turning, with the help of her magic tail, produced a splendid display of fireworks for everyone. Tiger and Dick barked with enthusiasm.

Ryan and his family stayed at the request of the King at the Palace for a long time, until Ryan grew impatient to go home to see his friends. He had so much to tell them about the marvelous quest and above all that he was a changeling! The young dwarf was very proud of it. This gift, he learned, had been in the family ages ago. For reasons unknown to them, it had gone and now had come back in Ryan.

The old Dwarf Wizard asked the privilege of returning the young hero and his family home. The Dragon Lord bowed. "They are yours, Wizard." Proudly the Dwarf smiled and bowed to the Dragon Lord. In a puff of light they left with a promise of returning soon.

***

Daryl restlessly paced in his room and mumbled, "It's time I become an Elf again. With all the festivities in the Realms I couldn't bother Paddy, but now, all is normal." Decision written all over his face, Daryl walked to the door of the chamber of the Prince, and opened it. Nervously, he pulled at his doublet, entered the apartment of the young Wizard. Paddy read Daryl's mind and was chuckling inside.

"Ah, here you are, man, come in. Today is the day where you are going to be an Elf."

The young human looked at Paddy and said, "I came to talk about that."

The wizard's brows went up. "Good."

Surprised, Daryl looked at him. In his mortal state he had difficulty comprehending that his old friend from Earth was a Wizard. He sighed. "When will you do it, Paddy?'

"Now?

"Now, oh boy, where are we going?"

"Nowhere, come here." Paddy took Daryl's hand and lead the poor reluctant human to the middle of his study. The young Wizard lightly touched his friend's head and shoulders, whispered, and raised his arms above the young human. A veil of glowing mist fell softly upon Daryl. Thousands of stars surrounded him. Then, it was over. A little dizzy Daryl stood in the center of the room. His sharp Elfic eyes and pointed ears were back.

"Wow, man, I am an Elf," he cried. "I can hear sounds coming from far away."

"Of course you are. I am a wizard, remember?" replied Paddy slapping Daryl's shoulder. "Come let's join old friends. They are anxious to see you, waiting at the academy, impatient to have you again as one of us." The two young Elves left arm in arm laughing. Their three dogs arrived barking and jumping.

Chapter 31

Paddy and Daryl had now been back for four elfic years from their quest, a long time for the earth. Paddy was now thinking about the future. What will it hold for him? *Being KING is a big responsibility*, he sighed. In long strides his legs took him to the stables. There he called a boy to bring his horse, Kalyste . He was going to explore the south border where he had never been before. The air was sweet with the smell of lavender. He rode for a long time, much longer than he intended to.

He and Kalyste arrived at the site of a ruined castle standing sadly upon a hill. It was truly old, brooding over its glorious past, where, surely, battles for love and honor had been fought. Now only the wind was whistling through its once proud towers and halls. The collapsed fortified walls showed the remains of a garden encircling the castle. Thorns and thistles had invaded the once lovely place. Through a hole in the wall he could see a broken fountain. A marble statue in the middle was the sad witness of a genteel past.

The sadness of the site and Paddy's own curiosity prompted the young elf to cross the crumbling drawbridge and enter the cobblestone courtyard. He dismounted and tied his horse to a rusted ring. With awe he walked into the remains of what had been a garden. "Wow, where am I? Never heard of this place," he whispered afraid to make any noise. A handsome white marble fountain and a beautiful pergola of wild red roses greeted him. Quietly he sat on a marble bench facing the dry pool and pondered the fate of the people who had lived here.

Dreamlike, he gazed around and noticed at the center of the basin an enchanting sculpture of a young girl in pink onyx sitting on a water-lily pad of white alabaster. Surprised, Paddy admired the delicate piece of art, so well conserved for a so long period of abandonment. To his astonishment, as he looked again, the girl gently smiled. Alarmed Paddy scrambled to his feet whispering, "How could she have smiled? This, of course, is an illusion, a fancy of mine. Onyx statues don't smile." Defying his sudden fear Paddy sat down. A soft breeze played in his long blond hair. His large green eyes were still fixed upon the girl. Was it a caprice of his imagination? For a second he could hear her sing a sad Irish ballad. Was this a trick of the wind and if it was not? His mind went wild wrestling with conjecture. How could he solve this mystery? Quickly he walked into the basin and looked directly into her eyes. They were dead, carved in the onyx. Disappointed, he stepped out muttering, "What was I expecting, anyway?"

At nineteen you can dream. With a sort of regret he got ready to depart walking away slowly, leaving the girl in the lovely old garden. Before passing through the garden's gate, he turned around and looked one last time at the girl. What! His eyes were playing tricks to him! She was not smiling anymore, she was crying. Baffled he cried in the wind, "But it's only a statue!" Heart pounding, Paddy ran back and jumped into the dry basin and touched her cheek. Tears were rolling down her onyx face.

Chapter 32

"What is the meaning of this? Why do you cry, girl?" Of course, no reply came from the statue. Disquieted, Paddy went back into the courtyard mumbling, "Was I expecting something else?" Unhappy with himself he whispered," I better leave this place, I am getting confused."

Paddy untied Kalyste and sprang into the saddle. Her hoofs breaking the silence, hammering sharply on the cobblestones, they left, riding slowly over the drawbridge. It was already late afternoon. The ruins had an eerie look with the sunset shining onto the old stones through the blind windows. Paddy's mind was deeply troubled by the crying girl. The elf had a hard time leaving the castle site.

Puzzled, he looked over his shoulder. This was strange. Honestly he couldn't even tell where he was at the present time. The only certitude he had was that he had never come to this part of the country before. He loved riding Kalyste, exploring his father's realm, but getting lost like this, never! To clear up his mind, Paddy, talked to his horse.

"What do you think of the crying statue, Kalyste? Do you know where we are, girl?" Kalyste whinnied softly. Paddy stopped and listened intensely, and his delicate pointed ears heard in the wind the girl singing. "I am not dreaming or crazy, how can it be?" he shuddered.

This time she was telling the story of her plight. “The crimson shield, the crimson shield, only the crimson shield can make me free.” The plaintive voice repeated the ballad again and over again.

Paddy rode to the edge of a beautiful lake, hours away from the ruins. A perfect moonlight gently brushed the dark water with its long silvery finger barely touching the surface. Paddy stopped. Incredulously he could see, written in silver letters on the black water, “She needs you.” Paddy was perplexed. “This message comes from the moon. I can hear her voice on the wind. Why?” He was baffled. “I know our elfic race has extremely fine ears, but not that fine.”

As he rode away, Paddy tried solving this enigma. Looking back he could still see the shining message written on the lake. Finally, he left the shore with a sigh. However, something else happened and it was far from reassuring. Suddenly, he was back at the king’s castle. Why and how by which mystery had he arrived home? Darkness covered everything. Large shadows created by the moon playing behind the turrets made the park spooky. It was late, and the guards heads were nodding. Some were even asleep, leaning on their spears.

The ride, for a reason unknown to him, had compelled him to go further and further away from his home. Paddy mumbled, “When I was there, for a moment I felt as if I was in another country. We don’t have desolate places like that in our realm. I can’t believe I got lost! I didn’t feel evil there, only loneliness and sadness.”

They rode directly to the stable. Paddy left Kalyste in the capable hands of the stable boy. Patting his horse on the rump, he said, “Good night, Kalyste.” Paddy smiled, as she whinnied back.

In long light strides he went quietly on the soft sand of the alley. The stars were now up in the beautiful night, shining like thousands of diamonds on a blue velvet rug. He stopped for a minute to admire and ponder on how lovely and peaceful his realm was. The crickets, in the tranquility of the night, were chirping. The frogs in the pond croaked loudly breaking the stillness of the night. The strong perfume of jasmine and gardenia filled the air. With a pang of sadness in his heart he remembered the desolate ruins and the crying statue.

Quietly he entered in the sleeping palace and smiled, looking at the sleepy guards leaning upon their spears. Yawning he went directly to his room and rang for his valet. The sleepy boy arrived, dragging his feet. Sluggishly he undressed Paddy.

"Would you like something to eat, Sir?"

"No, thank you, Aloza You may now go to bed. Sorry I woke you."

The young valet bowed and left.

Paddy, exhausted by the long baffling ride, went to bed. Hours later he suddenly sat up in his bed. The plaintive voice of the girl was singing her sad song. Amazed he whispered, "What is the meaning of this?" He dropped back onto his pillow trying to return to sleep, but without success. He tossed for the remainder of the night.

The next morning, roused by the sun playing in his hair, Paddy, with no help from his valet, dressed promptly. He rang the bell for his father's counselor and asked him to summon the wizard, Yanik.

Daryl heard the nervous pacing of his friend in the next room. Still drowsy, he rapped at Paddy's door.

"Enter. If you want to hear something odd, come in, man."

Daryl's foggy eyes went to Paddy. "What do you mean?"

At that instant the wizard arrived and found the young Prince overly agitated, pacing his room almost incoherently, talking way too fast. The old wizard watching him, frowned, and sat in a comfortable deep chair. Calmly he spread his long blue robe over his gold slippers and waited. Quiet, interested, he watched the young elf with sharp inquisitive eyes and said, "Please slow down, my young Prince, and repeat your story. I cannot make head or tail of what you are saying."

"Neither can I. All this is incredible," said Daryl.

Paddy calmed down, and recounted the fantastic story of the amazing statue and her strange song. The old personage listened gravely and pulling on his long white beard repeated several times, "Yes, it makes sense. It makes sense."

"I am glad it makes sense to you, Wizard, because it surely doesn't make any to me," shouted the elf angrily, and resumed his pacing.

"Will you please sit down. You make me dizzy. When I tell you the story, it will make sense. However, first learn this. You passed through the rainbow and went into the Earth Realm where the old castle stands. That is the reason you felt you were in a strange land."

Paddy bemused sat up brusquely. "How did I do that without my knowledge? If I want to go there, I know how to do it, I am a Wizard, too, you know." Paddy got up and started pacing again. The old Wizard looked at him angrily. Daryl, amused, watched the Wizard and Paddy arguing.

"I am certain this is Neph's doing. He is the powerful wizard of the Emerald Forest. Believe me, Prince, he has reasons of his own, and you will know them soon. Now listen, and please don't interrupt me, and sit d-o-w-n!" thundered the Wizard." Daryl jumped at the interjection The Wizard's sharp eyes turned into the past, and pensively he stroked his beard and started his tale.

"This happened many hundreds of years ago in the Mortal's Realm, which means decades for us. It was a battle between a gentle king and Zoltar, a wicked young sorcerer."

Both young elves jumped screaming, "Zoltar! The one we fought? How can it be?"

"Silence! Yes, it was long before you met him as an old man. Power and love for a beautiful young girl were at stake. The sorcerer was madly in love with the young princess Ida. One day he came to the castle and boldly asked the king for Ida's hand. The answer was no! Zoltar left with fire in his eyes and menacing words on his lips. The king, in his righteous anger, chased him away and had him pursued by the royal soldiers to his lair in the mountains.

Time went by peacefully. No one gave much thought anymore to the sorcerer's threats. King Tyson and Queen Natasha lived a happy and quiet life with their daughter Ida, and the younger children,-Prince Michel, and the two young princesses, Isabel and Leona. But one morning, they were rudely awakened by a terrible heat wave and people screaming in the courtyard. The palace was in an uproar. Quickly, king Tyson went to see what was the cause of such great commotion. He was greeted with the sight of flames as high as the outer wall encircling the castle. The water in the moat prevented the blazing furnace from coming closer to the buildings. The king and his counselors hurriedly climbed up the tower to find out who had attacked the castle and caused this catastrophe.

Down below, Zoltar was laughing fiendishly. Once more he shouted his proposal to the king. Of course, he received the same answer. No!

The incensed Zoltar then attacked the castle with all the forces of hell. The battle raged for days. The gallant king died with his wife and the children. All the people in the kingdom were destroyed. Only Princess Ida escaped. Desperately she was crying in what had been a lovely garden, now in ruins and ashes. Zoltar found her and with a sardonic smile came to her and for the third time asked for her hand. The reply was the same. Screaming, she answered "No! Leave me alone!" Then, the evil one said to her, "So my dear you will be. You will stay here alone, in these lovely ruins of yours, forever."

Chapter 33

Zoltar smiled cruelly and gently touched the young princess's face. As his fingers came in contact with her cheek the thunder growled, lightning flashed into the dark sky, and she was at once frozen in time into an onyx statue, sitting upon a lily pad in a dry basin. However, the evil one didn't notice the girl's tears on his hand. The strength of her love for her family went through the tears, and unknown to him weakened his power. He left the princess imprisoned in an onyx shell.

Demented, out of control, screaming, the sorcerer returned to the battlefield and there in a fit of rage removed the Crimson Shield from the king's hand.

"Centuries before, my young prince, your ancestor Shane, gave the shield to King Tyson as a token of love and friendship. It's an elfic shield with magic power. However, the sorcerer didn't know that, and took it only by vengeance and malice as a trophy of his victory. He knew how much the king cherished it. Now Zoltar is long dead, and the princess is still a prisoner of his spell in the garden of the Mortal Realm.

"That's incredible. But how did he come to our realm? He was in the Mortal Realm," asked Paddy, baffled.

"Greed, my young Prince. With the help of his friend Xary of the Elfic Realm they plotted to take over the Realms and be masters of our

right man, I will go. I am as insane as the old wizard. I don't even have the excuse of being dotty." Paddy chuckled nervously. Daryl joined him in his moment of jest and the two friends laughed.

"Don't be so merry man, you are coming along."

Daryl jumped out of his chair and danced. "Good for a moment, I thought you were leaving me behind like old useless baggage you didn't want any more!"

"No way. You are my squire." Paddy gave a big slap on his friend's back.

Before leaving the castle early next morning the young Prince went to see King Ariol his father to say goodbye.

"Yanick visited me last night. I know of your quest. You are a knight of The Shining Sword and a powerful Wizard. Be stronger than evil. Don't let fear overcome you, son."

"I won't father. I will take Daryl with me. We will be fine," he replied with a grimace.

King Ariol smiled, "I know sorcerers have never been your best friends."

Paddy and Daryl had carefully prepared their gear, choosing well what to take along for the journey. The magic elfic capes, their rucksacks, in which they had tucked a spare suit, a cape, a pair of boots, and of course a provision of biscuits so loved by Daryl. Elves always travel with these during a prolonged journey. Only a bite, and the pang of hunger was gone. In their pocket was the precious silver vial of magic pink water. One drop on the tongue and thirst is quenched. Paddy had put in the small pocket of his rucksack the magic balm, and two little elfic stones. And last, but not least, at their side they secured in the scabbard their faithful magic Shining Sword. This was all they took along for the quest.

The young elves left the palace with Paddy riding Kalyste, and Daryl riding KumKuat. The weather was crystal clear, and soon the Palace gates were behind them. Kalyste spiritedly stomped the ground and champed at the bit. Paddy laughed and let her go. Her beautiful red mane and her long tail flew brightly in the wind. Daryl's horse didn't want to stay behind. In a powerful thrust of his strong legs, he challenged Kalyste. The black mane and tail flew behind him like a dark standard.

They were happy for the quest, even if they didn't know where all this was taking them. Paddy realized that he had been cooped up in the palace much too long. The winds of adventure were calling him. He didn't like the idea of an encounter with sorcerer dead or alive. Paddy smiled. He was going to enjoy every minute of the quest, good and bad. Thanks to the wizard they were on their way to great exploits with his old buddy Daryl.

The ride in his father's realm was, as usual, wonderful. In the fields the elves, working joyously, were singing. The charming little stone cottages with flowers were a peaceful sight. Laughing, they stopped sharply, leaving a cloud of dust from their horse's hooves, as they watched a mother goose, her neck stretched out, proudly walking her offspring to the pond for their morning swim, while mama duck was being noisily pushed by her stumbling, scrambling little brood anxious to splash into the clear water.

At noon they stopped by a bubbling brook. Dismounting they stretched and let the horses loose, then sat eating their biscuits, as the horses quietly munched the green grass. The warm sun and the buzzing insects in the grass lulled Daryl to doze. So did Paddy. Much later Paddy woke and jumped up. The sun was slowly disappearing on the horizon. Galloping in the sunset they approached a thick green forest, and the horses slowed to an easy pace.

Chapter 34

Unexpectedly the plaintive singing voice of the girl startled Paddy. He had forgotten the girl and her plight. Nervously he pulled on the reins. This frightened Kalyste who jolted and pranced. Soothingly he whispered, "Whoa, whoa, girl, it's all right."

"Did you hear that, man?"

Daryl, puzzled, shrugged his shoulders. "Nope."

Reflecting on the conversation with the old Wizard, pensively he mumbled, "Her voice will guide me. So far so good, we are going in the right direction."

They entered the forest. Darkness had spread its black coat. This didn't bother their elfic vision, and they searched for a shelter. The majestic grandeur of the trees was most impressive. Their high canopy of branches and the soft moss on the ground were a pleasure.

Suddenly, Paddy's ears perked up. Something had alerted his sense of danger. Quickly he pulled on Kalyste's reins and stopped to listen. The sound of trampled branches cracked on his right, and a loud grunt made Kalyste fidgety.

Daryl tensed then relaxed when in the gathering darkness his sharp eyes discerned a small bear watching them from behind a tree. "Look, Paddy, it's only a young bear." They resumed riding in the calm forest.

The nocturnal wild life, unafraid of the intruders, romped around. The birds getting ready for night chirped, flying from bush to bush. Kalyste, her ears flat, was still nervous. They arrived in a clearing with lots of grass. Paddy quickly jumped down and removed Kalyste's saddle and bridle. Daryl with a tap on KumKuat's rump sent him free. Reluctantly the horses moved away. The boys sat under a big evergreen with boughs touching the ground. "Wow, this is a perfect place to sleep, man." Daryl stretched his legs on the moss.

Paddy, his ears picking up the quiet sounds of the night, sat comfortably beside Daryl on the needles by a big tree. After eating their elfic biscuits, Daryl lay down to sleep. Paddy quietly went to check the horses. At his coming they whinnied softly, but Kalyste's ears were still flat on her head. "What are you worried about girl?' KumKuat came and rubbed his nose on Paddy's shoulder. He stroked them and returned to the tree. Daryl was sound asleep. Paddy yawned and crawled under a bough, wrapped himself in his cape, pulled the hood over his face, and went to sleep.

The next morning Paddy woke with an ill feeling. It was cold. Troubled he looked around for Kalyste. Usually she playfully nuzzled him as he pretended to be asleep, but this morning she was nowhere to be seen, and neither was KumKuat. Disquieted he called several times, but the horses didn't show up. A little irritated, he said, "Kalyste stop that at once and come." But she didn't come, and neither did KunKuat.

With all the noise Daryl woke up. "What the matter, man?"

Paddy was distraught. "The horses have disappeared."

Daryl jumped up looking around. "What did you say, man?"

Paddy didn't answer and sat for the longest time, sadly waiting, hoping Kalyste would come back.

"What's happening? KumKuat is not here either." Daryl checked all around looking for signs of the horses, but the meadow was quiet.

"She has never left me like this. Where is she?" Paddy called again and again, "Kalyste, where are you? Come girl, we must go." Paddy noticed that her saddle and bridle had disappeared. "Could they have been stolen? KumKuat's gear is gone, too."

"What the meaning of this, man?" asked Daryl upset.

"I don't know. We have to leave, man" said Paddy, but he couldn't resolve himself to going without Kalyste. In despair they slowly moved away, turning around every minute, glancing inquiringly over their shoulders, thinking they could hear the horses running after them.

***

Their afflicted minds seemed to have changed the aspect of the beautiful green forest. The contrast was incredible. What had been lovely bushes were now thorns, briars, and thistles that scratched them unmercifully. The forest had become hostile. The soft mossy ground disappeared replaced by stones, roots, and pitfalls. A cold rain slapped their faces cruelly. Numb, they pulled their hoods down. A strong wind blew pushing them further away from where they had lost their horses. They felt miserable, sick at heart, and they bitterly missed their horses. The same painful question was torturing their minds. "Where are they? What happened to them?"

Trudging along, head down, immersed in their sad thoughts, the young adventurers were a perfect picture of dejection. Many times Paddy, distracted, tripped on rotten roots. A mournful wind howled around them bringing a strong smell of decay. Their progress in this infernal stormy weather was very slow. Adding to their discouragement, the voice of the girl had stopped.

Gloomy thoughts invaded Paddy's mind. "I wonder if we are lost, just like my poor Kalyste?"

Puzzled, the same question kept turning round and round in Daryl's head. "But why are their saddles and bridles gone, too?" asked Daryl, obstinately. A gold dust flew over him. "Goldy," he whispered with a big grin, feeling much better.

"I don't know, man. I didn't feel any evil in the meadow. Why do you smile?" No answer came from Daryl. The howling which Paddy had confounded with the wind was coming closer, and a heavy thumping steadily following them. Frightened, the friends ran as fast as elves can (and that is fast). The terrible thumping puffed and growled on their heels. Paddy turned his head to look behind. Terrified, he saw a horrible creature coming after them, a man-like monster with a huge round head. The beast had a long snout from where he shot slimy ropes, trying to ensnare them in a sticky gluey net. Paddy realized that they had no chance of escaping by running. Promptly he drew his magic Shining Sword and lifted his left hand throwing bolts of fire. At his side Daryl had pulled his sword, too.

The battle raged. The huge round head ferociously attacked and spat the sticky stuff to trap them. Nothing affected the evil thing. The elves light as feathers hopped endlessly to evade the deadly net. Paddy was getting extremely tired, but Daryl, stronger, was fighting endlessly. Paddy in a supreme effort threw his magic sword at the beast. The magic weapon became red flying in the air like an arrow. Shrieking it darted at the beast, spun around making a bright red crown of sparks about the monstrous head and severed it from the body. An incredible howl of pain filled the forest and at that very moment a pile of ashes lay at Paddy's feet. With speed of light the sword was back into the elf's hand.

"Wow, you never stop amazing me, man."

Badly shaken up, Paddy, slowly cleaned his magic sword and with a trembling hand put it back into the scabbard. Heavily he dropped on a rotten piece of log. "Farmit, man! That was an evil creature, or I don't know any thing about the dark side and certainly not from our realm." Paddy frowned, and whispered, "From where?"

Then, without warning, through the gloominess of the forest a white twister came down and picked them up from their log. The elves hardly had time to collect themselves to realize what was happening. They were sucked into a deafening noise and plunged into a deep darkness that even their elfic vision couldn't pierce. Tossed in all directions, completely disoriented, and Daryl sick, they were carried above the forest in the twirling funnel.

Dizzy from being whirled around, they landed on wobbling legs at the summit of an extremely large flat tree with a well cared lawn. Astonished they were facing a magnificent palace made of strange green materiel, something Paddy had never seen before.

Many tiny people were busy doing various chores and caring for beautiful suspended gardens of blooming flowers and shrubs with hundreds of colorful birds flying around. They looked at everything, completely dumbfounded, and Paddy noticed a lovely tiny girl curiously watching him. Paddy smiled thinking, “That girl has probably never seen anyone as big as I am.” He smiled back.

Chapter 35

At that moment a tiny man arrived, obviously in a hurry, dressed in a red velvet coat. The little fellow bowed deeply to Paddy. As he bent down, his long beard touched his gold sandals. A gust of wind came up and made the beard brush his nose. His dignity obviously offended, he gesticulated and pushed away the bothering thing. Daryl turned his head discreetly. Paddy knew why and touched Daryl's shoulder, killing the offensive noise in his throat. Bowing a second time he said, "Prince, would you be kind enough to follow me? Our wizard is expecting you."

They hadn't yet recovered from the battle with the monster and the incredible ride in the twister. Paddy was absolutely mute. He nodded, followed by Daryl. No words were exchanged as they walked in the man's footsteps. As they passed near the young girl, he looked at her. She was observing him intensely and smiled again. Paddy, breaking his silence, curiously asked to his guide, "Who is that girl?"

"Which girl, Sir?" asked the man looking at Paddy.

"Here, this one," replied Paddy turning his head to were she was standing. The girl had left and no longer was there. Daryl chuckled silently. He, too, had seen the girl and had been impressed by her beauty.

"Never mind," replied Paddy promptly returning to his silence.

They passed many halls full of flowers and soft music coming from unseen musicians. Through the transparent walls they could see the gardens and small houses tucked between branches. On the limbs fearless children were laughing and chasing each other while their friends bounced on small suspended bridges. Paddy broke his silence once more, curiously questioning the guide,

"Don't you think that it must be very embarrassing to have people looking into your home? How can you tolerate that?"

"No one can see through from outside inside, Sir," replied the man soberly.

"Ah," Daryl looked to Paddy with rounded eyes. They arrived in front of a splendid door. Gently the man's hand touched a carved leaf located at the height of the man for his convenience. It opened quietly on a rotunda. The man bowed and left. The beauty within was overwhelming. Paddy, even as a prince, had never had seen anything like it. The sun freely entered through immense bay windows, and the room, like a large green crystal bowl, shone with hundred of facets. Colorful birds were freely flying from flowers everywhere on stands of gold.

A tall handsome young man was sitting upon a throne of transparent jade. His extraordinarily large green eyes kindly regarded Paddy. A cascade of gold hair softly fell upon his broad shoulders, and a short beard touched the collar of his green and gold brocade tunic opening on a long white robe. On his chest hung a large gold chain where a huge emerald, like the same precious stone on his right hand, was set on a heavy ring of gold. The long white robe partly covered his golden oriental slippers, which had, set on the tips, two large emeralds.

"Greetings Prince Patrick and Squire Daryl, elves from the Promised Valley. My name is Neph, a wizard, and I am Lord of the Emerald Forest, and here is my dearest daughter, Soledad."

Paddy looked at her with surprise, realizing she was the tiny girl he had admired outside in front of the palace. Now, she was very tall and about eighteen. She smiled. An uneasy feeling crept over the elf. He bowed. Why had he been brought to the wizard's palace? Then indignation gushed into his heart. Politely he said, "I am delighted,

Lord Neph, to meet you and your charming daughter. However, as you know, my squire and I are on a quest. I deeply regret to have little time at this moment for a social visit." He felt trapped and didn't like it. Daryl sensed that Paddy had been tricked into something he wouldn't like.

"Of course, prince. I brought you here because I am godfather to Ida, Princess of the Mortal's Realm. With your help I want her brought back to life. Only you, or King Tyson, her father is capable of retrieving the Crimson Shield."

"But I thought he was dead." No reply came from the wizard. Paddy surprised asked, "Why, then, doesn't the King recover his shield if he is not dead?"

"He can't for the moment. He needs your help. Later you will understand. The shield is his. He received it as a token of friendship from one of your ancestors."

"Yes, yes I know. Yanick, our wizard, already told me that. Is my kin Shane still alive?" asked Paddy curiously.

"Of course, your uncle dwells in the north by the Blue Mountain Realm of the Dwarves. It is with his consent that I am sending you on this quest."

"How could you! How could he without even consulting me!" Paddy was incensed. "Why, after so many centuries, have you and my kin decided to bring king Tyson and his daughter back. If, by magic, he is still alive, that is. Mortals don't normally live that long."

"It was an oversight on my part. As you know for us, one century, ten centuries, or ten days for that matter, does not make much difference," replied the wizard.

Paddy literally jumped. "But what for her! She will be living in a foreign world lost for her friends," replied the elf.

"Wow, slow down, man." muttered Daryl standing behind Paddy's chair.

"Nothing is lost. Prince, look outside through that window, you, too, Daryl," said Neph smiling gently.

Paddy followed, Soledad showing the way to the window. She hadn't said a word. Paddy politely looked as told. Startled he jumped.

There on the flat top of a giant tree two tiny horses were grazing in a small green pasture. One voice was heard from the two elves, “Kalyste! KumKuat!” The horses replied, whinnying joyously. Stunned Paddy asked, “How come they are here? We thought them lost forever.”

“I am a Wizard, my young friends. Didn’t I say nothing was lost? You couldn’t go through the evil forest with them and through the other things waiting for you along the quest. So, while you were asleep, I brought them here and changed them into the size of my people. When the quest over, they will be here for you and back to their normal size.”

Paddy mellowed and lost his stiffness. “Thank you, Lord Neph. Kalyste and KumKuat are very dear to us.”

“Yes, I understand”

The Wizard continued his story. “Without knowledge of why he did it, the sorcerer made sure the Crimson Shield was well guarded, even after his death. On the battlefield when he took the shield from the king’s hand, he was not destroyed by the magic within. Against his knowledge his evil power had protected him. However, he couldn’t feel the magic in the shield. He took it as a trophy, by vengeance, knowing how much the king cherished it. The shield hangs among his artifacts. Many great dangers await you during the quest. Here is a powerful magic emerald. When you look into the jewel, you may ask for anything, and you will receive it. In urgent need of help or protection rub the stone with one finger. But remember, don’t use it foolishly.”

The wizard handed Paddy a beautiful pendant of pure gold. An enormous emerald was embedded in a large circle of fiery rubies set in the precious metal. When the wizard handed the locket to the Prince, sparks flashed. Startled, Paddy backed away from the wizard’s hand.

“Don’t be alarmed. The stone has made a bond with you. Now, when you command, it will obey. Put the chain around your neck. Under no circumstance remove it! Remember don’t remove it!”

Paddy, baffled, looked at it. “But my Lord, I too am a wizard. I don’t need it.”

A strange light appeared in the Wizard’s eyes. “I know boy. Listen, the power within it is beyond your imagination.”

Hesitantly, Paddy put the heavy chain upon his neck. A wave of heat went through his body, but strangely enough he couldn't feel its weight.

"Another thing, prince, my daughter, Soledad, has manifested the desire of going with you. I have granted her wish."

"Here we are. I knew something was behind all this," mumbled Daryl.

Paddy courteously replied, "No, thank you, My Lord. We can manage alone. Besides I don't think a girl can help." Paddy smiled at Soledad.

"You will be surprised of what she can do. Soledad is an accomplished archer and swordswoman," replied the Wizard. He moved his hand. Green sparks whirled round about him and his throne. Paddy heard a faint voice going away saying, "Farewell, Prince and Daryl. Good-bye, Soledad. Keep well, dear."

Through the window came a strong swirling wind taking the young people above the Emerald Forest. Hurled about by the wind, the prince, Daryl and Soledad, landed brutally in a dreadful looking landscape.—A desert with sharp high rocks covered with briars, thorns. and prickling bushes. With dismay Paddy looked around. On the ground were all sorts of small and big creeping creatures, snakes, lizards, huge tarantulas, salamanders. and scorpions.

Paddy whispered, "Where are we now? This must be the sorcerer's antechambers."

"I think you are right, man," replied Daryl.

"Whatever it is, it's not a nice place," replied a clear voice.

Paddy jumped surprised. He had completely forgotten the wizard's daughter and didn't think that she would have come along anyway. But there she was, beside Daryl, dressed like an elf, with bow and arrows upon her shoulder and sword at her side. Paddy, stunned, said, "You came."

"Of course. Long before you left your realm, I asked father to let me go on the quest with you and your squire."

"But you are a girl."

A joyous light shone in her splendid green eyes. "So?" she smiled.

Chapter 36

"Girls don't go on quests," replied Daryl solemnly as he remembered his sister asking why she couldn't play with boys.

"Ah, and why not, Sir?" she asked Paddy, who shrugged, put his rucksack upon his back and moved away.

Every step they took put into motion a repulsive army of venomous creeping things.

From the corner of his eye Paddy observed the girl, waiting for her screams, but no, she moved quietly pushing away the snakes crawling upon her boots. Daryl winked at his buddy and whistled. Paddy smiled at him.

Large spider webs were spread on every bush and scrawny tree. Dark clouds pierced and zapped by lightning in the obscure sky made the party walk faster. The thunder growled in a menacing way like a mad beast. Paddy was grateful for his high elfic boots. They walked silently for hours in the company of the creeping creatures. Unexpectedly, the sun showed up through the dark clouds. The heat from the scorching rays reflecting off the rocks became unbearable. Paddy looked at the girl, and finally he broke the silence.

"Soledad, you better pull your hood over your face if you don't want to be burned."

"Thank you, I will, Sir."

Daryl glanced at the girl and grinned, she gave him a bright smile. \

No shade was in sight, no trees, only the tall formations of rocks and no water either. Paddy took out the wee silver bottle and offered some to Soledad, explaining that she must pour only a drop of the pink liquid onto her lips and her thirst would immediately be quenched.

"This is amazing. What is it? Thank you, prince."

"Elves never travel without it," answered Daryl.

They trudged endlessly for hours. The hot haze of the desert under the ardent sun, lingered around them. They fought the creeping vermin with their swords until their arms were ready to fall off their shoulders. The girl never complained and always had a smile for Daryl.

Wow, she is gorgeous with those green sparkling eyes, thought Paddy watching her, obviously fascinated by the girl.

Finally, the sun disappeared below the horizon. Night was at hand. It became bitterly cold with a sharp wind blowing. Paddy quickly wrapped his magic cape snugly around him saying at the same time. "Wrap your cape tightly around you, Soledad, and you will be warmer." She didn't answer.

Paddy's elf eyes could see into the dark, so could Soledad's. Nothing appeared hospitable. "If you want to help Soledad, we can clear a place to put up a small cabin where we can go to sleep. Give us a hand, man. "

"Certainly, my prince," Daryl bowed down laughing.

Soledad smiled as she replied, "Of course, Prince Patrick.

"My name is Paddy. Please stop calling me Sir, or Prince."

Her green eyes shone "As you wish Prin…Paddy."

The elf smiled. They dropped their gear and worked with zeal using their swords to cut thorns and thistles, and one by one turned over the stones for unwanted tenants, chasing away the creeping things hiding underneath.

"There. Now we have a place to put a shelter and sleep away from those crawling things," said Paddy.

"Tell me, man, why didn't you use your wizard tricks to clean up this mess?"

"Don't you remember the Wizards rules?"

"Yes, I do. Use your hands first. Too bad, man, I prefer your tricks." He grinned at Paddy. "Remember, hard work has never been my forte."

"I know." The place cleaned up, Paddy moved his hand. A nice small shelter appeared. Inside was a cheery rustic fire burning between big stones. On a wood table was a steaming meal.

Daryl rubbed his stomach. "Ah food!"

Quietly, they sat on the bench. Soledad, smiling, pushed Daryl away to sit beside Paddy. Surprised the elf looked at her. They ate silently and rolled in their capes on the floor by the fire.

"Keep your gear close at hand, Soledad, you may need it. You never know what could happen during the night."

"I will. Thank you, prince."

"My name is Paddy. Good night." he said dryly. He was annoyed. "And don't forget to put the hood over your face."

"I won't. Good night Pr…Paddy." To herself, she muttered, *Do you think you are my mother?* She didn't know that Paddy's Wizard ears heard her comment. He smiled at her childish rebellion. Seconds later they were sleeping like babes.

In the darkness eyes shone like burning amber. Giant scorpions and salamanders crept closer and closer to the cabin. The door mysteriously opened. The tired young wizard had forgotten to protect the house. Paddy, breathing with great difficulty, suddenly woke up. A heavy load upon his chest was smothering him. He looked through the hood of his magic cape to find the cause of this awful feeling. The door was wide open, and a monstrous scorpion had crawled upon his chest. The horrible beast with its gigantic pincers tried tearing apart his cape. The weight was formidable. Paddy, mumbled, "I can't move. I should have conjured spells to protect the house. How stupid of me"

His hands under the enormous weight upon him were locked. He couldn't move to fight the monster. He tried to conjure it with word, but the evil in it was too strong. Then he remembered the big gold chain around his neck and with a supreme effort he freed one hand, pulled up the magic token and rubbed it. He remembered the extraordinary power within promised by the wizard. Out of the emerald flashed a formidable green light, a great sizzling sound, and a terrible stink reached his nose. For an instant his vision was veiled by a large cloud of smoke. The heavy weight upon his chest was gone. The magic stone had fried the monster.

Quickly, Paddy, jumped upon his feet, removed his cape, wrinkling his nose, he shook off the ashes. With a brief move of his hand he chased the bad odor. He looked for Soledad. The gril had disappeared. The door was open. Terrified, he called her. The idea of the young girl being killed by one of the evil beasts made him shiver. Paddy yelled, "Soledad, Soledad!"

Daryl woke up, rubbing his eyes. "What's the matter, man?"

Suddenly the girl appeared in a shaft of light. "Here I am"

Paddy, startled, looked at her.

She laughed and said, "Don't look at me like that. My father is a wizard, too. Sometimes I borrow a bit of his power, that's all."

"Sound's nice," replied Daryl. "I wish I could do that."

Stunned Paddy looked at her angrily. He couldn't get over the fright she had given him. "Didn't Father tell you I could do lots of things?"

"Yes, but don't do it again, girl. I thought a monster did you in. Without your father's locket, I would be history by now. A giant scorpion almost killed me." Then Paddy's spirits suddenly soared, and he laughed at the adventure. It was good to be alive and have Soledad still with them. "Well, Daryl, my boy, once more we have escaped. I wonder who's after us? The sorcerer is dead." He stretched his arms upward, smiling at Soledad, his anger gone.

Daryl astonished by his sudden change of mood looked at him. Quickly Paddy bent down, pulled his rucksack, and, like a magician, smiling triumphantly he brought out a healthy breakfast.

With a chuckle, Paddy said, "Here, friends, enjoy!"

Daryl pulled his cape off. With a grimace he held his hand out then his eyes shone. "O good. Thanks, Paddy. I was expecting a ration of elfic biscuit."

Soledad, surprised, looked at Paddy. "What a strange fellow you are Prince Patrick."

"Ah, not really." He winked at his buddy.

Paddy gave a big slap on Daryl's back and laughing they walked out into the still dark day. With a twist of his hand, Paddy dismissed the cabin. Soon they were on their way. Soledad secured the quiver upon her shoulder, and in long strides left, not looking behind her. Paddy felt invincible with the powerful stone now in his possession. Lightly his long legs sailed over the creeping creatures as the three of them went happily on their way.

Chapter 37

The first light of dawn appeared on the horizon. The young Prince, grateful to the wizard shouted, "Thanks, Neph, for the marvelous stone."

In the wee morning, came the voice of the wizard. "You are welcome."

Surprised Paddy looked around expecting to see Neph. "Where are you, Lord Neph?"

"Nowhere and everywhere, man," Daryl replied, with a chuckle, kicking off a large lizard stuck on the top of his boot.

Paddy smiled and said, referring to Lord Neph "That's right you are a wizard and a great one. I fear no more the sorcerer's tricks however well he has left his lair protected by evil magic."

The weather was the same as the previous day. The sun, with its darts of fire passing through the occasional black cloud was scorching. Hoods down, they trudged on. The lizards and snakes were still crawling on their boots. Paddy and Daryl's sword slapped their legs, swishing like the tail of angry cats. Soledad still walked fast, without a word.

"What's wrong with her?" asked Daryl, frowning.

"Don't know, man."

After several hours of trudging in sand and rocks, they arrived in rolling hills with meager trees. At last the desert and its repulsive creatures was behind them. What a relief to see green trees, even though scrawny. Exhausted they collapsed under a tree to rest. The growling of thunder through the black clouds in the distance, announced a coming storm. Soledad came back to join the boys and flopped down beside Paddy. She stretched her legs, squinted, and drowsily watched a very bright light coming toward them. Exhausted by the heat she fell into a deep sleep.

Two hours later she woke up. Paddy, and Daryl were gone. Astounded and panicky, she called upon her father. "Father, Paddy and Daryl are gone. I am scared. Where are they? How could have they left me here?"

Neph reassured her. "A wicked fairy has abducted them. They will be back soon. Don't worry, Soledad."

"Where is she keeping them father?"

"Beyond the clouds is her realm."

"Thanks, father. But how can I rescue them?" No reply came from Neph. She searched through the clouds for the fairy's dwelling. Because of the approaching storm, the task proved to be a major problem. Lightning zapping the dark sky blinded her.

***

Paddy and Daryl awoke in a room, on sofas of silk. Warm sunshine flowed through windows which opened on a beautiful garden.

"Gosh, what is the meaning of this, man. I don't like it at all," whispered Daryl with frightened eyes rolling in his face. Paddy didn't reply. With his mind's eye he was watching the young women giggling in the room, seated on colorful pillows spread on the floor. They were dressed in gauze of light pastel colors. Jewels adorned their hair, arms, legs and feet. They whispered curiously looking at the elves who prudently kept their eyes closed. Paddy was still observing the strange scene.

A girl noticed that Paddy had moved his eyes. Quickly, she approached and said, "Prince, you are in Fairyland, Queen Sheba's realm."

"I am in what! Where is this Fairyland? How did we get here?" exclaimed Paddy.

Daryl had jumped to his feet. "I don't like Fairies," he cried red in the face. "We have had bad experiences with you people."

Paddy was quite upset, too. "I don't like to be abducted by anyone, Fairy or other. This is outrageous! I demand to be returned immediately to where we were."

The young girls in the room chuckled. "You are here by the will, pleasure, and power of our Queen," the girl replied to more snickering from the young ladies. The girl who had approached them softly advised, "Beware prince. The queen is vain, jealous, selfish, and can be cruel, too." Interested in Daryl, she winked at him. He ignored her completely.

A door silently opened. A gentle rustle of silk and a flow of perfume filled the room. Then, a sweet voice said, "Welcome, Prince Patrick of the Irish Elfic Realm. We brought you here by our own pleasure. I am Sheba, Fairy Queen of this Realm," said a beautiful young woman moving toward Paddy. She gave a quick glance of disdain to Daryl.

Her slender shoulders were covered by a mane of lustrous black hair, and a magnificent tiara of diamonds scintillated upon her delicate head. She wore a robe of silk as light as the breeze, that was the color of a magic sunset. The hem of the gown was touching her tiny bare feet, where diamond rings sparkled on her toes. Playfully smiling she touched, with her wand, flowers, changing them into butterfly, and candies into precious stones.

"I am on a quest, your Majesty, and have little time for pleasure," said Paddy.

"I know that can wait," she replied, smiling.

Surprised by the reply, the prince saw flashing into her dark eyes a strange light. Then, he realized that she didn't care about what he had just said. Daryl in silent elfic tongue spoke to Paddy, "Gosh, man, here we are again in the claws of a nasty one. What are we going to do?" Daryl was frightened.

"I am afraid we are. We'll see, man. Relax."

The queen couldn't hear them, and much absorbed in her plot she didn't noticed the brief exchange between the young elves in their tongue.

***

Meanwhile, under her tree, Soledad was still searching through the clouds and projecting her mind into space. She finally whispered, "Here they are." She laughed at the sight of them being beset by the girls. "I think I will wait for them right here. Paddy will love all this attention to his person, and Daryl will hate it even more." She chuckled joyously. "They are well off right there." A little worried she added, "I hope."

***

However, at the fairy's palace, Paddy and Daryl were being spoiled by the girls. The queen clapped her hands. A young fairy immediately responded by singing and dancing. Some others silently brought fresh pastries, fruit, and cool beverages.

In elfic silent talk Daryl said, "Wow, I think I will like it here, at least for a while." Gourmand Daryl smiled with his mouth full of pastries. Paddy admitted that the delicacies were much appreciated after days in the dessert, and he smiled at the queen.

This sort of life continued on for days. They became restless. All this attention showered upon them became tiresome. Something more pressing than being fed by the girls, like exotic birds in a cage, awaited them. One morning Paddy announced to the queen his desire to depart, and said, "Your majesty, as much as we appreciate your hospitality, we must now take our leave."

"Come, come prince, enjoy yourself as much as I do," she replied smiling wickedly, and laughed as she fed him with a soft chocolate. Daryl was being stuffed by giggling girls with pastries. But even the gluttonous elf had enough of this treatment.

***

Soledad used her borrowed power to observe the scene, and murmured, "I think Paddy has had enough, and so has Daryl, even with all the goodies at hand." She chuckled.

***

The young prince, now irritated, realized that indeed they were prisoners of the queen. "We have to escape," Paddy said to Daryl in elfic tongue.

"But how do you propose to escape from a fairy, man?" Daryl replied.

"Well, I am a wizard, and she doesn't know that. The problem is, I don't know where we are." Paddy, exasperated by the impossible situation, while the queen was busy chastising a girl, whispered to Daryl. "Be prepared. We have to get away from here, pronto."

The Prince, preoccupied, wasn't paying much attention to the Queen. She felt his lack of interest in her precious person. A cruel light shone in her eyes and, now irritated, she thought, "I will have to teach you a lesson, young Prince. Goodnight." She left followed by the young fairies.

Paddy's mind was racing for a solution. Daryl, worried, whispered, "Do something, man. We can't stay here forever."

Chapter 38

Soledad, tired of watching the comedy played beyond the clouds, rolled into her cape, and went to sleep under the unleashed storm.

***

The elves at last were alone. They stretched comfortably into deep sofas sipping cool glasses of exotic juice, enjoying the peaceful twilight. Paddy lost in his thoughts, played with the locket around his neck. Daryl was munching some fruit beside his chum. Suddenly, they were caught in a flash of green light. Amazed, they found themselves under a tree flat on their backs with the rain pouring on their faces. Lightning was flashing in the rolling hills. While Paddy was playing with the stone, they had been freed by its magic power. Soledad was at the foot of a tree bundled up in her cape.

"Goodness, Soledad, what did you do all those days alone here?" asked Paddy, worried.

"O, I was well entertained, extremely busy watching you and your courtesans." She laughed merrily. "You had a good time, boys?" A wicked grin shone into her sparkling green eyes.

Vexed Paddy replied, "As a matter of fact, yes, I did enjoy that very much, girl." Daryl winked at Soledad.

"O, just teasing. Goodnight Paddy, goodnight squire"

"Good night, Soledad," said Daryl. "Goodnight, man." Paddy, still miffed by Soledad's remark, didn't reply. He rolled into his cape and went to sleep.

Daylight was up and Paddy woke. Soledad and Daryl were sound asleep. The black clouds were rolling fast, promising more heavy rain for the day. A feeling of danger came to him. "Hurry up, man. Let's move."

Daryl from under his hood screamed, "What, without eating."

Paddy shrugged his shoulders. "Hurry, Soledad. We'll eat some biscuits. No fancy food, man. We must move quickly. The fairy could be after us again."

"Good morning. Did you miss your feather beds, boys?" she chuckled.

Paddy, with fire in his eyes, abruptly said, "We don't have time for jokes"

The young Wizard knew the danger they were in, to be again captured by the queen, and brought back to her realm. He gave biscuits to Soledad and Daryl, who made a terrible grimace.

Paddy laughed. "You had enough sweets for a month. Move, guy." Munching, quickly he started running. (When Elves run, they run.) Paddy's feet hardly touched the ground. Soledad with Daryl closed the rear. They had a hard time keeping up with him.

"What's the rush, man."

Paddy, not looking behind, replied, "Here is why the rush. Listen."

Mingled with the sound of the rain and the wind Daryl's pointed ears caught the sound of laughter and the smell of a garden of flowers. The fairy queen, with a train of dancing stars arrived, followed by the young fairies.

"Watch out, Paddy, she is after you!" cried Soledad.

Daryl stopped, turned around, and threw his heavy body upon the queen. She laughed and quickly, as if chasing an importuning insect, she gestured. Daryl found himself with his nose in the mud flat on the ground. This gave time to Paddy to recover his wits. "*I am a Wizard. Why am I running?*" Abruptly he stopped his flight, turned around, laughed, and shouted, "I am a Wizard. You are going to experience it,

Lady." A shower of sparks flew out of the prince's hands. The Fairy, startled, stopped. Soledad raised her arms, and long flames came from her fingers.

The queen laughed. "Do you think, silly girl, you can stop me?"

"Move, Soledad." Paddy quickly took from his tunic the magic emerald and rubbed it. He held the stone in front of him. The queen and her party braved Paddy with a triumphant smile. At that instant a large green beam shone, encircling the fairies. With cries of despair they disappeared into an explosion of light. Lord Neph had sent them back to their realm.

Paddy, smiled, "I received a great gift from your father. The fairy was too powerful for the two of us. I had to call upon Lord Neph's strength."

They all collapsed onto the soggy ground. Paddy said, "The time lost at the fairy's palace is great. Sorry, friends, we have to move on." They got up. Shaking the water and mud from their capes they left. Even a teeny weenie minute was not taken to have a good meal. Daryl was trudging in the rain, head down eating his biscuit on the run. After an exhausting walk, a muddy lake blocked the way. A belt of noxious weeds girded it, and a haze spread over it. They searched for an opening which would make it possible to continue.

Paddy mumbled, "Nothing. We must go across, but with what?"

Daryl said, "As much as I love water, I am not going in this muck"

"Neither am I, said Soledad, wrinkling her nose.

"Maybe we will find something. Let's continue looking," said Paddy.

They searched and Paddy's sharp eyes caught something hidden in the high weeds. "Look, there in those weeds, I see something."

Soledad stretched her neck out, "I see nothing."

"Yes, yes, I think it's an old barge," said Daryl.

The elves ran to find what Paddy saw. Daryl excitedly jumped into the shallow water. With great satisfaction he announced that it was an old barge buried in the weeds. Soledad rushed to them.

"Stay where you are! If it's safe, we will call you," said Paddy.

The girl bit her lips. Paddy always treated her like an infant. She didn't like that at all.

Carefully the boys approached to inspect the safety of the thing. However, after a closer look it passed the test. Paddy jumped in while Daryl pushed it out of the weeds. Paddy called to the girl. "It's all right, you may come."

Vexed, she replied sourly, "You are very kind. Thank you for the invitation. Maybe you suppose I could walk upon the water."

Paddy laughed. "Who knows, you do so many things. Don't be ridiculous, Soledad. You reacted like a spoiled child." This, of course, was the wrong thing to say,

"You think so." She kicked hard at the water with her boot splashing him wet from head to toes. Chuckling, she joined them on the deck. Underneath the bench of the antique vessel, Daryl found two oars. He grabbed them, and with effort he rowed the old heavy barge out from the muck. Soledad sat quietly watching the maneuver. Daryl determinedly used his strong muscles to row.

The dark lake looked as if it were brooding over some sort of bad deed and had a greenish haze floating upon its water. Suddenly, an unexpected strong wind blew fiercely. High waves rocked them dangerously. It became tempestuous. Daryl had great difficulty controlling the barge. As if things were not bad enough, Paddy discerned in the middle of the lake a large turmoil with something boiling into it. Muscles taut, Daryl desperately tried to get away from the troubled water. Paddy joined him in his efforts. An invisible force sucked the barge slowly toward the funnel. To escape, the young men rowed till their hands were bleeding.

"Hang on tightly, Soledad. It's going to be rough. I feel evil. What can this be? I don't like the look of it." Tensed to the extreme, they looked at the churning water. The fight against the unleashed elements was fierce. The barge came closer to the turbulence, but even with Paddy's and Daryl's determination, they were caught in a terrible turmoil. The young wizard fought with all his might, strength, and power to stay at the edge of the whirlpool to avoid being sucked into the watery grave.

Chapter 39

Soledad looked into the funnel and put her hand in front her mouth, horrified by what she saw. At the center of the funnel a terrible creature was watching the elves fighting. Its cruel eyes were set upon them with jaws wide open showing menacing double rows of teeth waiting for prey to fall in.

The skinny arms of the creature brutally stirred the water to make it go faster. The funnel got deeper and steeper. In spite of the young men's efforts, the boat was slowly being drawn in. Paddy's two hands were not strong enough to control the barge. Neither were Daryl's strong arms. Sweat ran over the bodies of the two friends fighting for their lives. At the bottom of the watery pit the monster's eyes were gleaming, rejoicing in the anticipation of a good meal.

Terrified, Soledad quickly took an arrow from her quiver. A bit unsteadily she set it into the cord of the bow, aimed, and shot at the eyes of the creature. The monster shrieked and for one minute stopped stirring.

Paddy muttered between his teeth, "I was completely out of my mind, to leave my quiet realm for this evil quest. Those old Wizards have all power within them. They have it easy. My power is still not strong enough to fight such evil things. I can't even grab the Magic stone," he continued grumbling angrily. Then, he realized that Soledad had injured the monster. "Good girl," he yelled at her, and she smiled.

Their courage was renewed resumed their terrible fight with much ardor. They struggled to keep the barge at the edge of the watery pit. The beast, due to its injury, had slowed down. As Paddy was struggling to keep the barge from sinking and being swallowed by the monster, his tunic had opened, and now the locket dangled out. A bright green flash shone right at the creature's face. In seconds it was consumed by the power of the stone. Instantly, the lake returned to its calm dark muddy appearance, the funnel had disappeared. Exhausted, Paddy and Daryl collapsed onto the barge's floor.

"Gosh, what a fight, man," said Daryl with a trembling grin on his pale lips. Paddy looked at Soledad seated on the bench looking at him with a trembling smile. Paddy smiled back. "Thanks, Soledad, for your help. I don't know how long I would have hung on. My arms were getting numb. I am glad you came along." Daryl made a sort of grimace. "Me too, Soledad."

Paddy took Daryl's hands, which were bleeding. "Show me that, man. Looks nasty." Paddy touched each palm and Daryl's hands were like new. "Yes, it was starting to hurt badly." Paddy did the same to his hands.

However, even tired, they grabbed the long oars, and they rowed with energy to reach shore. With a sigh of relief, the elves pulled the old vessel onto the beach, and as they dropped on the sand Paddy threw his rucksack beside him.

Soledad came, kneeled, and kissed Paddy who immediately turned red. She smiled and lay at his side. Exhausted Daryl watched her and gave a mischievous smile to Paddy.

They stayed silent for a while, enjoying the moment of rest. The fight with the elements and the monster had taken hours. Since their flight from the fairy, they hadn't had any rest. Soledad moved away from Paddy and rolled into her cape. She fell asleep.

The boys backs were very sore. The elf took from his pocket a small jar of bright orange salve and gave some to Daryl in his hand. Gently he rubbed it into his palms with Daryl doing the same. A few minutes later the pain was gone.

"Gosh, that's fantastic, man." Both went to sleep. Daryl didn't complain about being starved. For once he was too tired for that.

Next morning Paddy woke everybody. "Let's have a bite and go. We have lots to do. Get up Soledad." He gave her a smile as she yawned,

"Food," screamed Daryl.

"This is the best thing I have heard for days." They ate a nice breakfast and left quickly. Soledad grabbed her bag. She didn't look at Paddy. The rolling hills where they encountered the fairy were now disappearing into the mist. The Prince decided to continue to walk for a while. They had to rest but the battle on the lake had left them hyper. The best thing for them was to keep moving.

Night had come quickly. The sky was dark with no stars or moon, and only lightning scarred the night in the north. After two hours of trudging sluggishly, dragging their feet painfully, they despaired of finding a place to rest. Then Paddy discerned in the darkness the silhouette of a large cluster of scrawny trees. "We will sleep here. I don't think that any of us can go further."

"Daryl muttered, "Nope." Soledad shook her head. Drained of all energy, they dropped heavily at the foot of a tree, pulled their hoods down onto their faces, rolled into their capes and fell instantly asleep. In the middle of the night, into the depth of his slumber, Paddy's sharp elfic ears heard a strange buzzing and flapping of wings around him.

Quickly, he opened his eyes to check what caused that sound. Looking up he saw a huge white cocoon hanging down from a tree with a moth busily at work laying larva inside Soledad's body. Horrified, he saw that she was trapped in the cocoon suspended in the air by strong threads. A gigantic moth up in a tree was working on Daryl weaving a cocoon around his body. The insect was giving him the same treatment while he fought trying to reach his shining sword. The huge insect diligently threaded its web of death around him. Finally, he freed himself. Quickly, Paddy drew his sword to cut the threads around him. Daryl hung moaning in the air. With a zap Paddy freed him, and he fell with a heavy bump on the ground screaming a loud "OUCH!" Paddy moved his hand to loose him from the web. Dizzy from the venom injected, he wobbled on his legs. The young Wizard touched his hand,

and the malaise was gone. Then gently he brought down Soledad. He waved his hand to unravel the girl from the horrible net she was trapped in.

Furious at the loss of their prey, the moths attacked. The long stingers they bore at the tips of their pointed noses pointed toward Paddy like swords. The elf, indignant for the treatment they had given to Soledad and Daryl, furious at being awaked by those insects, raised his blade and with a strong blow severed the three stingers. The moths shrieked in pain and flew away.

"That will teach you, nasty things. You are lucky he didn't kill you," screamed Daryl with his sword menacingly up in the air.

Paddy laughed.

"You can laugh, man. It was not you prepared for a meal."

"It was worse than that, man. They had put larva on you so you'd be slowly eaten by their offspring."

"What!" Daryl was sick.

Soledad was busy getting rid of the sticky cocoon. Paddy moved his hand cleaning up the mess from her. Frowning he said, "What next. Indeed, that sorcerer has a wicked imagination."

Soledad disgusted replied, "You can say that. That insect had me well prepared for its table, and Daryl was going to be the dessert." She giggled.

"Yes, but I only appreciate dessert on my own table, and when I eat it myself." Daryl chuckled. Paddy laughed at the thought of Daryl being eaten as dessert. "Good night Soledad. I don't think the moths will come back. Anyway, I will cast a spell around us."

"Thanks. Good idea. Night Paddy. What a night." Daryl sighed.

"Goodnight Prince, 'night Daryl," Soledad said yawning.

No reply came from Daryl. They all had returned to sleep. The remainder of the night was quiet. The next morning they were awakened by the sound of a strong north wind blowing through the meager trees, and a nasty rain fell upon them in piercing needles. Instantly they were back into the evil world in which they painfully toiled.

After eating a hot breakfast, the young Wizard smiled, stretched his legs and got up admitting that after all he was appreciating the silent fight with the sorcerer. He turned toward Daryl, and with a loud laugh, said, "I will beat him. I will bring back the Crimson Shield and free the Princess."

"Of course you will, man"

"With my help." Soledad gave him a great shiny smile.

"Absolutely, Soledad. Thank you," said the elf winking at Daryl.

With this cheerful thought they left for their new exploits. Paddy's fear of the sorcerer's power was less. However, he was surprised because he hadn't heard the girl's voice now for a while. Concerned, he said to his friends. "I hope we are still on the right path."

Daryl replied with a grin. "We must be. Too many bad things are standing in our way.

Paddy, surprised by the simple logical reply from his buddy, said, "Right, man."

The wind pushed and tossed them fiercely. It was miserable weather. The rain was unmercifully beating their bent backs. Paddy's light frame had a hard time being shaken by the ferocious wind, and so did Soledad's, but Daryl's strong legs were anchored onto the ground, and the wind had no grasp on him. They joined forces by holding hands. The country, completely drowned in water, made the visibility nil. Paddy and Daryl, with the help of their elfic vision, couldn't see a thing through the opaque veil of rain. They didn't know where they were except in a gully full of water. Suddenly they bumped onto a rock. The rain eased up a little and revealed with what they had collided. They faced a huge, sleek rock, standing right up and blocking the gully entirely, a dead end with no way out

Chapter 40

"Wow, how are we going to get out of here?" Daryl was looking puzzled

"Now what?" whispered Paddy.

A voice that he recognized as Lord's Neph's said, "Fly."

"Yes, I know, but what about Soledad?" replied, Paddy.

"Leave it to her, Prince."

The girl had followed the conversation between her father and the elf. "Don't worry about me, Paddy, I will make it, you'll see," she gave him a push toward the wall. "Go."

"You are sure?"

"Yes, go."

The elves unbuttoned their capes, grabbed the two sides, opened their arms, kicked the ground with one foot and off they flew upwards. It didn't take then long to reach the top of the rock. From there, they looked around and below for Soledad. The girl had left the bottom of the cliff. They looked on the other side. The weather was clear and the visibility excellent. The valley below was a desert with not a speck of rain in the air. Small twisters there quickly picked up dust from the ground which was as dry as an old bone. "It's not too inviting, man."

"Well, it will dry up our soggy bones." Daryl amazed by the brutal contrast of land rubbed the back of his neck. Worried they looked for Soledad.

"Where is she?" asked Paddy.

"Don't know."

Capes extended like wings, they jumped. However this time they flew downward. Slowly the ground came up to greet them with arms of prickly bushes.

"You chose a bad spot for landing, Paddy," said a cheery voice.

"How did you get here," asked Paddy dryly, annoyed by her remark.

"Remember, I am a Wizard's daughter," she said with a chuckle.

"Yes, I know. You already told me that once," he replied, not amused.

Daryl enjoyed the little conflict between them. Diplomatically he didn't say a word, but just smiled and looked elsewhere. Sensing Paddy's bad mood, Soledad silently moved on. After that unfortunate landing, the young elves were mighty glad for their high elfic boots that nothing could pierce. Night was almost at hand. Time to look for a shelter. They walked endlessly with the wind at their backs pushing them into a cloud of dust flying all around.

The ground had changed. Now it was made of small mounds. In one of those, made of a little pile of rock, Paddy, found a providential cave, almost like a burrow, but large enough to host all of them. Satisfied, they walked in, dropped their packs, and sighing with relief, collapsed on the soft sand. From his packsack Daryl took out some biscuits. Making a funny face, he smelled it, sighing.

Soledad was watching him. "What's the matter, Daryl?"

Paddy laughed. "Even after so many years in the Realm my friend doesn't like elfic biscuits."

She patted him on the shoulder. They ate, drank a drop of magic liquid, and ready to sleep, rolled into their capes.

It was a dark night. Paddy, listening in the silence, tried to hear the soft voice of the girl, but heard nothing. "Oh well. Goodnight, Soledad, goodnight, man." No reply came from the girl. She was already sleeping. Only Daryl's loud breathing came to him. Paddy smiled and with a sigh of pleasure rolled himself into his cape. The nights in the desert were cold. He pulled the hood over his face and went to sleep.

A few hours later a big rabbit, the size of a large man, approached his burrow to spend the night in comfort. Astonished, he found Paddy, Soledad. and Daryl asleep. Perplexed the rabbit scratched behind his ears. "Well, well, well, I don't want to wake these people. But on the other hand, I don't want to sleep in the cold, either. Maybe if I moved this one a bit, I could sleep beside him." Gently he moved Paddy.

Paddy was too tired to hear the rabbit and didn't feel the gentle push. As usual, that night Paddy's, elfic cape provided its warmth, but with the heat from the rabbit's fur, he was extremely hot, so this induced him to sleep late. However, the rabbit was long gone before the elves woke up. The only evidence found of the furry visitor was the hairs on Paddy's cape.

Soledad opened her eyes, curiously looked at Paddy's cape, and asked, "Where did you get that?"

He looked where she was pointing her finger. "I don't know."

"Gosh, man, your cape grew hair during the night," said Daryl impishly.

***

The rabbit, atop a pile of rocks, watched them from a distance. Paddy's face was covered during the might by the hood of his cape, and the rabbit hadn't seen him. In the daylight he now saw Paddy's face and said to himself, "I like him. If I can, I will help them."

***

One more day had passed and gone. Paddy had the uneasy feeling of going on and on forever. As they walked, nothing changed in the landscape. The wind continually stirred the dust erasing their foot prints. Insouciant young rabbits, played hide and seek, disappeared swiftly behind piles of rocks. Amused Daryl and Soledad watched the little guys having fun.

"Aren't they nice," said the girl with a bright smile.

"Yup, I like rabbits, nice insouciant fellows."

Paddy, preoccupied, didn't reply. Disquieted he said, "I have the feeling of being always at the same place." He frowned, looking around. Then the clear voice of the statue rang into his ears. Paddy joyously said, "Guys, we are going in the right direction. I heard the voice of the girl singing."

The heat in the desert was intense, even under a pale sun. Several times, Paddy took the little flask out for them to drink. After a terribly long walk, the girl hoping for a little rain looked up at the cloudy sky. Then she screamed, "Look out, Paddy!" Her hand quickly grabbed an arrow, and at the speed of lightning it flashed into the sky killing a huge buzzard which was diving on the elf.

"Wow, that was a mighty shot, girl." Daryl whistled giving her a glance of admiration.

"Thanks, Soledad. I understand what your father meant, when he said, that you will be of great value in the quest." Paddy smiled with respect to the young archer. He could have deflected the bird with a wave of his hand. He thought, *The girl is great.* Paddy looked at her with a different frame of mind, and a butterfly of love fluttered in his heart.

She laughed and didn't give a look at the carcass lying on the sand. They walked for few hours more and dusk was upon them. At last it was cool. Daryl found a cave in which to sleep. Paddy, stupefied cried out, "But this is the same cave where we slept last night. We are walking in circles!"

***

The rabbit, upon his pile of rocks, watched them from afar.

"I must help, otherwise they are going to turn round and round in these forsaken hills for ever. How can I do that?"

***

Like the night before, the rabbit came down from his outlook post to his burrow and moved Paddy aside. The next morning the prince woke up early. He muttered. "Today I'll watch carefully where we are going." Anxious to be on his way, he quickly got up and was brutally pulled backward falling on his buttocks. Astounded, he realized that he was trapped and couldn't move. His cape was caught on something very heavy. He grabbed the side and yanked trying to free himself. He pulled again and felt under his hand warm soft fur. Flabbergasted, he turned his head to see where that fur came from. Amazed he saw beside him a huge sleeping rabbit!

"Goodness!" he cried.

The rabbit instantly sat up. So did Soledad and Daryl. They rubbed their eyes still foggy and incredulously looked at the rabbit. Paddy struggled to get free.

"Who are you? What are you?" asked Paddy, still trapped in his cape. To get loose, the wizard moved his hand.

"My name is Tyson, King Tyson, of the Mortal Realm," replied the rabbit.

"A king in a rabbit suit, who's talking. I am going out of my mind!" cried Paddy.

Daryl beside him pounded his forehead. "It's insane."

Soledad, who had recovered her wits and had followed the conversation shouted, "King Tyson, I am so glad to see you, even in a rabbit suit."

Chapter 41

"Gosh, you know that rabbit? How could you? He lives in the desert," said Daryl still holding his forehead.

"Tyson! Are you the dead king?" asked Paddy.

"A dead king in a rabbit suit. Oh, la, la, what's happening, man, are we getting crazy?"

"Yes, boy, she knows me. She is the daughter of my friend, Neph. Alas, you are not insane. I am king, or I once was. The sorcerer, after destroying my castle and my family, as a vengeance turned me into a rabbit, and one of my beautiful daughters into a statue."

Soledad said, "Centuries ago, Ida was my friend. That is why I am here, Paddy. When father talked about sending you on a quest to free Ida, I wanted to help her. I didn't know you were still alive, King Tyson. It's wonderful."

"Thank you, Soledad, but your father knew."

"He didn't tell me."

"I thought the king was dead." replied Paddy.

"Not quite. The sorcerer came back to the battleground and got my shield that he had coveted for a long time. Then he conjured spells around me and took me into his lair, nursed me to health, and turned me into what you see. His vengeance was terrible. I would stay this way forever and never leave this place."

Daryl, totally flabbergasted, followed the conversation and asked, "Why into a rabbit, Sir?"

"That was his sense of humor. I was a great king, and a gallant soldier. The rabbit, poor little thing, as you know is not the emblem of courage."

"I don't understand. The sorcerer is long dead. His spells should have died with him," replied Paddy.

"Oh, no, he made sure of that. That is why Ida is still a statue and I a rabbit."

"Tyson, excuse me, if I don't call you, King Tyson. It is a big title for a rabbit."

"I understand. I have lost the use of that title long ago," replied Tyson sadly shaking his ears.

Daryl felt sorry for the poor rabbit. "Paddy, can't you do something man?"

The Rabbit, surprised by the question, sadly asked, "What can he do, boy"

The elf thought a moment and replied to his buddy, "Unfortunately, no, Daryl. The spells binding the king are too strong for me to undo." The elf turned to the rabbit and introduced himself. "I am Prince Patrick of the Elfic Irish realm, going on a quest with my squire and friend Daryl. We are going to retrieve the Crimson Shield, given to your ancestor by one of mine, named Shane. I was told, by our Wizard Yanick and by the Wizard Neph, the shield, with my help, will free Princess Ida. Do you know where it is?"

"Yes, I certainly know, but it will be extremely difficult to get it." The rabbit sadly added, "I won't be able to pass through the barrier of spells, however, I will show you the way."

The elf scratched his forehead. "I don't understand. Tyson, a few minutes ago, you said the sorcerer was dead."

"Not quite. You will see when you get there," replied the king.

"What do you mean, not quite? It is what Neph said about you." Paddy, plainly puzzled, looked at Tyson and pensively rubbed his forehead. "My power is not strong enough, yet, to make you human. Maybe the magic stone could do something."

Neph's voice whispered, "Tyson must look at the stone while you hold his ears up firmly in your right hand. I will be there with you."

"Thank you, Lord Neph." Paddy addressed himself to the king. "Tyson, I am going to ask you to do a strange thing, but please do it. Lord Neph will help me. See this Emerald?"

"Yes, of course. I have had many in my time. It is a beautiful one."

"It is a magic stone. Don't be offended, Tyson. I must hold your ears up while you look at the stone," said Paddy to the bewildered rabbit. A bit worried, Tyson scratched behind his ear, looked at Paddy and said, "You are sure? I am really afraid of magic after what happened to my family centuries ago." The poor rabbit was scared.

Paddy smiled at Tyson reassuringly. "This is good magic. Don't worry. In my realm, magic is a great part of our lives, and Neph will be with me."

Soledad took pity on the poor rabbit and said, "King Tyson, this magic is from my father. He loves you and wouldn't hurt you. You know that."

Nevertheless, Tyson was not convinced. Uncertain the big rabbit still balanced his furry body from foot to foot.

Daryl encouraged him. "Come on, King Tyson. You have been through worse things than that," he said cheerfully.

"Yes, but I was not a rabbit. With the rabbit suit I have inherited, it has attributes of shyness and cowardice," sighed the poor rabbit

However, after much dilly-dallying, Tyson, decided to let Paddy grab his ears. Still troubled, the rabbit, with hesitation, looked into the stone. At that instant a cloud of silver stardust came down upon him. Paddy let go of the ears and backed up. They couldn't see the giant rabbit, now bathed in sparkling lights. A few minutes latter a handsome man in his forties, was standing in the place of the pathetic rabbit.

Amazed the elves asked, "King Tyson?'‘

"Himself!" replied the King, touching his body in wonderment.

"King Tyson!" cried Soledad running to embrace the king. "Only my father could do such a miracle!"

A loud voice said, "Welcome back, Tyson, my friend."

The king recognized the voice and replied, "Thank you, Neph."

The king hugged Soledad. "Yes, child. I can't believe it! I am human again," he said, laughing nervously. Tyson was dressed the way he had been centuries ago, in silk and lace. Paddy with a chuckle said, "Not too practical for the journey, King Tyson."

Patrick. These will have to do. They are the clothes I wore under my armor while fighting the sorcerer. When I left the palace, I didn't take any baggage along. Beside my rabbit suit, I don't have a wardrobe with me, friends," replied Tyson, smiling.

"Ah, but I have one, Tyson. Don't jump to conclusions," replied Paddy.

The elf fumbled in his rucksack. Fortunately, the king was the same size as he, and for the quest he had brought a spare suit in his sack. Paddy quickly took it out and proudly handed him the suit. "Here, Tyson."

"I am glad your spare suit will fit him. Mine would float around him like a standard," Daryl laughed.

Accustomed to four legs for centuries, Tyson awkwardly walked to the cave and changed his lacy garments. A few minutes later the king came out looking like an elf.

"That's much better," said, Paddy, satisfied.

"You are superb, King Tyson," said Soledad laughing.

"And one of us, a real elf, King," added Daryl smiling.

Chapter 42

"I feel great. It's so good to be in my human body! But I have to learn to keep my balance on two legs. I am ready for the quest, Paddy. Let's go," said Tyson, enthusiastically.

Paddy laughed at Tyson's remark. "I wouldn't know. I've never been a rabbit." They laughed.

Soledad, Paddy, and Daryl grabbed their gear, and the four of them left with Tyson holding onto Daryl for dear life. They walked in the desert for a while, and when they reached a certain place, the king stopped and said, "Here is the portal to get out of here that you missed each time you passed."

"I don't see anything," replied Paddy.

"Neither do I," said Daryl, his nose pointed to the ground like a hound.

"I know. That's the point. Come along. You'll see." The King followed by the three young people passed between two small stones deeply set into the ground. "You would have always come back to the cave," said Tyson "that was one of his curses."

"Gosh, nasty beggar," whispered Daryl looking suspiciously at the embedded stone. As they went through the spells, the earth shook, the thunder growled, and lightning scarred the suddenly dark sky.

Tyson, laughing, cried loud and clear, “We are free at last, friends, and he is not happy.” After crossing the spells, they continued their journey in the desert. Dark clouds rolled above, promising an approaching storm. A fierce wind blew.

“To be drenched will do us good after that terrible desert,” said Daryl cheerfully.

“Yes, I didn’t like that much either,” said Tyson.

Suddenly they were shrouded in heavy darkness with groaning and weeping around. “Wow, it is spooky.” Daryl shivered.

“This is evil country the sorcerer still has a strong hold of power upon it,” said Tyson.

“We must find a shelter soon. The company of these things, whatever they are, gives me the creeps,” replied Paddy.

They battled through the darkness pierced by striking lightning. Late afternoon they found a refuge in an old stone hut, abandoned long ago by shepherds. A heavy door hung on half-broken hinges. The weather was getting worse. Grateful, they entered into the providential hut.

The three men heaved and pushed to close the massive piece of coarse lumber. In a corner of the small room was a pile of wood and twigs, enough to start a fire in the rustic chimney set along the wall. The girl excitedly ran to the pile, grabbed the twigs, and touched the wood. Sparks came out of her fingers. Soon a bright flame burst upward, cheering the place. She called to the men, “Look, tonight we are going to be warm.”

“Good girl. Come, Paddy, let’s eat some of your biscuits,” said Tyson.”

“Oh, no, man Serve a good human meal to the king, a royal one that he will enjoy by the fire.” At the thought of such a treat, Daryl licked his lips.

Paddy laughed and winked at his chum. “Okay, man, here it is.”

To Tyson’s amazement he found a meal like he hadn’t had for centuries. “How did you do that, Paddy?”

Daryl with a chuckle replied, “Magic, King Tyson, and good magic, in many ways as you see. Paddy is a wizard, and a powerful one.”

A good meal on their laps they sat by the fire and ate silently. The king, having forgotten human, food savored every bite. Outside, the rain poured, and the wind wildly howled accompanied by the terrible sound of thunder and the frightening lightning.

"I am glad you made a fire in that chimney, Soledad. I am not used to the cold any more. Without your clothes, Paddy, I would have been frozen in that weather. By the look of it, we are here for a while. With good food, I don't mind, do you, Daryl?" Tyson smiled observing the big elf, mouth full as he replied, "Nope."

Tyson's face became taut and his eyes worried. "This is no good Paddy. The sorcerer has spells everywhere and this is one of them."

Daryl making a face replied 'You are probably right, King, but let's enjoy the fire." He put his hand in front of his mouth, stretched his legs, and a few minutes later he was snoring.

Paddy, watching the flames dancing in the hearth, smiled as he realized that along the quest his character had changed. The sorcerer didn't terrify him any more, and he was sure of himself. He felt that his power had grown much stronger.

Soledad, wrapped in her cape, silently observed the young elf. She was getting very fond of Paddy and Tyson, and she quietly enjoyed this moment with new friends.

Sadly, Tyson said, "It may sound odd, but I haven't seen a fire since I was captured and turned into a rabbit. I forgot how restful watching the dancing flames can be."

Paddy noticed a strange bright red light burning in the fire. It moved heavily from side to side. Daryl had woken up, and he watched the strange thing, too.

Paddy was tense. "What's wrong, man? What's that?" said Daryl.

"I don't know, man. Something is coming, something strong, something evil. Let's be vigilant," he replied. They rolled into their capes and went to sleep. In the middle of the night, Paddy's sharp ears heard a queer sound approaching and definitely getting closer. Gently he touched Soledad and Tyson, and immediately the king woke Daryl. The companions at once were on their guard.

"Listen," Paddy whispered.

"What is that? It sounds like a huge crawling beast," said Tyson.

"It is, believe me," replied Paddy.

"How do you know?" asked Tyson.

Paddy didn't answer. He pursed his lips with a finger on his mouth and soundlessly moved to the door. Through a hole in the wood he looked outside. It was very dark, still raining abundantly. With the help of his wizard's vision he could see through the darkest night.

"Farmit!" whispered Paddy,

"What is it, man?" asked Daryl coming near Paddy.

"Will you believe me, man, if I tell you that we are being visited by a dragon crawling on short legs toward our shelter?" replied Paddy.

Tyson moved to the door and tried to see something, but it was too dark for his human eyes. The king opened his mouth, but the elf anticipating his words whispered, "Hush."

Paddy, tensed like Soledad's bow, was watching every move of the monster, who sniffed the presence of enemies and was getting ready to attack. Its long snout went up, and it let out a terrible sound something between the roar of a lion and the grunt of a bear. Its carapace shone with water dripping from every crevice of the terrible armor.

Paddy, whispered, "I am going out. If we stay inside, we will be killed like mice in a trap."

"I will come with you," said Tyson.

"No! You can't see in the dark, and your human sword wouldn't even scratch the beast."

"I am behind you, man."

The two young elves silently opened the door and quickly slid between the heavy planks. Soledad, unnoticed by the elves and Tyson, slipped outside.

The beast was huge. The monster's beady eyes couldn't see the elves, but its acute sense of smell alerted its feeling of danger. Paddy, anticipating the attack, braced himself and sure-footed waited with Daryl at his right side. In a surge of raw power, the beast struck. The magic sword, feeling evil, shone and sparks flashed from it when flames came out of the dragon's mouth.

The boys were used to fighting. At the academy they had learned many tricks with their friends and teachers. All of the young elves had to master the art of battle. The thing the Prince Wizard feared the most was evil he couldn't control. Paddy smiled, "It will be a great fight, Daryl, but we will win."

"Yup."

Chapter 43

Calmly they sized up the beast, evaluating their chance to kill it.

Surprised, Paddy whispered, "Strange this kind of beast never attacks at night. They have poor eyesight. The sorcerer must have cast a spell upon this one to protect the approach of his lair. The only chance we have to destroy it is the soft spot above the eyes. This is going to prove a bit hazardous, buddy." Paddy moved toward the monster. The elf's feet barely touched the ground.

The beast was relying on its acute sense of smell, which right now screamed, "Danger approaching!" Furious, it let out a long jet of flame. Agile, like wild cats, they jumped aside and were missed by the deadly spurt. The elf knew that the only way he could reach the soft spot between its eyes was to ride its back.

Paddy signaled to Daryl to keep the monster busy wile he was going to attempt to ride it. Feather light, and avoiding making any sound Paddy walked beside the huge body and arrived at the end of the long tail. The beast roared searching for its antagonist, then Daryl made a little sound to divert its attention from Paddy. Not making any unnecessary move, the elf climbed up the tail, grabbing the rough scales as handholds. The beast, feeling an intruder upon its tail jerked. The sharp scales badly scratched Paddy's hands. With bleeding fingers he hung on for dear life. He had a terrible time trying to stay on board. The monster desperately shook its huge body rocking the elf. Paddy, at every step he made, was flirting with death. Daryl tried to distract the beast by flashing his sword at it. If, by mishap, Paddy's foot slipped and he fell, the thing would crush him to pulp, like an insect, under its huge paw.

Soledad watched Paddy's every move. Tensed, she was ready to fire her bow. Tyson, hopelessly tried to see something, his mortal eyes stretched to the limit. The king, frustrated, grunted like a bear. He couldn't see what was going on, and for a soldier, staying away from a battle was terribly hard. As the beast turned its head toward Paddy, it blew a jet of flames hot enough to roast the elf. Tyson finally saw the young prince riding the monster's sharp spine. The king holding his breath whispered, " Brave young fool! Goodness, you are going to be killed, boy."

The monster suddenly swung its long neck backward, and tried to catch the elf in his jaws.

Soledad and Tyson cried at the same time, "Look out!"

Petrified, helpless, the two friends watched the terrible battle. Daryl had come to the side of the beast and in a mighty jump was upon its back. Paddy almost lost his balance, and Daryl grabbed him just in time.

"What courage. Those boys are crazy," muttered Tyson.

In a tremendous leap Paddy reached the top of the monster's head which was roaring in rage. Shaking its neck violently, the monster tried to get free of Paddy. Quickly, in a mighty thrust, the magic sword, now red with flames, pierced the scale above its eyes. The monster grunted fiercely, huge sparks came out from every part of its body, and Zoltar's evil spell was destroyed. The elves rapid as vultures diving upon their prey, opened their capes and flew down.

Paddy's strength doubled. Running, he grabbed Soledad in his arms. Daryl pulled Tyson, who was blind in the dark and tripping on the rough ground. The boys without explanation entered the shack and with Tyson's help quickly heaved the huge door and closed it. Outside a terrific burst shook the ground. Through the little window and cracks of the wood they saw the sky turn red.

"What happened?" asked the king, shaken by the adventure. His quiet rabbit life for centuries hadn't prepared him for such thing.

"I am sorry, Tyson. Our realm is a realm of magic. The beast was the sorcerer's creature. My magic sword of light recognized evil at once. Then with power, she destroyed it.

Tyson looked at the elves and Soledad with awe. The young girl smiled at Paddy the Wizard. A light of admiration and love shone in her beautiful green eyes. Paddy felt warm as he looked at her. "What a girl," he thought.

."Your Realm is quite a realm, Prince. I have to get used to it." The king sighed. The battle had been long and fierce. They all were exhausted mentally as well as physically.

A livid light appeared at the small window. Paddy said, "I think we should rest here for a while and then move on. Who knows what is waiting for us."

All agreed. Soledad revived the embers glowing softly in the cinders, and soon a cheery flame burst into the hearth. She quietly rolled in her cape and lay down beside Paddy. One by one they went to sleep. A couple of hours later they woke up. Outside the weather was still bad. They ate a brief breakfast and warmed their hands before going out in the wind and rain. Paddy, Daryl, and Tyson joined forces to pull on the huge door. A strong gust tried to push them back into the shack. Heads down, hoods over their faces, bent under the wind, rain beating them, they left going away from the dreadful place, into the raging storm. With the howling wind, it was impossible to talk.

Paddy came close to Tyson and yelled. "Are you sure we are going"—

Suddenly he disappeared into a pit followed by Soledad, who was walking behind him. The ground gave in under Tyson's and Daryl's feet. They all fell deep down into the earth. It was frightening for Tyson who couldn't see in the dark. The terrible howling of the wind had stopped. A complete silence shrouded the party.

Fortunately the crevasse was large enough for the elves to spread their arms, and they grabbed Tyson on each side as they passed him and slowed his descent. Soledad disappeared in the darkness. Paddy said to Tyson, "Grab the sides of your cape and open your arms." Tyson was terrified, regretting his quiet rabbit life. "Don't be scared, Tyson. I see you. I will guide you."

Approaching the bottom of the crevasse, a wave of sticky heat slapped them in the face like a wet blanket. "What is that?" asked the king.

"I don't know, yet. We are still too far away."

Unlike Paddy, Tyson was not used to the realm and its mysteries. He got very nervous as he heard gurgling water. "What is that sound?"

"We have arrived, whatever that means," said Daryl.

"Ah, here you are, Soledad. I know you are capable of taking care of yourself, nevertheless, it's unnerving when I don't see you." He smiled.

"How did she get there?" asked Tyson.

"Remember, King, her father is a Wizard," Daryl said with a chuckle.

"Ah." The poor king was lost in all this magic. After all, he was only a human. Paddy winked at Soledad, and she answered with clear laugher.

"Please, Tyson, give me your hand. There, now put your right foot in front of you and bring the left beside it. Good, don't move."

Trembling, Tyson replied, "Trust me, I won't, my friend."

Soledad smiled. Eagerly Paddy searched in his pack and found what he was looking for. "There, I found it." Daryl chuckled, remembering, only too well, when years ago he had received from Paddy the blessed stone. Now, being an elf, he didn't need it.

"What did you find? What is it?" asked Tyson.

"Tyson, my friend, you are about to see where you are."

"How so? I don't know how, Paddy."

"Ah, but you will. You are in a magic realm. I will put a band around your forehead with an elfic stone embedded in the strap. As soon as it touches you, you will see. There, how is it?" Paddy had done what he explained to he king he was going to do.

"Incredible, I can see!" said Tyson.

"Of course you do." said Daryl with a chuckle. They looked around. It was a cave with a small lake of hot bubbling water. The walls were dripping and slimy with algae.. "Be careful, don't fall in. You would be cooked."

"I don't intend to. Charming place, your realm, Paddy." Tyson began to relax and laughed for the first time.

"Don't worry, you will get the knack of it, Tyson," Paddy laughed.

From out of the water came a strange sound, and it suddenly increased. A giant lizard rose from the depth of the boiling lake. Terrified, they looked for a way to escape. Paddy's, sharp eyes scanned the cave and found a ledge along the side where they stood. Soledad left, running for safety. The elves urged Tyson, "Hurry, follow us."

The king ran behind Paddy, and Daryl was closing the rear. In dismay Tyson asked, "How this can be? It should be cooked."

"You can be sure this is an infernal creature of the sorcerer," replied Paddy, almost flying on the ledge.

"But the evil one is dead!" cried Tyson, puffing behind Paddy.

"I know, however, not his spells. He left them behind to protect his lair." Perspiration dribbled on their faces burning their eyes. "Hurry, cover your faces with the hoods of your capes," shouted Paddy. The king, still not used to running like that, stumbled several times. Panicky, he grabbed Paddy's tunic. His mortal body slowed him down.

Chapter 44

The lizard, galvanized at the thought of a good meal, flapped its long tongue like a whip behind Daryl. Tyson, terrified, turned his head and saw the monster, erect on its hind legs, catching up to them.

"Look out, Daryl," shouted Paddy. Exhausted, Tyson couldn't run any faster. The beast was closing in on them.

"I can't make it any more, Paddy," he said, out of breath.

Paddy promptly halted and cried, "Hurry, all of you hold onto me." With his hand, Paddy made a circle around them. A brilliant light filled the cave, and they were gone.

Tyson found himself lying flat on his back on the grass, panting, wet with perspiration.

Soledad whispered, "Thank you, Paddy."

The young wizard grinned at her holding her shaking hand for a second. "You are welcome. I had to use my power, or we couldn't mak it."

"I am glad you did, man. That lizard had us on his noon menu," sa Daryl, nervously.

The place was quiet, too quiet, not a sound of birds. The silence w oppressive. Paddy anxiously looked around. "Are we on the right pa

Tyson?" The meadow was beautiful, no more storm, no growling thunder. A welcome breeze cooled them off teasing their hair.

"Yes, but it is difficult for me to remember anything after so many centuries. The aspect of the country has changed. I was almost dead when the sorcerer brought me to his dwelling. When my strength returned he wished me into the desert as a rabbit."

Nearby a whispering brook flowed over shining stones in the silvery water. Many fish shone like precious jewels.

"What a lovely place for fishing," said Daryl. Suspicious, Paddy looked around. Then it dawned on him. The brook was a trap. Soledad dropped her quiver and her bow beside her on the grass and pulled off her boots, splashing the cool water with her feet.

"No! Soledad," cried Paddy.

Soledad, feet up in the air, stopped. "Why, Paddy?" Suddenly out of the brook rose a huge snake angrily showing its fangs dripping with venom. It tried to coil its slick body around Soledad's legs. Terrified, quickly she made a backflip. Screaming. she ran to Paddy who grabbed her with his left arm. He lifted his right hand and zapped the monster. Angrily, it hissed and slid into the brook. "Thank you Paddy," she said in a shaky voice.

"Farmit," swore Daryl. "Is there any place which is not evil, man?"

"I guess not, friend," replied Tyson. "When I was a rabbit, I couldn't go through the circle of his infernal spells. That was part of his vengeance. I would have loved to go away from the hot desert sun."

Paddy looked at him sympathetically and said, "Tyson, if you are rested, we should leave. And you, Soledad, please put your boots on. You could walk on poisonous insects. Don't forget we are trampling on evil ground, and who knows what tricks the sorcerer still has in store for us?" Paddy picked up his rucksack from the grass and left with Daryl walking beside him. Soledad quickly put her boots on, ready to follow Paddy. She secured her quiver on her shoulder and the bow in her hand. Without a last regard for the wicked creek they left the meadow and the deceiving singing brook.

"Tyson, do you know approximately how far we have to go?" asked Paddy.

"Unfortunately I don't have a clue. As I told you, I was brought into the desert under a sleeping spell."

"Don't worry, we will find it," said Paddy."

"You are right. Look at the sky getting dark." replied the King. Once more the weather had turned sour. This time large hailstones bombarded them. Quickly they covered their faces with their hoods. Soledad, ignoring the bad weather, walked faster anxious to arrive and get the shield to free her friend. The elves and Tyson closed the rear. Paddy, shouting in the storm, reminded her of the king's human body. "Not so fast, Soledad. Tyson can't follow us." She slowed down.

Trudging in the meadow with the hail pounding upon their heads, they entered an oak forest. The brook had followed their course with the hail thrashing the water furiously. Between the trees appeared a lovely stone bridge crossing the beaten water. It was covered with moss and tiny white creeping flowers.

"I wonder what this lovely bridge is doing here?" said Daryl.

"I don't recall it," replied Tyson.

"Probably built long ago by shepherds. Soledad, please come back. Let's stay close together," asked Paddy. Carefully they set foot on the stones one step at a time. Too late Paddy saw a hand crawling on the side among the creeping plants. The thing grabbed Paddy and with a tremendous force pulled him into the water. Paddy was held in the weeds by two arms locked against his body. The elf struggled fiercely against a huge demon fish trying to drown him. In a desperate effort he freed his right hand and grabbed the locket on his neck. Bright green sparks came out of his fingers holding the emerald. A spell of death was sent by the stone . Paddy was free. Short of breath he appeared on the bridge. Soledad rushed into his arms, and the elf held her fondly for few seconds.

Daryl hugged his buddy saying, "I was scared to death, man."

Shaking Paddy's hand the king replied, "So was I."

They were shocked at all the terrible things that were happening. A forbidding silence was about and a presentiment of calamity shrouded the forest. The sound of falling hail on the leaves was unsettling and the feeling of the evil presence of the sorcerer was extremely strong.

Beads of sweat appeared on Tyson's forehead. "He is here. I can feel his presence," whispered the king.

"How could he? He has been dead for centuries." replied Paddy.

"You'll see, you'll see," repeated Tyson, terrified. Soledad came closer to Paddy. She grabbed his hand, and he smiled reassuringly and thought, *Of course the king is still under the shock of the awful circumstances he has been through, but after so many centuries, this is strange, very strange."*

The forest turned dark. The hailstones spared no one. Even under the trees and their elfic capes, they were bombarded. Unexpectedly a horrible howling, enough to freeze the blood in one's veins, resounded in the depth of the wood. Even the hail seemed motionless, suspended in the air.

"What on earth can make such a cry," asked Tyson, feeling the hair at the back of his neck standing up.

"I hate to repeat myself, Tyson, but here you are not in earth realm, and we are intruding on evil ground. Even we elves fear it," said Paddy.

"I know, boy, this is not earth, but what was that?"

Daryl answered shivering, "A demon, King, one of Zoltar's pets."

Soledad came closer to Paddy, holding his arm. Frowning, he replied, "I don't know. I think that you are right, Daryl. However, we are not going to stay here to find out. Night is coming. Let's go. We are going to sleep up on the highest and biggest tree we can find, and right now," Paddy moved away, pulling Soledad with him.

The king followed. "You are kidding! I am past the age of climbing up trees. This is fine for you, Soledad, and Daryl boy, but not for me. Youth has left my stiff joints long ago, Paddy."

"All right, you made your point, but listen don't try to fool me. You are not an old man, either. Simple, we won't climb up, we will fly," replied Paddy.

"Fly! Have you lost your mind, Paddy?" Tyson was pale with fear.

The elf had stopped at the foot of a huge tree. Looking up he assessed its height. "In few minutes we will be sitting at the top of this big fellow," Paddy said.

Daryl, with a chuckle, replied, “Yup, this reminds me of when on earth I wanted to escape from my father’s strap.”

Soledad laughed. “You can do it, King Tyson.”

The king sighed. “I am not an elf, girl.”

“See my cape? Yours is the same. They are elfic capes, magic capes. Grasp each side of it, like you did going down the crevasse. Spread your arms, kick the ground with your right foot. and you fly, that’s all.” Paddy slowly rose.

Chapter 45

Tyson, uncertain, was looking up. Then, once more, the terrible howling resounded, but this time much closer.

"Hurry up, Tyson! Whatever is after us is getting nearer," said Paddy. Frightened, the human opened his arms, kicked the ground, and rose. Up on a branch, Paddy watched in case he would fall and need to be rescued. Tyson arrived and sat beside Daryl. Soledad used only her mind.

"All right, lets go higher," said the elf.

"Fine with me, man." Tyson astounded and pleased asked, "Was I really flying?"

"Of course you were. Stand up on the branch, kick, and follow me."

Soledad had already reached the top and waited for them. Down below a heavy shuffling cut the silence of the night. The trees shook. Paddy's sharp eyes pierced the darkness and saw a formidable creature, half man half beast with four horns around its head. It tried uprooting the tree. Paddy quickly sent a spell of heaviness. Furious, with much grunting, the monster continued pulling on it.

"Farmit! We won't sleep. Let's move to the next tree," said Paddy.

Daryl, with a chuckle said, "The creature will be busy for the night while we will be sleeping quietly next door."

They left and quietly settled down upon a large branch on the next tree. After eating a biscuit, they rolled into their capes and went to sleep. Tyson didn't sleep easily, his mind much too busy reflecting on the wonderful things happening to him since he returned into his human body. Early in the morning a horrible howling woke them up. The first light of the day was chasing the frustrated evil creature. "I am glad the beast is leaving us," said Paddy.

Tyson looked worried. His eyes were going from Paddy to the forest.

"We better go now," said the elf.

Tyson, fear in his voice, asked, "How are we going down?"

Daryl laughed "The same way we came up, flying."

"What? You want me to jump down from the tree? Never, boy," replied Tyson, horrified at the idea.

"Sorry, friend, there is no other way, except if you come down by yourself," said Paddy, looking at the worried king.

"Come down by myself? I haven't done this since I was a wee lad."

"Then, fly, do what you did in the crevasse. Watch me."

Paddy walked to the end of the branch, took his cape by each side, opened his arms and jumped. He was gently flying down.

"Come on, Tyson, you have been through worse than that," encouraged Paddy.

"Okay, we jump together" said Daryl beside him.

The human, terrified, muttered, "And if I don't fly, on the other hand, I can't stay here forever."

"Right, King, let's jump," Daryl boldly punched him.

Tyson let out a yell, then delightedly realized he was gently flying down. He arrived safely beside Paddy. The elf gave him a big slap on the back.

Daryl cheerfully said, "See, nothing to it. You are becoming an elf king."

During the night the storm had stopped, leaving on the ground an awful crop of crushed leaves.

The big tree they had left the previous night was badly battered by the monster. Paddy moved his hand to repair the damage "There, it's like new." He smiled to his friends. The ground around them had been trampled as if an army had camped there. An oppressive silence reigned. Their steps were hushed by the moss covering the forest floor.

Suddenly, Paddy heard the voice of the girl singing her sad song. She had been mute since his encounter with the rabbit (her father). The elf thought, *Her voice is so clear we must be close to the sorcerer's lair.*

The trees were thinner. They had reached the edge of the forest and left the large oaks and the monster behind. A burning sun shone through a haze upon a field of high weeds swaying strangely under an invisible breeze.

"I don't like this. I feel evil all around us," said the young Wizard.

"I do, too, but I can't see anything threatening," replied Soledad walking closer to Paddy.

An unusual quietness floated in the mist covering the weird area. As they entered the field, they were pulled down by their boots and thrown on the ground. The long green blades moved, ensnaring their necks with an unusual force, choking them.

"Farmit," swore Paddy, falling on his knees.

A few seconds before, Soledad had moved away from Paddy. She now saw him with Daryl and Tyson, flat on the ground, and she heard the elf swearing.

Suddenly Daryl was covered with gold dust. The weeds ensnaring him shriveled and died letting him go. "Thank you. Goldy."

Soledad quickly levitated herself. Paddy and Tyson battled furiously in a supreme effort, and the young wizard managed to free his hands. Flames burst from his fingers burning the weeds around. The elf pulled out his sword from the scabbard. Smiling, he helped Daryl chop at the weeds. Teasing, he said, "It's nice to have connections." Daryl shrugged his shoulders. However, Tyson's earthly blade had no effect whatsoever against evil. Quickly, Paddy conjured a magic elfic blade for him. "Here, friend, now you can fight." Paddy cleared the weeds still upon him. Shaken, Tyson was pale.

"What else is this diabolic character preparing for us?" asked the human rubbing his neck. Soledad had come down and was standing beside him.

"Daryl and I will clear the way with our magic swords. Both stay close to us," said Paddy.

"I will help, Paddy, with my new sword," said Tyson.

The weeds were tough, and they tried constantly to pull them down. Progress was slow, and their arms became sore from slashing the weeds. Daryl, tougher for this type of work, said, "Stop, man, rest for a while. You, too, King Tyson. I will continue."

Adding to their misery, the sun burned through the mist unmercifully.

"We must put our capes on if we want to keep cool, because I think we still have a long way to go," said Paddy.

Soledad moved her hand, and immediately a transparent shield covered her. The elf smiled, asking, "Is there anything you can't do, Soledad?"

"O, yes, Paddy, many. I am just an apprentice, and, as I told you, I borrow magic from father," she replied with a little laugh.

"Nice to have a powerful father wizard." Daryl winked to Soledad.

Paddy resumed his cutting with Daryl and Tyson. As soon as Paddy stopped hacking at the weeds, he was caught by his boots. Exhausted he said, "We must stop, Tyson. I can't feel my arm any more."

"How can we do that with the weeds all around us?" asked Tyson worriedly.

"Just don't move, stay where you are," replied Paddy.

"I'll help you, Paddy," said Soledad eagerly.

"Please do."

Soledad stood where Paddy had already chopped the weeds. She brought her arms forward. and with her hands burned all around.

"There," she said satisfied, looking at her work. She gave Paddy a big smile.

"Good, Soledad, but I still have a bit to do," Paddy replied. With his sword extended in front of him, like a dervish wizard he started to turn going faster and faster. He had brought a spell of safety upon the ground.

"Now we can relax. We are well protected."

Tyson, watching all this magic, asked the elf, "Is there anything you can't do in your realm, Paddy?"

The young Wizard smiled, slapping Tyson on the back. "Yes, my friend, there is." With the haze, the sun had disappeared over the horizon. It was now almost dark.

Paddy sat heavily beside Soledad. She took his hand. "You are wonderful." Abashed he smiled at the girl. Tyson looked at the elf. Paddy got up and laughed. "Come on, Tyson, sit down. You, too, Daryl. The weeds are dead. Well, friend, we have a good spell to shield us against evil. Let's eat and have a good sleep."

Reluctantly the King sat facing Soledad, and she kindly smiled. Tyson didn't reply. The human ate silently and rolled into his cape, pulled the hood down, and went to sleep.

Paddy whispered to the girl, "Good night Soledad."

She replied a soft, "Good night, Paddy." Daryl was already asleep.

Paddy woke with a strange feeling that something, or someone, was trying to overpower him. He opened his eyes. Evil hands weighed down upon him. Tyson had wakened and was watching. Paddy said, "Those hands are absolutely evil."

"I don't see them, however I feel their presence."

"Tyson, don't stay close to me. My magic circle protects you. It's after me, whatever it is."

Suddenly, Paddy was caught up in a funnel of fire. Tyson could see him fighting some elusive forces of hell. They were all over him. In a supreme effort, the elf drew his sword and destroyed the satanic adversaries. The funnel disappeared. Exhausted, Paddy collapsed onto the ground. Soledad quickly grabbed his hand to give him some strength, borrowed from her father.

"What on the green earth was that?" asked Tyson.

Chapter 46

"Before his death the sorcerer called upon the dark forces of hell to protect his lair." replied Paddy.

"Wow, man, you scared me out of my wits. That was horrible," said Daryl. Soledad, exhausted by the transfer of strength from her father, quietly lay beside Paddy and fell asleep. The elf, now almost well, sat with his friends munching his biscuits. At the horizon the sun showed a pale face. With the mist a stench rose from the weeds.

"Wake up, Soledad. Time to go," said Daryl shaking her. "You have to eat your biscuit on the run, girl." Paddy pushed his friend away and helped her to get up. Looking into the sparkling green eyes, they smiled at each other. "Thank you, Soledad."

Paddy, canceled his spell, and they left. The young Wizard opened the way in front of them by burning the weeds. In his fight against the dark forces he had used lots of energy. Sluggishly, he dragged his feet, swishing his sword in front of him to direct the fire. "Let me take over, man."

"No, Daryl, you can't do it. Your magic sword is not powerful enough. Thanks, man." Gradually he recovered his full strength. Tyson put his hand on the elf's shoulder affectionately. "You have been shaken up, boy."

"I guess so," replied Paddy.

With a sigh of relief they left behind the awful stinky place to walk through briers and thorns. In the distance huge mountains suddenly appeared in the mist. At the crest of one of them they could see the sorcerer's lair.

"But it was not there before," said Tyson stupefied.

"Probably before joining his evil friends from hell, the Sorcerer moved his lair into an inaccessible spot," said Paddy.

"Possibly. It must be long after he transported me from the valley when I was wounded," replied Tyson.

"Well, I don't think we will be there soon," said Paddy.

"But those are the Blue Mountains, Realm of the dwarves," said Soledad, surprised.

"You mean where my kin Shane lives?" asked the Wizard, stunned at the news.

"Yes."

"Farmit! This is incredible," whispered the elf.

"Gosh, I hope the evil one didn't kill him," replied Daryl worriedly.

Without more comment the party moved toward the mountains. Tyson plunged into his melancholic thoughts and closed the rear. They toiled, fighting through brushes, rocks, thorns, and briers. Finally, a narrow trail was found which led up. Without losing any time, they ascended the mountain. Rocks rolled under their feet. Tyson fell more than once. The young people smiled.

The trail was rough and narrow. It became more treacherous with the change of weather. Snow had started falling. Concerned for Tyson, the elf often looked over his shoulder and finally asked his buddy, "Daryl, walk behind Tyson, please." A strong blizzard howled in the mountains.

"Okey-dokey, replied Daryl."

After a bend in the trail, Paddy, suddenly found himself in front of a deep chasm breaking the trail. They looked at each other. Tyson, terrified at the sight, asked, "Goodness, what are we going to do?"

"I don't know yet, Tyson. Soledad, Daryl, and I, can jump to the other side. That's nothing, but it will leave you here," replied, Paddy, unhappily.

"What about the magic stone?" asked Tyson.

"I must use it only in a case of great emergency. I have to first find a solution by myself, then, if I don't succeed, I use magic. Magic is always the last resource. This is the way we Wizards do it in our realm."

"I see." No, he didn't. If he had that power in his hands, he would use it right now. The mortal sighed. Paddy searched for a possible way of going across. The snow violently pushed by the strong howling wind jostled them around.

"We are going to fly over the chasm," said Paddy.

"What? Are you out of your mind, boy!" asked Tyson.

"Tyson, it's the only way. You can do it. If you can't, I will magically transport you on the other side," said the elf.

Tyson, utterly terrified, replied, "It's easy for you to say and do. I am not a youngster any more, and I don't trust that flying cape of yours. It could let me down. I am not an elf."

"See how easy it is," said Paddy.

The elf held his cape, opened his arms, pushed off, and he flew. The snow in connivance with the strong wind pushed him. Tyson watched him. "Now do the same thing. I am waiting for you on the other side, Tyson."

The King looked desperately at Daryl and Soledad. Closing his eyes, he spread his arms. The girl smiled and gently gave him a push.

"Good, man, think you are flying, and the cape will do the rest," said Daryl encouragingly. The king did what he was told and reached the other side. Exhausted he lay down on the snow. The wind was howling like a hungry beast into the canyon. Paddy helped the king to get up. "I am sorry, Tyson, but we must move. We can't stay here. Night will soon be here."

Paddy was ready to go. Tyson stretched his legs and arms and without comment followed the young people. Paddy was worried about his human friend. He was going through many hardships after having been so long in the skin of a gentle rabbit.

The weather turned for the worse. The wind, now loaded with ice pellets, beat them fiercely. They moved slowly, heads down, on the slippery trail.

Discouraged, Tyson looked up at the menacing sky, which showed no promise of change for the better. The human screamed a warning to Paddy as a huge turkey vulture dived upon Paddy at the speed of an arrow. Neck and claws stretched out, the huge bird lifted the elf like a feather into the air. Trying to get free Paddy battled the raptor furiously.

Soledad quickly brought from under her cape the bow and arrow and aimed at the neck. With a shriek of pain the bird opened its claws. It dropped Paddy and flew away leaving a trail of blood behind.

In the raging tempest, the light elf, tossed like a piece of straw in the furious wind, had a hard time flying down. Tyson, Daryl, and Soledad watched helplessly as their friend fought the unleashed elements. In spite of all his efforts, Paddy couldn't keep control and drifted away, precipitated into the abyss like a rock. He lost consciousness.

How long he was out he couldn't tell. His head was sore, and all his body ached. Painfully, he opened his eyes. Amazed, Paddy, looked around. He lay on a bed with a thick red comforter upon him. The chamber had colorful tapestries hanging on the stone walls, with well polished heavy wood furniture. Paddy, heard the door squeak and a blond-bearded face appeared.

"Ah, you are awake, my boy," said the thin old man.

Paddy immediately recognized him as an elf. His green eyes shone with concern. He was warmly dressed in a dark green woolen coat with a big collar of white rabbit fur on which shone his long blond hair. From under his coat showed a pair of white rabbit fur boots. A large gold chain hung around his neck.

"Paddy rubbed his aching forehead and asked. "Where am I? Who are you, Sir?"

"One question at a time, please. Where are you? In the Blue Mountains. my dwelling. Who am I? Your uncle three times removed. My name is Shane. and you are Paddy, Prince Patrick."

"Shane! You are the one who gave the magic shield to King Tyson, and the same, who with the Wizard Neph, plotted the quest I am embarked on."

Chapter 47

"Precisely," replied Shane laughing loudly.

"How did I get here? How do you know my name?"

"You see, with the help of the dwarves, my squire and I were looking for an injured deer, when I saw your foot sticking out of a mound of snow. We found the deer, and you. We brought both of you to safety. Now, how do I know who you are. I simply called upon Neph, who told me all about you and your party who right now are caught in a terrible blizzard on the trail."

Paddy said "I am worried sick about them."

"Don't be. If you feel strong enough, boy, get dressed and join me in my parlor for a hot chocolate. Pull the chain which is at the door. It will ring a bell, then a page will come to guide you." Shane left.

Paddy, still a little dizzy, stepped down from the bed and gingerly sat on a wooden chair covered in red velvet. For a few minutes the young prince stayed still, calling upon his power to stop his head from swinging. Then, still uncertain upon his legs, he started to dress. When he finished he was feeling fine, and he walked to the door and pulled the chain. The soft sound of a bell echoed in the distance and then hurried footsteps in the hall. Gently, someone rapped at the door.

"Come in."

The cutest little dwarf boy entered and bowed to Paddy. Under a bunch of flaming red hair shone two large, bright, intelligent blue eyes, illuminated by a splendid smile. The wee fellow was dressed in fine leather. His coat was yellow and his pants purple. On his tiny feet he wore small brown boots. With a grin, he proudly announced. "My lord Shane has put me at your service, sir. My name is Kortis. If you please, Sir, follow me." Paddy smiled. Escorted by his guide he left the room.

The somber and silent halls were lighted by torches upon the stone walls. The giant shadow of the little dwarf was dancing on the walls. Kortis, used to it, didn't even give a look at it. However, Paddy, in this crypt-like environment felt uneasy. How come he could feel evil near? In the gloom something or someone was watching his every move. Then in the darkest corner of the hall, Paddy was grabbed by tentacles with spikes trying to strangle him. He fought, and blood was running on his hands as he tried to pull out the spikes digging in his flesh. All the wizardry he used was not strong enough to neutralize his adversary. Terrified, he realized he had left his magic sword in the room.

The little dwarf didn't see or hear anything. It was only at his master's door that he saw the prince was not with him anymore. All etiquette forgotten, Kortis quickly entered screaming into the chamber of Lord Shane, "Master, Prince Patrick has disappeared!"

"What do you say boy? How could it be, within these walls?"

"I don't know master. The Prince was with me, and then, he was not, anymore!"

Precipitately, Shane left his chair and went to a beautiful tapestry which he punched and touched a stone on the wall. Quietly, a secret door opened and closed behind him.

Shane entered into his laboratory where he kept many old manuscripts bound in gilded leather. The old elf ignored them and went directly to a small table with a black silver top. The Wizard muttered secret words, and his hands lit as they flew over the table. The little boy couldn't hear. Beyond his master's knowledge he had quietly followed Shane and was curiously watching him. To Kortis surprise the silver top shone brightly and upon it appeared the face of Lord Neph.

"Neph, my friend," said Shane. "Paddy has vanished within my walls. Where is he?"

"He is still within your walls, bound by the sorcerer's ropes, and invisible to you, but he is there."

"But how can that be? The evil one has been dead for so long now! How can I help him? I am not a wizard like you, Neph."

"I know, friend. You don't need to be. Do only what I am about to tell you, and soon Paddy will be with you, unharmed."

Shane sighed. "All right, Neph, tell me. I am ready."

"Fine, listen."

Kortis, disappointed, couldn't hear anything. Shane stormed out of the chamber and rang the bell calling his Intendant. Shane smiled at Kortis, "You may go ,boy. I don't need you, for now."

The little dwarf left running. He had plenty to tell his friends about all this strange business of the prince's disappearance and his master talking to a silver table.

A little short of breath the Intendant arrived and bowed.

"Ziurga, I have work for you to do. Go to the shepherd's house. Bring me the youngest lamb you can find, hurry." Surprised the elf opened his mouth to talk but judged better and left immediately as he was asked. Shane nervously paced in his chamber. At last Ziurga arrived, carrying in his arms a little white lamb.

"Perfect," said Shane. "Give it to me, and go to fetch seven young children." Baffled, the elf looked at Shane, and without a word, left. A few minutes later, he was back in Shane's room with the seven giggling children.

"Now, please follow me." Escorted by the whispering children, the old elf left the room. They arrived at the bend where Paddy had disappeared. Like everywhere in the halls, a torch burned. Shane waved to the little folks to approach and make a circle. Seven pairs of curious eyes attentively watched every move he made. The lamb, still in the arms of Shane, was quietly asleep. Without disturbing his slumber, he gently put the little animal on the ground in the center of the circle made by the children.

From the ground rose a delicate mist, and the hall started shaking.

The lamb woke, terrified, bleated and frightened the children, who attempted to run away but couldn't. A huge tremor shook the mountain, and a terrible cry of rage filled the halls. Then Paddy appeared in the middle of the circle. Monstrous spiked ropes, like serpents of fire, were about Paddy. The elf, bleeding, was fighting with all his might to get free. Shane promptly pushed the children away. The little ones left running in every direction. The lamb, lying petrified on the ground, was softly bleating. Then the wizard's voice echoed into Paddy's ears. "The stone, Paddy, the magic stone." Paddy grabbed the chain around his neck and quickly aimed it at his neck. A sharp green beam burst out of the stone, destroying the evil thing ensnaring him. Paddy, covered with blood and exhausted, fell to the ground.

"That was a fierce battle, Paddy," said, Shane, a little pale. The young prince smiled and bent down to grab the poor terrified lamb. Silently, the two elves walked back to Shane's chamber. Speechless they sat. The little lamb resumed his interrupted nap, on the rug. Paddy cleaning the blood and closing his wounds broke the silence and asked, "What about my friends, Shane. Have you any news?"

"Yes, right now they are resting at the dwarves lodge. Soon they will be here with us."

A little later, Tyson, Daryl, and Soledad were announced by a page. Paddy bounced out of his chair, arms outstretched to greet his friends. Soledad kissed and hugged Paddy a little longer. Eagerly the men grabbed his hands. "Oh, man, I thought I had lost you again," Daryl hugged his old pal. Paddy smiled and told the story of how he was found by Shane and the dwarves in the snow. They talked for a long time. A fabulous meal, to Daryl's delight, awaited them. Then, very tired, they retired to their rooms. The next morning, after many thanks to their host, they left to continue their quest.

It was miserable, rainy, weather. The party, heads down, fighting the gale, was happy being together. Tyson, followed Paddy, Daryl was right behind. Soledad, closing the rear, was watching Paddy with glowing eyes.

The trail they laboriously plodded upon was a river of slush and loose gravel. Their feet were constantly sliding backward, and discouragement was gnawing at their hearts.

With night almost upon them, and no shelter in view, Daryl asked, "Well, man, what are we going to do?"

Paddy's sharp eyes perceived a niche in the rock big enough to shelter them. He yelled above the noise of the storm, "There, we will be safe for the night."

They nodded and hurried to get into the protection of the small cave. Numb, they ate a hot thick stew provided by Paddy's power and wrapped themselves in their capes. Soledad, without a word, cuddled against Paddy. Hoods over their faces, they went to sleep.

When they awoke in the morning, the weather had cleared up. Spirits uplifted at the thought that the end of the trail was almost there, they talked and laughed. Quickly, Paddy provided a hot cereal breakfast. With renewed courage they walked in the slush left from the storm. With laughter Daryl and Soledad fell on their hands in the muck. Finally, they arrived at the top of the mountain. Stupefied, they looked around. The sun shone, no gale, no more snowstorm. The contrast with the trail was astonishingly incredible.

An immense plateau covered with high weeds swayed in a warm gentle breeze that faced them. It was more likely an overgrown lawn, probably well cared for by the sorcerer's minions, centuries ago.

"What's the meaning of this, man? We are in summer here," asked Daryl, delighted.

Paddy suspiciously looked at this sunny scene and replied, "I don't like it. Don't be fooled by this. Evil surrounds us. It's everywhere. I feel it in my very bones, man."

Chapter 48

An alley of majestic oaks made a splendid archway at the entrance to the field. Cautiously they moved under the trees, remembering how they had been ensnared previously in the field of tall weeds. Proceeding with extreme prudence they advanced. Suddenly they were engulfed into a dark void with screams of pain and despairs. Long arms tried to grab them. Terrible moaning and growling encircled the party trapped in the large branches of the trees. Even with all their efforts, they couldn't get free. A sardonic laugh resounded as the branches steadily squeezed them. Paddy uttered some magic words which were not strong enough to overcome the powerful evil the sorcerer had left here.

"He is here," whispered the king terrified.

Paddy reassured the poor human. "No, Tyson, what you heard was only his evil spirit lingering around his lair. He has been dead a long time. But he can still hurt us through the spells he left behind." Paddy, to free himself from the deadly grip, pulled hard scratching his doublet against the rough bark of the branch holding him. He reached his neck and felt the chain from were the stone hung. With one finger he pulled on it and brought the stone out under his chin. Holding it there with his free finger he gently rubbed the emerald. A bright green light cut the darkness, and they found themselves free on the ground breathing heavily.

"Wow, I wonder what else that horrible sorcerer is going to do," said Daryl.

"I am glad Lord Neph gave me this magic stone. Without it we wouldn't have come this far. My power is not yet strong enough. Neph knew it." They entered a splendid alley of cypress standing on guard side by side, facing each other like gigantic sentries. At the end of the alley, standing out of the weeds, a huge black torch burst into flames. At the same time a small black and white onyx castle emerged, shining under the setting sun.

"Wow," whispered Daryl.

"Here it is. The sorcerer's lair." said Tyson, with anger flashing in his eyes. Strong emotion filled his heart. The loss of his family, friends, and all his possession was too much for a man to bear, and he wept. Paddy sympathetically patted his shoulder. Soledad held his hand. Daryl, touched by the anguish of the King, couldn't say a thing.

"Come friend. Nothing is lost." Paddy said.

Tyson didn't reply. He only shook his head, with a strangled sound coming out of his tight throat.

The castle made of white and black onyx was sinister facing them in the evening light. They arrived at the bottom of elegant black marble stairs. Paddy opened a path, carefully touching each step with his magic sword as they climbed up. He pushed open the unlocked door, made of precious black ebony with heavy gold hinges. Time had not damaged it. Evil was protecting it.

A great silence shrouded the castle. Warily, they entered.

Soledad excited and curious held to Paddy's doublet. Daryl, knuckles white, nervously kept his sword tight in his hand. Dusty spider webs covered everything. Some fat black hairy spiders hung from the gold chandeliers above their heads. They cut their way through the sticky webs, protected by their elfic capes. The strong evil presence made their skin crawl. Making no sound, they advanced cautiously. They crossed the small hall to reach the door on the other side. No word was exchanged. They were much too tense to utter anything. A pale evening light came through the dusty high windows giving to the place an unquestionably evil look.

"Wow, it's weird here, whispered Daryl. His hair rose at the back of his neck. Soledad gave him a funny look. She didn't know what weird signified. She held tightly onto Paddy. The sorcerer terrified her. Quietly the young wizard opened the door. Still tiptoeing, they entered into a splendid room filled with all sorts of gold artifacts. Gold was everywhere. Paddy, even in his father's palace, had never seen that much.

"Wow, gosh, the guy loved gold," Daryl whispered in dismay.

Suddenly whispers were all around. They froze, as they saw at the center of that incredible room a man (or what was left of him) seated on a throne of pure gold. The personage was completely mummified, his skin like parchment. "He is horrible, a perfect mummy out of a sarcophagus from the pyramids," said Daryl nervously. "What are the pyramids?" Soledad asked in a whisper. No answer came from any of them. Spider webs hung from the sharp bony nose, his stringy white hair was covered with webs. His dried hands were curled on a gold lion's mane, like raptors claws grabbing its victim. The finger nails were huge as talons with hanging webs. Webs, webs, were everywhere on the precious pieces of gold trimmed furniture.

In a low husky voice, Tyson, whispered, "The sorcerer."

"He surely loved gold," said Soledad, impressed by the scene.

"For what. He is dead. Look at him, an empty old carcass!" replied Paddy loudly. A tremor shook the castle.

"Hush, man," Daryl shivered. A menacing glow flared in the sockets of what had been the Sorcerer's eyes.

"Look! Here is the Crimson Shield." said Tyson. On the wall behind the Sorcerer's skeleton was the shield. Daryl ran to get it.

"Don't touch it!" cried, Paddy. "It will kill you!"

Petrified, Daryl stopped dead. "Why man? I am an elf"

"Yes, but not of Shane's house." Paddy moved toward the wall. At that instant a horrible roar came out of the dry corpse. Surprised the elf turned around.

"Look out! The sorcerer's carcass is on fire:" cried Tyson, terrified.

Soledad, who had let go of Paddy's doublet, lifted her hand. A formidable charge of lightning zapped the flaming corpse, and in return the carcass sent a terrible jolt which threw her unconscious to the floor. Quickly Paddy pulled her behind a desk.

"Wow, look. He is even more than ablaze!" Daryl shouted. Petrified, Tyson watched oozing out of the dry body a horrible thing, a sort of Dragon which roared with anger. The beast was green and slimy, getting bigger every second.

"How disgusting and repulsive." said Paddy.

Under the insult, the monster roared with rage. The young Wizard, light as the wind, ran to the wall, jumped and grabbed the Crimson Shield, threw it to the king and screamed, "Catch Tyson." The human caught the shield just in time and lifted it in front of him. A jet of flames struck the metal and bounced back onto the beast. Furious, the dragon turned its fury on Paddy and spat fire upon him. The Prince rolled so fast onto the floor that the jet missed its target and passed above his head.

"Keep the shield in front of you, Tyson. The dragon can't harm you. The shield's power is too strong for him. The beauty of it is, the sorcerer never knew it," Paddy laughed.

Daryl quietly eased behind the throne and lifted his magic sword above the Dragon's head. Paddy, still crouched on the floor, opened his tunic and quickly took out the magic Emerald and held it up to the dragon's gaze. Daryl's sword severed the monster's head. Simultaneously, a green beam of light flashed, striking the Dragon's carcass. In seconds it was reduced to a pile of cinders.

"Wonderful, good job, Daryl. Zoltar is now dead for good! Hurry, Tyson, let's get out of here!"

The elf ran to Soledad, who was just coming back to her senses. Paddy helped her up. Daryl sped out from behind the throne of gold. The walls cracked, the floor heaved, dust and fumes were all around them. The noise was almost unbearable. Bouncing from side to side, unsteady on their feet, they reached the heavy black door, which was slamming shut and opening with a terrific bang. They jumped outside. The sun had disappeared; the dark sky was scarred by lightning. A strong wind blew and the earth shook violently. Tyson, burdened by the

Crimson Shield and his mortal body, was going as fast as he could. Paddy saw his difficulty. The elf grabbed the king by the arm and pulled him along.

They arrived at the far edge of the lawn. There the tall cypress bounced under the furious gale. Then a tremendous explosion deafened them. They witnessed the total destruction of the little castle engulfed in an enormous crater of flames, rocks, and smoke. At the same time the setting sun appeared in a blue sky.

"Look at the beautiful sky." said Tyson.

"Evil has left the Realm for ever. Too bad, it was a pretty little castle." said Paddy.

Tyson didn't answer. For him it was the total destruction of his nightmare. Sighing he asked the young wizard, "Now what, Paddy?"

"Patience, friend. Everything in good time."

Chapter 49

The return trail was now pleasant, the chasm had disappeared, and once more they went through the high weeds, this time with no trouble. The forest and the lovely meadow with the singing brook invited the party to cool off and stop there a moment to have a good meal. The birds had returned singing around them as they passed by. Soledad mischievously removed her boots, jumped in the water and laughing threw them at Paddy. Surprised he looked at her and with a loud cry jumped in beside her, boots and all. Daryl, the water lover, couldn't resist joining the splashing party. Tyson watched the young men and girl having fun. After months of tension they needed that. Paddy leaped out shaking himself like a wet hound and gave the signal to depart. "We haven't had that much fun for a long time, man," Daryl laughed, pushing his buddy in the ribs. They were all wet.

After a long walk they arrived in the desert where Tyson had spent so many centuries of his life as a rabbit. Everything had returned to its natural beauty, no more creeping things and spiders. Several more days of walking brought the party to the meadow where they had lost Kalyste and KumKuat. They waited for a few minutes, then, whinnying happily, the horses arrived, running to their masters.

Soledad, with a bright smile, said, "I am home, Paddy."

"Yes, you are, and I am glad you came along with us." The Prince took her in his arms and passionately kissed her lips." She threw her arms around him and held his long blond silky hair in her hands. Paddy smiled and let her go. Very princely-like he bowed his head to her. "You have been a great help for us in the quest Soledad. I will see you and your father later."

He turned toward his horse to hug her. "Kalyste, my friend, how are you? I am so glad to see you. King Tyson, here is my Kalyste, and Kum-Kuat, Daryl's horse. We thought we had lost them. Lord Neph, the good Wizard of the Emerald Forest, Soledad's father, was wise. He knew they couldn't make the journey, so he kept them safely for us. I thank him from the bottom of my heart."

"I do too. I wouldn't have accepted the loss of my Kum-Kuat without a broken heart." said Daryl.

Soledad, her beautiful green eyes shining like morning stars, smiled and said, "Prince Patrick, Daryl and you King Tyson, I am going home now. I do thank you, for helping me to develop my skills and my courage. I will see you soon, Paddy. Good-bye." She disappeared in a shaft of light.

"Wow, what a girl," said Daryl.

"Yes, she is." Paddy smiled with, a dream in his eyes.

Kalyste joyously ran to the other end of the meadow whinnying, and prancing proudly. She came back with another horse, a beautiful chestnut stallion with a brown mane and a long brown tail touching the ground. He was dressed up with saddle and bridle, ready to be mounted. A note was attached to the blanket.

"To King Tyson of the Mortal Realm, with the compliments of Lord Neph, Wizard of the Emerald Forest. The horse's name is Bow. Thank you for taking good care of my Soledad. This quest meant a lot to her."

"Thank you, Lord Neph, for the wonderful gift. Bow and I are going to be very good friends," said Tyson. Bow answered, whinnying with approbation.

"You are welcome," replied a voice in the wind.

Paddy, concerned for his friend said. "Tyson, I am deeply sorry, but in your realm, you will find only the ruins of your castle, and your daughter as a marble statue."

"I know, Paddy, but I want to see her."

"Then let's go, friend."

The three cavaliers jumped on their mounts, and rode as fast as the wind. The king was so impatient to see Ida. He couldn't restrain his joy, even knowing that she was in marble, he had to see her. They rode through the elfic realm for many days. No more evil to fear. Paddy's heart sang at the sight of his beautiful and peaceful realm.

"Wow! What a realm you have, man!" Daryl said laughing joyously.

"It's yours, too, Daryl. You have helped so much to restore it that way, man."

Daryl was so happy that Paddy called the realm his realm, too. Goldy danced in front of his eyes. "Hello, Goldy. When am I going to see you?"

He heard a soft chuckling, "Soon, my human."

One fine morning they reached the bright rainbow, went through the veil and arrived in earth, the mortal realm. After traveling through the beautiful Elfic Realm, the King's heart sank at the sight of his land. Ruins everywhere! Only dust and tumbleweeds rolled under the push of a gentle breeze. Then, afar, upon a lonely hill, etched against a light blue sky, they saw the dark silhouette of his castle (what was left of it). The once proud towers were broken and the blind windows sadly looked onto the desolate countryside.

Tyson's spirits received a bad blow. Slowly they rode to the castle. The King went across the drawbridge still holding the crimson shield. Heavily he dismounted. Mute he walked in the courtyard, leaving Bow to himself. Staggering he took the path leading to the garden.

***

Daryl, after tying up the three horses, quietly followed Paddy and Tyson. Heavyhearted, afraid of looking up, Tyson sat on the bench facing the pond. The white onyx Princess was sadly brooding on her lily flower pad. Suddenly she saw her father, then a radiant smile shone on her onyx lips. Tyson, looked up and saw her smiling at him.

" Ida," cried the King jumping off the bench. Joyously he ran and stopped. "How can it be? You smiled at me." Tyson started again for the pond. Paddy cried, "Tyson one minute! One minute:"

Tyson stopped "What's the matter, Paddy?"

"Listen, not yet. Don't touch her. Wait, please. You will soon, but not now."

"Why? Why?, Paddy." The young Prince Wizard didn't answer. Daryl, hypnotized was looking at the young girl. Never had he ever seen such beauty. His heart wildly pounded in his chest. Softly he whispered, "Ida." she heard him and smiled. Goldy heard him too, and with anger threw a heavy load of gold upon him. Under the weight Daryl fell upon his knees. "Whats the matter Goldy? How come you are here in the earth realm?" She laughed and left in a gust of angry wind.

Paddy pushed Tyson back. His pointed ears quivered. Tensed he was listening as if someone was talking to him. Slowly he bent down, picked up the shield which had dropped at the feet of the king. The elf quietly moved toward the fountain. Smiling at the girl he walked into the dry basin and dropped the shield on the lily.

Apprehensively Tyson watched the young Wizard, wondering what was going to happen. Paddy, overwhelmed by the power surrounding him, bent one knee, bowed his head and put his two hands on the shield. Sparks came out encircling his body. The young elf prince stood up, his whole being luminous as a bright lamp. Quickly he held the Crimson Shield above Ida's head.

At that very moment, from the core of the shield, lightning flew up into the clouds chasing the darkness which shrouded all things. A brilliant sunbeam flashed back from the sky, went through the Shield and touched the frozen girl. The statue shone brightly. In an incredible ballet, myriads of stars danced around her. With a sharp sound the onyx cracked like an egg shell. At last the spell was broken and the Princess was free of her prison.

Chapter 50

Thunder and lightning struck the ground and vapor and fog shrouded everything. Zoltar's evil was trying to take back what it had held for centuries. But this was the end of evil in Tyson's realm. The castle was engulfed into huge clouds. Sparkling stars gently fell from the sky. Unexpectedly, all this spectacular display disappeared. The sight was incredible. Daryl's eyes almost popped out of their sockets. The castle, in all its beauty, appeared. The garden was restored. People, children were all about running and laughing.

Ida joyously hugged the Prince and said, "I remember you. In the garden you wiped my tears, and asked, 'Why are you crying girl?'" She laughed nervously, then seeing her father, in one breath she leaped out of the pool and flew into his arms.

Daryl's eyes shone, full of the magic he just witnessed. Even after many centuries in the Efic Realm he had a hard time accepting such marvelous things. He smiled at Ida.

Tears of joy ran down the King's face. Paddy and Daryl discreetly fell back. Nothing had changed. Everybody was the same as they were when the terrible tragedy happened. Lord's Neph good magic had brought that wonderful miracle.

Queen Isa arrived, followed by her young ones bouncing with joy around her. They entered into the castle. Prince Patrick, the hero, was followed by Daryl. Ida, glowing with joy, walked beside her royal parents.

In the great hall the Wizard Neph, Lord of the Emerald Forest, waited with his daughter Soledad. The two young girls joyously fell in each other's arms. The Dwarves were there, too, and Shane, Paddy's relative, the elf who centuries ago had given his mortal friend, King Tyson, the Crimson Shield.

For weeks the Kingdom rejoiced. Tyson showed the elf the beauties of his realm. He sat with the children on the soft rug cuddling their pets and their friends. With eyes shining with excitement, the youngsters delightfully listened to the story of the incredible quest and of Paddy's courage. How those little heroes would have liked to be the young elf Wizard. Prince Shane Tyson's son, asked, "Prince Paddy, are you going in a quest soon? I want to go with you."

Tyson and Paddy smiled at each other. Daryl seriously replied, "Certainly, my Prince, we will let you know."

Tyson didn't want to see his friends go, but one day Paddy said, "It's time for me to leave. I must return to my Realm."

"So soon?" pleaded the King. "Come again."

"We will, Tyson."

Kalyste and KumKuat waited for them on the front lawn. Ida was holding Daryl's hand whispering, "Don't go."

"I will be back, Princess."

In a burst of light riding the rainbow, the young elfic Prince and his squire left the mortal realm.

***

This extraordinary tale happened in the Elfic Realm, where time, as we know it, does not exist, and where imagination is reality without limit.

Do you hear my friends, Paddy the young Wizard and Daryl his friend, laughing? Listen closely. They are in the Elfic Realm where youth, life, and friendship really exist, some say forever.

When you have a dream in your heart, seek and follow the elusive rainbow.

The End